CETI

REACH FOR THE STARS - BOOK 3

JOHN WEGENER

Ceti

Written by John Wegener.
Published by John Wegener.
© Copyright, John Wegener, 2019. All rights reserved.
© Cover designed by Fiona Jayde Media.

To those who ask the question, "Where did we come from?"

1

FAMILY

"Ethan? Where are you Ethan?" Jade Powers said, raising her voice, as she looked out through the sliding doors at the back of Ethan Richards' villa. The villa sat in the foothills of Los Angeles, overlooking the sea in the distance on one side and the mountains behind Los Angeles on the other. Ethan had a deck on the side with the view of the Pacific Ocean and a grassed lawn area at the back of his residence.

"Out here," Ethan replied. "On the lawn." The sky sparkled with the vastness of stars on the moonless night with not a cloud anywhere. Being late spring, the balmy temperature made outside activity comfortable to do. He enjoyed being outdoors on nights like this. He could think of nothing better than lying down on his back and looking up into the vastness of the universe.

"There you are." Jade walked over to him.

Ethan looked towards her and smiled. Her slim body silhouetted in the light shining from the villa as she walked over. She stood over him momentarily, blocking his view, but he had no problem with that. Looking at her excited him much more than any stars. He frowned. Or did it? The thought left him as Jade lowered herself to the grass and lay next to him, joining him in his observations. He felt her warmth as she sidled up next to him.

"What are you doing?"

"Just looking out there. We've been to one of those." Ethan said as he pointed to the sky.

"Can you see Alpha Centauri from here?"

"No, you can only see it in the southern hemisphere, unfortunately. Almost every one of those has at least one planet orbiting it, though. Huge Earth-like planets and small Jupiters, mega Jupiters, and any other variation you could dream of, all waiting for someone to explore it."

"You can't live on most of them though. We were lucky to find the ones we did at Alpha Centauri."

"It was more than luck. We had a fair idea we would find something suitable for human occupation. But you're right, of all those stars, we would not survive on many of the surrounding planets." Ethan sighed.

"What's wrong?"

"Nothing, I don't know, something…"

"You just want to live among the stars, don't you? Would you really step into the unknown?"

"Maybe."

Jade raised her torso and leaned on one elbow, looking at Ethan, studying his face to read his mood. "You sure you're not just bored."

"I'm not bored. It's just…"

"Aren't you excited about getting married?"

"Of course I am. You've seen me. I can barely sit still for five seconds when we try making plans. I just want it over with, not that I don't want the wedding, I just want you, us, alone and moving on to a future. Feels like I'm in limbo. Nothing's happening at work. John has mentioned nothing about going to another star. What did we build that ship for, if we're just going to park it in Earth orbit?"

"I'm sure they're thinking about it. Anyway, we're off to Adelaide next week to prepare for our wedding."

"Yeah, that will keep me busy. I'll meet all the relatives." Ethan frowned.

Jade laughed. "I'll protect you as much as I can." She leaned over and kissed him sensually. "It might be time to go to bed."

"I'm not tired."

"Who said anything about sleep?"

"Oh." Ethan rose, lifted Jade up, who screamed in pleasant surprise, and carried her inside.

∼

∼

∼

ETHAN SAT NEXT to Jade on the plane to Adelaide, Australia, the following week, the excitement and tension of the approaching wedding prominent in his mind. They flew overnight, so the view out of the window displayed the stars in sharp detail at the altitude they flew. They glowed more than sparkled. Even with the joy of publicly announcing his love for Jade, his desire seemed to pull his eyes out of the window, and towards the vast emptiness of space. He wondered if humanity's yearning to escape the confines of Earth. Was it programmed or if it was just him? Looking over at Jade, asleep in her seat, he sensed a need to protect her, a need to prevent something similar to the disaster on Chariclo. He knew he couldn't live on if she died, as she nearly did there. He sighed. It was all irrelevant at present. They were flying to their wedding, and no trip was in the wind. Not that he knew of, anyway. He suddenly panicked, sitting up straighter in his seat. Maybe they were planning a trip without him. Relaxing again, he realized John would still have told him about it, if that were the case. He also felt certain that John would want his involvement in some capacity, if they planned on doing something. Deciding not to worry about it, he sat back and closed his eyes.

Jade and Ethan pulled up at her parent's residence five hours later in the hire car they rented for the duration of their stay, Jade in the driver's seat. They both hopped out and went to the front door, but it opened before they reached it and Bernice, Jade's mother, rushed out to greet them.

"Oh, Jade, it's about time. Come in. Don't stay out here and freeze," Bernice said in quick succession. They arrived early in the morning to a cold late fall day. She finally reached Jade and wrapped her arms around her in a hug. Holding her at arm's length again, she said, "You look thinner. Have you been eating enough?"

Jade laughed at her mother's fuss. "Yes, I have. I'm the same weight as last time you saw me."

Ethan looked on, amused and a little envious that she still had family to care for her. He wished he still had his mother and father to fuss over him on such a joyful occasion. He suddenly found himself in a hug from Bernice, almost overbalancing from the movement. He smelled the lavender scent that she always wore.

"And how are you, Ethan? All ready for the big day?"

"Yes, I am," Ethan said, looking to Jade for help. Jade smiled, but let Bernice complete her welcome.

"You lot coming inside?" Clyde, Jade's father, spoke loudly from inside the house. "You're letting the cold air in."

"Oh Clyde, why aren't you out here," Bernice retorted.

"I can greet them just as well in here as I can out there in the cold."

Ethan and Jade both laughed. "Let's go in," Jade suggested as she started moving towards the door.

They all entered the warm interior of the house, and Bernice closed the door behind her.

"Hi Dad," Jade said as she went up to him. They kissed each other on the cheek.

"You can see Mum's a bit excited."

"I am not. It's not every day there's a wedding, that's all."

Clyde chuckled. "Welcome Ethan. Hope you both had a pleasant flight." He reached out to shake Ethan's hand.

Ethan reciprocated. "Yes, we did thanks. I admit I'm getting nervous though."

"You see, Clyde. It's a special event. Hope you're ready for it on the day."

"I'll be ready. Listen, if we're going to have a panic, let's organize one."

Ethan smiled at Clyde's little proverb of wisdom.

"Well, let's go sit down and have a cuppa. Have you two had breakfast?"

"Yes Mum, we had something on the plane."

Jade and Ethan followed Jade's parents as they went to the dining room. They sat down while Bernice went into the kitchen to prepare the beverages.

Ethan felt a little overwhelmed and claustrophobic with all the attention he and Jade were receiving. He almost wanted to escape, but sat stoically as he took in the excitement of Jade's parents.

The morning passed quickly. They had lunch, and he brought in their luggage and put it in their rooms. Ethan had a separate room to Jade, Jade saying she didn't want to upset her parents.

"Why are you in separate rooms?" Clyde commented. "I know times have changed."

"I just feel more comfortable, that's all," Jade said.

Ethan heard a knock on the front door in the late afternoon as he sat in the family room reading a magazine. A commotion of activity erupted as three children appeared through the door, running through the house and out the back. Lorraine, Jade's sister, appeared in the doorway shouting, "Come back here and say hello, you brats." She looked at Ethan and smiled. "Sorry about that, you know what kids are like."

"That's fine," Ethan said as he rose from his seat. "Good to see you again."

They both gave a small kiss on the cheek.

"Where's Gavin?"

"He's just getting a few things out the car. He'll be here in a moment."

Footsteps came their way from the front of the house and a man appeared in the doorway moments later, his arms full of things. Ethan did not understand why he'd brought them, but he was sure he wound find out in time. He had some toys and also clothes and had a bag full of food and drinks over each shoulder.

"You look like you could use a hand," Ethan said as he moved to help.

"Won't say no," the man said. Ethan grabbed the toys and clothes while the man disappeared into the kitchen. He reappeared moments later with his arms unloaded of their previous burden. "Now, welcome to Hoffnungthal." He held out his hand.

"Thanks Gavin," Ethan said, shaking hands with him.

"Where's my sister-in-law?"

"She's somewhere in the house with Bernice. They could be out the back though, I'm not sure."

Gavin disappeared again, and Ethan heard him greet Jade. He came back in moments later, "Want a beer?"

"Sure."

Gavin went into the kitchen and came out with two beers in his hands, handing one to Ethan. "Cheers."

"Cheers."

"I'd better get the old man one before he complains."

Ethan laughed, "Yeah, keep on his good side."

Gavin did his duty, Clyde coming back inside with him, a beer in hand, "Well we've got a bit of peace and quiet for a while with the others out the back. Better enjoy it while we can." Clyde sat in his favorite armchair and the others sat, talking and sipping their drinks.

The women came in half an hour later and went to the kitchen.

They all had a large lamb leg roast for dinner, the aroma of the rosemary and garlic making his taste buds salivate before they started eating. Ethan felt like he would burst afterwards. He had eaten so much, not wanting to offend Bernice. The meal ended with apple crumble and cream for dessert. Wines accompanied the meal for the adults, while the children had a soft drink.

They all sat talking as they finished their desserts, when Clyde spoke up with a glass of red wine in his hand, to gain the others' attention. "It's good to be here and have my other daughter here tonight, and now Ethan too. It's rare the entire family is together. I hope you two can relax in the days ahead, amongst all the business of preparing for your wedding. I must say, it brings a little tear to my eye to see my young daughter finally tie the knot, but I welcome you into the family. I don't think she could have found a better man." He raised his glass.

Ethan choked with emotion and a little embarrassment at the attention, as he found his glass and raised it with all the others.

"Oh, Clyde, you're embarrassed him now," Bernice said. "He might change his mind."

Ethan almost spluttered his mouthful of wine as he half coughed. "I don't think there's any chance of that. We might elope though."

Everyone laughed. They continued talking around the table for some time until Lorraine and Gavin went, having to put the children to bed. They left and Ethan felt exhausted by the long day. He said good night to Jade's parents and Jade followed him to his bedroom. "Isn't your bedroom over there?" Ethan asked, a teasing smile on his face as he pointed to her room.

"I just wanted to kiss you goodnight."

"Is that all?"

"Not in my parents' house."

Ethan sighed. "The sacrifices we make," he said, as he pouted with widened eyes and a slight smile.

Jade huffed and hit him on the arm before embracing him, as he did her. They kissed. "I love you," she said.

"I love you too." Ethan stroked her cheek with the back of his forefinger. "Goodnight."

"Hope you have a good sleep."

"I will."

Jade left and he prepared for bed, slipping between the sheets ten minutes later and turning the light out. He lay on his back looking up at the ceiling, reflecting on the day. It warmed his heart to have a family again, even if it was Jade's.

He rose late the next morning since he had no commitments. He came into the family room at nine thirty.

"Hello sleepy," Jade said.

"First sleep-in I've had for ages."

"Well, sit down and I'll make you some breakfast," Bernice said from the sink, a dish in one hand and sponge in the other, as she cleaned the plate in soapy water.

"It's OK. I can make something," Ethan said.

"Nonsense. Let me pamper you while I can."

Ethan looked at Jade, who had a snigger of a smile on her face. He knew by the smile she would not support him. "OK, then." He sat at the table and waited.

Bernice made bacon and eggs with toast for him and some piping hot coffee. He ate the meal and thanked her. She made it just how he liked it. He wondered if Jade had mentioned anything to her beforehand. It didn't matter. He enjoyed the savory taste immensely. Jade disappeared while he ate, but he presumed she had things to do to prepare for the wedding. Clyde seemed to be absent too, so Ethan went to the lounge in the family room and caught up with the latest news on his tablet. He heard a knock on the door at twenty to twelve, but didn't get up. He presumed Bernice would answer it. Voices filtered into him from the lounge room a moment later, the arrangement of the rooms preventing him from seeing who talked. He continued reading.

"Ethan," Jade said from the doorway.

"There you are. I was wondering where you'd gone."

"There's some people here to see you."

"Me? Who?"

"Come meet them."

Ethan put his tablet away and rose, heading for the lounge. He got halfway through the doorway and froze into a statue. General John O'Conner and Ching Hu, longtime friends and work associates of both Ethan and Jade, stood in the lounge looking at him with amused faces. Two others stood with them, a man and a woman. Tears started falling from his eyes. "Alice... Mark."

"Hello Ethan," Alice said from where she stood, appearing to be apprehensive over whether to come forward. Mark also stayed where he stood.

Ethan couldn't contain himself. He ran the few paces to them and hugged first Alice and then Mark. They too started crying. Ethan wiped his eyes. "Jade, this is my brother and sister."

"Oh," Jade said, approaching the group with tentative steps. "Pleased to meet you," she said to Ethan's siblings.

Mark released Ethan and went to Jade, giving her a hug. "It's good to meet you too. John and Hu have told us all about you and Ethan."

Jade blushed as she looked at Hu. "I wouldn't believe much of what those two say."

Hu gave a look of pretend shock.

Alice came over and gave Jade a hug too. "Well, it sounds like you are just what Ethan needs in his life."

"Does it then," Ethan said, also looking at Hu and John. He realized he should have suspected something was up when they had grilled him about his family recently. He looked at Jade. "You had nothing to do with it?"

"No. I'm as surprised as you are."

"Consider it a wedding gift," John said.

"What's all the commotion?" Clyde asked as he walked into the room, Bernice right behind him.

"Clyde, Bernice, meet my brother Mark and sister Alice. I haven't seen them in fifteen years."

"Well, I'll be. Ethan said he'd lost track of you. I know it's before noon, but if this doesn't call for a celebration, nothing does." He went over to Mark and Alice and greeted them, as did Bernice. He left the room and came back five minutes later with a bottle of champagne. "Get some glasses Bernice, will you?"

Bernice left to get the glasses, and Jade helped her. Clyde popped the cork, filled the glasses, and they all drank a toast. "To family," Clyde said.

"To family," they all replied.

They spent the rest of the day talking. Ethan felt emotionally exhausted by the end. He needed time alone to process everything that had happened, so he sat outside on a bench at the back of the house.

"You OK?" Jade asked as she came outside ten minutes later.

Ethan looked over to her, "Yes, I'm just exhausted. Come and sit with me."

Jade obeyed and sat next to him, wrapping her arm around his.

"It's just the last thing I would have expected, and the emotions unleashed in seeing them just drained all the energy out of me."

"You'll sleep well tonight then."

"Sure will. I just don't understand why they haven't contacted me until now."

"Did you try to contact them?"

"No, I didn't."

"Why not?"

"I don't really know. They were the ones that left. I thought they would come back when they were ready and then I lost touch with where they were. I can't explain how re-uniting with them makes me feel complete as a family again though. I started feeling envious of you last night, with all your family around you when I had no one. It's all changed now."

"It would overwhelm me."

"I'm so happy. I don't want today to end."

"But then we would never marry."

"No, that is the one thing that makes me want to fast forward time, skip all the in-between stuff, and bring the day finally into being."

"Oh, I love you." Jade reached over and kissed him.

They stayed on the bench and talked for some time. Bernice and Clyde came out at one stage and said goodnight as they went to bed. Ethan and Jade finally decided they had better retire.

The rest of the week entailed preparing for the wedding and meeting other family and friends that came by the house from time to time. Apep Chernakov and Galena Alvarez also came and visited as they attended the wedding rehearsal the day before. John was

Ethan's best man and Apep his groomsman at the ceremony. Lorraine was Jade's matron of honor and Hu her bridesmaid. Ethan felt exhausted by the time the night before the wedding came. He stayed in Adelaide that night so the men were all together to dress and make all the other preparations for the ceremony. John and Apep had a surprise outing for him too. They coaxed him into going to a bar with them for a few drinks, which he did.

2

I DO

Ethan turned when the organist started playing 'The Wedding March' on the pipe organ at the back of the church in Hoffnungthal. The church was the oldest in the town, built by the original settlers. People now only used it for special occasions and private bookings like Jade and he had made. Ethan stood in front of the altar with the priest standing in the sanctuary area. The altar stood behind the priest, blue and white, as did the reredos behind it, with the pulpit for preaching integrated into the structure of it at a higher level. His heart raced, and hands perspired in anticipation of the impending ceremony. Despite Apep's encouragement, he curtailed his alcohol consumption and Ethan fell into bed before midnight the night before, ensuring he could enjoy his wedding without a hangover. He wore a freshly tailored white English suit with jade green waistcoat and tie, a red rose pinned to his lapel. His eyes brimmed with tears of intensity as the essence of the moment hit him, the moisture threatening to escape. He gasped as they focused on Jade at the back of the church with Clyde. She wore a sleeveless pure white halter-top dress, her face covered with a veil, but enough of her face showed through the fabric to expose the sheer beauty of her presence. Her hands clasped a posy of red roses, matching the one in his lapel. John and Apep stood next to him and they too turned to face the bridal party.

A flower girl, Jade's niece, stood at the front of the procession, followed by Hu and Lorraine, all dressed in the same jade green he wore. He momentarily fixed on Hu's eyes and saw a radiant, satisfied smile on her face. He also saw a tinge of nervousness in the way she walked, which amused Ethan slightly, as Hu's composure always held, except under the most severe of circumstances. He refocused on Jade as her march to him started. His eyes flickered to his right, and he briefly focused on Bernice in the front row of the church, exquisitely dressed in a burgundy-colored outfit with chiffon sleeves as the mother of the bride. She had a handkerchief out to dab away any tears threatening to fall out and damaging her mascara, but she also had great pride in the event, emphasized by her posture.

They intended the wedding to be small, at Jade's insistence. He had no arguments there, as his guest list was short, apparent by the sparseness of people he knew on the side of the church traditionally reserved for family and friends of the groom, although the church was full, anyway. Jade's invitees grew as time passed, much to her displeasure, but her mother kept convincing her they just had to invite the people to prevent insult. They both compromised and the entire event grew to be a moderate size that seemed to placate everyone involved in organizing it.

Ethan's mind returned to the present as the bridal party continued their march to the front. His eyes solely focused on Jade and he saw that hers were for him. It seemed to take an eternity for her to pace the distance to him and yet it took no time at all, his mind and emotions being so honed. Jade positioned herself to the side of Ethan and two steps behind, her father next to her, his arm interlocked with hers. She looked at him with a nervous smile. Ethan chuckled inside. He presumed she was as nervous as he felt, and he smiled back before turning to face the altar and celebrant.

The music stopped, and the ceremony began.

"Who gives this woman away to be with this man," the celebrant said.

"I do," Clyde said, loudly and with pride and a slight croak of emotion in his voice. He let go of Jade, turned and went to sit next to Beatrice, taking her hand and patting it once he as did so.

Jade stepped forward to be next to Ethan. The celebrant proceeded with the ceremony as tradition dictated with what they had both decided the ceremony to be.

"You may now kiss the bride," the celebrant said.

Ethan turned to Jade, as she did to him. He felt immense joy, but also fear as the commitment they just made started sinking in. What if he couldn't live up to Jade's expectations? He then realized that it wasn't the time to think such thoughts. He lifted the veil from Jade's face and embraced her, Jade welcoming him into her space and they both kissed to the joyous uproar of the guests. They parted after a brief period and Ethan saw a tear in Jade's eye and realized he had one in his. They both laughed and hugged again.

"Ladies and Gentlemen, I present to you Mr. and Mrs. Richards," the celebrant announced.

Ethan and Jade faced the assembled crowd with smiles of jubilation.

The rest of the day passed quickly as Ethan and Jade performed the legal formalities and then whisked away for the obligatory holographs to commemorate the event.

Arriving at their reception party to celebrate, Ethan felt he could finally start relaxing and enjoying the rest of the day. They walked to their table at the head of the reception room in a vineyard restaurant that they had selected and sat with the rest of the bridal party. Not long after, someone in the room started tapping their glass with a spoon, the crisp noise resonating throughout the room. Ethan and Jade obliged with a kiss, to the delight of the guests as they clapped. They had to repeat the performance several times throughout the meal. John, Ethan and Clyde made speeches as did some others, the rest of the night being set aside for socializing.

"How do you feel?" John asked Ethan as they relaxed in their seats.

"Exhausted," Ethan said, "but I'd do it all again if I had to."

John laughed, "I can imagine." With that, he looked across the table to where Hu sat and a smile of a different hue developed. Ethan saw Hu looking at John, and her face exploded into a magnificent state of bliss at seeing his interest in her. "What are you doing for your honeymoon?" John asked.

"We're spending a few days out in the Pacific but not much else."

"That should be great."

"We wanted somewhere no one could get hold of us. Not even you."

"Oh, I would find a way, if I had too. Now, let's enjoy the festivities tonight shall we." John picked up his glass and rose from his chair, moving over to Hu and out into the crowd of guests.

"Hey, handsome," Jade said into Ethan's ear, tickling his lobe with her nose as she did so.

Ethan's attention instantly refocused on her. "Be careful who you say that to."

"I am," Jade replied, eyes sparkling with love.

"Tonight's gone well. The meal's finished, and the speeches are out of the way. Your father even seems happy."

"Ha! It must be a good night then. I think he is just happy to get his daughter out of the house."

"You're probably right."

Jade momentarily looked shocked, but then burst out laughing, "Yes, I'm probably right."

They both kissed, looking into each other's eyes afterwards.

"Let's mingle," Jade said.

Ethan allowed Jade to take the lead as they moved from their table into the crowd. They came to a familiar group, The other team members were still around from their expedition to Centauri the year before, Celeste Grüber, Marie Lorraine, Max Roberts and Angelo Soula, whom they both agreed they had to invite to the wedding. They stood talking as a group, so Ethan and Jade walked up to them.

"Hi Jade. I love your dress," Celeste said. "I envy you. How special you must feel."

Jade laughed. "It feels special now, but I was a nervous wreck earlier. But you're right, it is a special day and I wouldn't change it for the world."

Apep and Galena also conversed with the group. "Ah, if I were a few years younger," Apep said, "I'd give Ethan a run for his money. Your beauty becomes you even more than normal."

Jade blushed. "You are a charmer. No wonder you swept Galena from her feet."

"You can't imagine how hard it is to stop his eyes straying," Galena said.

"Ah, my eyes are only for you my love," Apep said to Galena. She giggled. "Where is Hugo, anyway? We need to plan our little schemes together."

"You may have lost her too, I think. She seems to have someone else these days."

"Never." Apep said in shock, a smile accompanying the expression.

They all laughed.

The others joined in the conversation and Ethan and Jade talked to them for quite some time before moving on.

"Can you see what I see?" Ethan asked Jade, pointing to a darkened corner of the room, where Hu and John stood trying to be inconspicuous as they interacted in what seemed like a very intimate exchange.

Jade looked to where Ethan was pointing and smiled. "They look so right together, don't you think?"

"They have grown very close from what I've heard. They're always very guarded when talking about each other, though."

"Well, John's different to the facade he portrays as a military man."

"Yeah. He's like me, really."

Jade laughed. "Like you were anyway."

Ethan smiled. "I hope things work out for them."

The reception continued until it became for Ethan and Jade to depart, but Jade had one last formality to perform before leaving. Ethan had Jade at his side and the women congregated behind Jade who held her posy bouquet, ready to throw it up and into them for one of them to catch. She faced away from them, so she couldn't see where she threw the flowers and tossed them over her head to the general screams and excitement of the group. Jade and Ethan turned to see who had caught it and stared in disbelief. Hu stood in shock with the bunch of flowers in her hand, as if wondering what she should do with them.

Ethan laughed. "That's the first time I've seen Hugo stumped about what to do."

Hu raised her head at Ethan's voice, blushing, but with a grin on her face. She raised the flowers above her head and did a little jig on the spot in celebration.

Ethan looked for John and saw him to the side, slightly nonplussed. Traditional superstition had it that the woman who caught the posy would be the next to marry, so Ethan could understand what John may have been thinking at that point. He changed his concentration back to Jade, "Shall we?"

"Let's," Jade replied, and they turned and walked out of the reception, into the waiting vehicle and off to enjoy the rest of the night alone.

ETHAN AND JADE quickly visited Jade's parents the next morning, before rushing to the airport for their flight to Tahiti, arriving at the beachside resort in the evening. Jade and Ethan sat in deck chairs out on the balcony of their room in the balmy night air, sipping champagne from the open bottle in front of them, finally relaxing after the bustle and excitement of the past week. The smell of frangipanis wafted by them in the gentle breeze. Ethan almost dozed as his body came accustomed to the relaxation. "I could get used to this," he mumbled as he took another sip.

"Mmm mmm...," Jade agreed.

"What do you want to do tomorrow?"

"Stay in bed all day."

"You can't sleep all day."

"Who said anything about sleeping?"

"Oh... we should do something else too."

Jade looked over at Ethan, pouting. Ethan laughed and reached over for Jade's hand, which she freely gave him. He caressed it in his as he thought. "You want to learn to scuba dive? There are some great reefs here."

"That might be fun. Let's go for a hike."

"What all tomorrow?"

"Nooooo... While we're here."

Ethan lay back, closing his eyes again. He couldn't explain the peacefulness he felt. He felt lucky to have Jade in his life. He didn't want the dream to end. He married the woman he loved, and she had a great family, and he finally reunited with his own siblings again after so long, completing the close family circle around him. Why had he let his brother and sister drift away? They said they wanted to give him space to reach his full potential after looking after them for so long. He wondered if there were other reasons, but it probably wasn't important anymore if there were. He knew they would keep in touch with each other. They were much alike but very different to him too, maybe because he was the oldest or maybe he just had a distinct personality. Whatever it was, he was happy to see them again, and didn't want to lose touch with them like before.

Clyde and Bernice always amused him when he saw them. They seemed to know each other so well. They didn't even need to ask what the other wanted most of the time. They seemed to know by instinct. He wondered whether he and Jade would get to know each other so well...

Ethan woke with a start as he felt himself being shaken.

"Ethan," Jade said. "Wake up."

"Huh...?" Ethan opened his eyes, confused, as he tried working out where he was.

"You were asleep."

Ethan stretched as his senses returned. "Must be more tired than I thought."

"Let's go to bed."

"Let's."

They both got out of the deck chairs and went inside and to bed.

Ethan rose the next morning, refreshed by the sleep. He jumped out of bed and went out onto the balcony, leaving Jade sleeping in peace. The sun, half risen above the horizon, beckoned a fine and clear day. The humidity, although tropical, felt tempered and controlled from its full potential of discomfort by the proximity to the sea. He breathed in the air, as a gentle breeze blew in from the ocean, the saltiness just noticeable in its scent as he leaned on the balustrade of the balcony, gripping the railing with both hands. The sea sparkled, light blue and aqua. It felt so tranquil. He thought he could stay there forever and just enjoy the serenity of the place. He heard Jade stirring behind him, but didn't turn around, arms encircling his waist moments later as she nestled up behind him. He felt her warmth and curves and smile with pleasure. Rotating, he held her, and they greeted each other with a kiss. "It's a beautiful day," Ethan said, once their lips parted again.

"Yes, it is."

"You want to go for that hike?"

"I thought you wanted to go scuba diving?"

"We can find out about it today and organize some lessons."

Jade nodded. "OK, then."

"Let's get ready and go have some breakfast."

They both went inside. Ethan asked if she wanted to shower first, but she pulled him in with her and they showered together, saying she wanted to conserve water. Ethan wasn't sure how much water they conserved though. They sat on a deck in the resort having breakfast half an hour later.

Consulting the staff at the resort about hiking trails, they arranged a picnic hamper and a map of the island showing various paths they could explore. They hopped on a jet boat ferry and used it to take them to another part of the island where they could start their hike. They arrived at the pier half an hour after getting onto the boat. Ethan asked the operator about arrangements for returning at another pier and, happy they could get back, they hopped off the boat and started their hike. Being in no rush, they started at a leisurely pace as they walked up the gradual incline into the island interior. Staying on the easily identifiable path with markers within sight of each other, they arrived at a stream with a waterfall and pool just after midday. A large grassed area next to the pool allowed people to relax and use it for meals and other activities. The grass looked frequently maintained to provide comfort and a suitable recreational area for the tourist who came there.

"Isn't this just ecstatic?" Jade said, a smile of wonder on her as she rotated on the spot with her arms out, head back and eyes closed.

Ethan looked at her, also smiling. He felt her excitement too. "It's out of this world." He looked around for a suitable spot to have their picnic lunch. Seeing a place under the shade of a tree, he put the backpack on the ground and ambled over to the pool of water. The purity of the water allowed him to see the bottom, and the sky reflected an azure blue from the mirror surface. The waterfall produced a rainbow, as the spray from it diffracted the sunlight in their direction. Tropical trees surrounded the area, tall and overarching as they jostled for sunlight. Various squawks of birds echoed through to him from the forest.

Jade came over to him and looped her arm in his, resting her head on his shoulder. "Inviting, isn't it?"

"Yeah, we should have brought swimmers with us."

"Who needs them?"

Ethan chuckled. "Maybe not, someone else might come along."

Jade sighed.

"What? I'm not that much of a prude."

"I know. I sighed because you're right."

"Hungry?"

"Yeah."

They broke from the serenity of their surrounds and went back to the backpack. He pulled out the containers of food and drink and they sat on the grass, relaxing as they ate the meal. Ethan looked at the map to check their route. The trail made a large arc up into the mountains and back down to the sea again. They were about a third of the way along. "We'd better get moving," Ethan said. "We've a fair way to go yet."

"I don't want to," Jade replied, pouting. "It's so beautiful here."

"I know. We want to get back before dark though."

Jade succumbed to Ethan's logic and helped pack up the waste and leftovers. They continued on their hike five minutes later. The trail weaved its way through the jungle, the sound of various birds singing and animals scurrying in the undergrowth joining them from time to time. They reach the highest point an hour later and walked into a clearing with a lookout, allowing a panoramic view of the island and surrounding sea. Ethan pointed out the jetty he thought they had arrived at, but couldn't see any other one for their destination. He presumed he couldn't see it from their vantage point. They continued the walk after about ten minute's rest and a healthy drink of water. Their pace increased from that point as the landscape predominately sloped downhill. It still took some time, and they arrived at the destination pier late in the afternoon. The boat came along after a half hour wait and they welcomed the sight of the resort as the sun prepared for its descent below the horizon, getting to their room soon after. They made love and had a shower and prepared for dinner, Ethan being ready long before Jade. He wore a plain mint short-sleeve shirt and gray pants.

"Why don't you go along to the bar?" Jade said, "I'll be another ten minutes."

"I can wait."

"No, it's all right."

"OK, then." Ethan kissed her and walked out, wondering why she seemed to want him out of the way. Ethan went downstairs to the bar adjoining the outside restaurant. He made a dinner reservation, just in case it became booked out, and sat on a stool at the bar, ordering a beer. Being westerly oriented, he saw the last of the sun's rays flicker as they disappeared over the horizon. He sipped his beer as he recounted the pleasure of the day. He wished time stood still and he could live in the place forever. He honestly couldn't think of another time he enjoyed more. He finished his drink and wondered where Jade was, as he looked at the time on his comm. He knew she took some time to prepare herself on occasions, but it seemed longer than normal. He started feeling hungry, and he considered whether he should order another beer, but waited. He sat playing with the card-board place mat his beer glass had stood on instead.

"I'm here," Jade's voice came from behind him.

Ethan swiveled on his stool and sat in stunned silence with his mouth half open, looking at Jade's appearance. She wore an ankle length jade-colored evening dress with shoestring straps, displaying the top of her breasts to perfection. Matching jade earrings and neck-lace adorned her with black high-heeled shoes. Ringlets of hair cascade on both sides of her face as her jade-colored eyes sparkled. She looked like a china doll, too fragile to touch in case she broke. Ethan's heart jumped into his throat. He didn't want to destroy the moment.

"Aren't you going to say something?"

Her voice brought him out of his trance. "You look beautiful."

"Thank you. I wanted to do something special tonight."

"You did that. I'd better get you out of here though, before someone else sees you and takes you away from me."

Jade laughed softly. "No chance of that. I only have eyes for you."

Ethan jumped off the stool and tidied his clothes. He held out his arm. "Shall we?"

Jade nodded, "Let's." She placed her hand on his arm and they both walked into the restaurant and to their table. They ate their meal and stayed late into the night, talking and drinking their wine together.

Scuba diving was on their agenda the next day, and they did other tourist activities throughout their week's stay. They sat in the restaurant the final night eating a delicious seafood meal together.

"It'll be hard returning to our mundane life tomorrow," Jade said.

"Sure will. I'll still have you to pamper me though," Ethan teased.

"You can look after yourself."

Ethan sighed. "Where did the week go? I've never seen such a beautiful place, both on land and in the water. Let's move here."

"You wish. Somehow I think you would get bored with it quickly."

"You're probably right." Ethan sat looking out at the ocean, watching the ripple of the sea sparkle to the reflection of the moonlight. He looked up. The clear sky displayed the heavens in a clarity he could never wish for with the light pollution in Los Angeles. His yearning returned and yet he felt at peace with his life, thinking he would still be happy if he never returned to space again. He wondered how true that was, or was he just deluding himself? Maybe the excitement of the honeymoon overwhelmed his desire, and the balance would swing back once he returned to his normal life again. Time would tell.

They left the restaurant and went on a walk together along the beach, removing their shoes in the sand. Ethan felt the particles squelching between his toes as they ambled next to each other, Jade resting her head against his shoulder. They returned to their room just before midnight and went to bed, going to sleep after exhausting themselves.

The next morning came, and they packed and caught the shuttle bus to the airport, catching their plane just after midday. With the transfers they had to make, they arrived back at Ethan's villa early the next morning. Ethan unlocked the door, and they walked in.

"This may not have all the excitement of a tropical paradise, but it's still home sweet home," Ethan said.

"Yes, it is. I wonder what's in store for us now?"

3

DISCOVERY

Professor Jacobson looked up from reading the report on his desk, adjusting his glasses as he did so, as Hendricks came barging into his office. He could have had his eyesight corrected, so he didn't need to wear glasses, but he preferred them. He thought they made him look more academic. Grey hair, last combed days ago, hung like haphazard wood shavings from his head and his drooping jowls highlighting the grumpiness he felt. He found the disturbance most irritating as they by-passed office protocols. "What is it Hendricks?" he asked, frowning. He hated being on the god-forsaken planet. They would discover nothing groundbreaking. In the meantime, his colleagues and competitors back on Earth continued making the big discoveries. Damn those blasted explorers that found the place, and those blasted skeletons. His only consolation was the wormhole portal. At least he could get back to Earth, without too much fuss, in excellent time when he wanted to. Who had the audacity to name the damn place Chariclo, a Titan of all things? It felt more like Hades. At least you can breathe on this one, not like the other planet they found. Another ridiculous name, Chiron.

Hendricks took a few moments to recover from the long run over to the offices, gasping to regain his breath. "Sir, they've found something." People never used the comm to communicate with Professor Jacobson. First, he probably wouldn't answer it and second, he would tell them to come see him, anyway.

"Found something?"

"Yes, they say it's a star map, or something, and they want you to come and have a look."

Professor Jacobson frowned, as he wondered what it could mean. The planet had already come up with several surprises with the skeletons and the virus and a few other minor discoveries, but a star map? He needed to have a look. It might make being on this backwater of a planet bearable. "Who found it?"

"Dr. Williams and Cassandra, Sir."

"Hmm. Are they back or on their way?"

"They just arrived back at the base and they told me to get you. They're very excited."

"Yes, well, I doubt that it's much once we look at it closely. We'd better see what all the fuss is about then." Professor Jacobson chuckled to himself. *They sent Hendricks instead of coming to see me themselves. They know how cantankerous I can be about false hopes when making new findings.* People had come to him excited about a discovery sometimes, only to find out it had little significance, and suffering Professor Jacobson's acerbic reprimand to check their facts before coming to him. He rose from his seat, put his jacket on and followed Hendricks out the door. They wove their way out of the office complex through to the vehicle parking area, where Dr. Williams and Cassandra stood talking.

Dr. Williams, the chief geologist on the archeological dig, was still climbing the rungs of the academic ladder, his blond hair accentuating his strong chiseled face and athletic body. Cassandra, his PhD understudy, idolized her mentor and followed him everywhere. Some gossiped that their relationship extended beyond the purely professional. Her brunette hair sat clumped into a ponytail as it cascaded halfway down her back and her round face and frumpish body didn't really convey the look of a geologist, although what should a geologist look like? Dr. Williams and Cassandra looked up as the others approached.

"So what is it you say you've found?" Professor Jacobson said.

"Let's go into the meeting room where we'll have more privacy," Dr. Williams replied.

Professor Jacobson raised an eyebrow in surprise, but followed Dr. Williams and the others to the nearby conference room. They entered, and Dr. Williams closed the door. "We went to the new cave site we discovered the other day. It's the same as the first one, skeletons interred and laid out neatly on the floor."

Professor Jacobson nodded, getting frustrated that Williams took his time getting to the point. "Yes, yes."

"The sonar operator found another cavity sealed up in another section of the cave. We opened it up and found this." Dr. Williams set up his holographic imaging device on the table and turned it on, bring the image they took into focus, hovering above the table. A view of a wall from the site shone out from the image.

Professor Jacobson moved closer, leaning over and lifting his head back to bring his bifocal vision into better focus. He moved around the table to view the image from various angles. "Interesting," he said several times, making no other comment. His heart started racing, as he considered what possibilities the discovery might provide for his Nobel Prize prospects, although he kept his excitement to himself and maintained a blank face to the others. He straightened up in thought. "This is all that was in the room?"

"Yes, it was bare except for these etchings on the wall. They look like some kind of star map, don't you agree?"

"Possibly."

"I think it'd be worthwhile for you to have a look yourself. This image doesn't really do the find justice."

Professor Jacobson looked at Dr. Williams for a second. He really didn't enjoy going out into the field these days, preferring the younger scientists to do the manual digging around and whatnot, but he thought Dr. Williams made a suitable point in this case. If someone would announce a monumental find to the world, it should be him. He deserved it after being sent there. He knew that they selected him out of jealousy. "Ok, I'll come with you tomorrow and we can review the finding together."

"Good. We usually like to set off about seven."

"Yes, yes, I'll be ready." Jacobson leaned over to inspect the image again, letting the patterns on display sink into his memory, so his gray matter could get to work on deciphering what they could mean. He left the room not long after, head bowed, deep in thought.

They started out to the cave the next day, soon after seven. The vehicle bouncing around as it navigated the terrain. Professor Jacobson brought along a few instruments he thought might be useful to take with, after spending several hours looking at star maps of the immediate area and manipulating some of them. He had retired after midnight, but he rarely slept more than a few hours, anyway. Hendricks also tagged along, as did Cassandra. They arrived at the cave ninety minutes later. Piling out of the vehicle, Dr. Williams led the party to the cave and the room they had discovered the day before. The cave walls were smooth and obviously artificially cut out of the rock, and the room measured five metres by five metres by three metres high. It too had smooth walls except for the one with the etched markings on it.

Professor Jacobson moved closer to the etching on the wall and scrutinized it for fifteen minutes. "Is it the same age as the other site?"

"Our analyzes say it is, yes."

Pulling out an instrument Professor Jacobson brought along, he made some measurements, careful to write each down once he made them. The others looked on in silence as he did so. He took a two-dimensional image of the wall, and overlaid it onto the star map he had, rotating the map to try matching the pattern on the wall with the orientation of stars. After experimenting with the map for ten minutes, he looked up at the wall again. "Well, I'll be."

"What is it?" Dr. Williams asked. "What have you found?"

Jacobson looked at him. "It's an area of the sky as seen from here two million years ago. These lines here," he said as he pointed to the arrow-type lines on the wall, "point to one star in particular. That must be it. There can't be any other explanation." He descended into retrospective thought as he placed his hand on his chin, turned and slowly paced around the room.

"Well?" Dr. Williams asked after a lengthy period of silence.

Professor Jacobson looked up, brought back to the present, "What? What?"

"Which star?"

"Oh... Tau Ceti," Professor Jacobsons said, waving his arm around, as if the information was inconsequential and went back to his pondering. His thoughts digressed to how best he could announce it to the academic world for his eminence to shine within the academia.

"But that's incredible. Don't you think we should tell someone?"

Professor Jacobson stopped again. "Yes, you could be right. The finding is beyond doubt. Let's get back to the offices."

4

ARGUMENT

Several weeks later, John contacted Ethan in his office. "All rested and ready to get back into some proper work again?" he asked over the comm, with a hint of mischief in his voice, as his mouth curved up slightly at the ends.

"I'd do anything to do something more exciting than what I'm doing now. Why? What's up?"

"Can you come over to the LA Hilton tomorrow, say around ten in the morning? Bring Jade with you."

"Aren't you a little busy?" Ethan asked, as he knew that Hu still lingered in LA, and she had been spending a significant amount of time with John.

"I'm never too busy for you two. Besides, work must go on with or without distractions, as pleasant as they may be."

"Why do you want Jade to come along?"

"I'll tell you both tomorrow."

"We'll be there, unless Jade has something important that she can't get out of."

"Tell her to get out of it, national security."

"National security?" Ethan responded.

"That should stop people complaining."

"And asking questions."

"Anyway, I'll see you both at ten."

The screen went blank.

I wonder what that's all about? It'll be something exciting to talk to Jade about tonight, anyway.

The rest of the day passed quickly as he speculated over what John might want to talk to both of them about. He felt it had to be another expedition somewhere with *Destiny*, their warp bubble drive spaceship, but where and for what purpose? He knew speculating wouldn't provide any answers, but he couldn't help himself. He picked up Jade after work and helped her move the final consignment of her furniture and belongings from her apartment to Ethan's villa, making it ready to finalize the termination of the lease.

"I had a strange call from John today. He wants us to see him tomorrow."

"Why?"

"He wouldn't say. He wants us to meet him at ten."

"Well, I don't have anything on, so that's no problem."

"He said to get out of it, if you did. National Security."

"Now he has me intrigued."

"It must be something to do with *Destiny*. He wants us to go somewhere."

"Let's just wait until we see him tomorrow, shall we?"

"You're right, but I just can't help trying to work out what it could be."

Having completed the move, they prepared a quick dinner and relaxed for the rest of the evening. They went to sleep late that night, not solely because of the work they needed to complete that day though.

The sun rose bright, and promising a glorious spring day, without a cloud in the sky. Ethan and Jade rose early and went for their ritual half hour jog together before showering, breakfast and preparations for traveling to their meeting with John.

They arrived just before ten and went to the foyer, Ethan sending a message to John when they got there.

Hu sat waiting for them when they arrived. She looked happy and flushed with the joy one has when everything is going right in their life. "And how are the newlyweds?"

"Nothing could be better," Jade answered for the both of them.

A distant stare of sadness momentarily touched Hu's face, as she remembered a past happiness, but disappeared as quickly as it had come. Not before Jade noticed, though.

"What's wrong?"

Hu looked at Jade and then Ethan, and looked down, a frown on her face. She finally confided in them. "I just remembered something from the past."

"Is that all?"

Hesitating more, Hu finally shared her current concerns. "It's John. Our relationship is going really well, but..."

Both Jade and Ethan looked at each other. "What do you mean?" Jade responded.

Hu remained silent for a few seconds, eyes staring in the distance. "I don't really know. He's holding back. It's as if... he's confused or not sure where things are going and how he feels about it. He has opened up to me about many things, but just this... it is annoying... frustrating."

Ethan, feeling for her, butted in, "Give him time, Hugo. You know he hasn't been in a relationship like this before, and there's no military training manual for it. As you said, his feelings may confuse him at the moment."

Hu thought about what Ethan said and looked at him in appreciation. "I think you are right. I will give him time to move at a pace he is comfortable with."

"Don't let him off too much though," Jade added. "You know what men are like."

They all laughed at the jest.

"I had better not keep you from your meeting."

"You're not going to be there?" Jade asked.

"No, this is official business. That is fine. I would do the same."

"Maybe we can have a drink afterwards?" Ethan said.

"I hoped that Jade would go shopping with me afterwards, if you can bare being apart from each other."

"I'd love to if I'm able."

"I will wait for you in the cafe over there then."

"Do I hear a conspiracy in progress," John said as he joined them, dressed in full military uniform, the others not noticing his approach.

"Oh, hi John," Ethan said as he turned to face him. "You've just saved me from these two discussing shopping plans."

"Really," John said, raising his eyebrow as Hu moved closer to him. She wrapped her arm around him. "I'll have to make sure the meeting goes all day then."

Hu looked at him in annoyance and jabbed his rib softly. Her face soon turned angelic though, as he returned a face of innocence.

"What was that for?" he asked while rubbing where Hu had nudged him.

She poked him slightly harder again. "You know very well what you're doing."

"I surrender," John said as he held his hands up, awkwardly, with Hu restraining one arm. "Let's retire to the meeting room for our discussion then, and I promise I'll keep the meeting as short as possible for you." John looked at Jade and Hu as he said the last words, a friendly smile on his face, which turned to adoration when he looked at Hu.

"Lead the way," Ethan said, "and as for me, we can take as long as you want. It will keep our bank balance healthy."

Jade looked at Ethan with feigned darts in her eyes, "I'll make sure I buy something expensive now." She smiled straight afterwards. "Let's go. I'll see you later," she said to Hu.

Ethan and Jade followed John to the elevators, up to the first floor and to the now familiar meeting room, having visited the room many times before. Celeste sat waiting for them when they arrived.

"John didn't mention you being here," Ethan blurted out before realizing it.

"Hello to you too," Celeste said with a smiling riposte as she stood in greeting.

"Don't take any notice of Ethan," Jade said. "How are you? You look well."

"I am. You two look bursting with vitality too."

Ethan blushed, "I just wasn't expecting anyone else here. It took me off guard. I hope you're looking after *Destiny*."

Celeste grinned at Ethan's concern for '*his ship*.' "*Destiny* is just fine and undergoing some alterations to improve it."

"What improvements?" Ethan paused and stared at Celeste for a moment and then at John and back to Celeste again. He turned to John again, "What have you asked Celeste to do to *Destiny*?"

Both John and Celeste laughed.

"She's still the same *Destiny*, I promise," John said.

"I have you to thank for the ideas," Celeste continued, "but let's get down to business, shall we?"

Ethan was still unsure about Celeste's seemingly meteoric development, giving her one last sideways look. He looked at Jade for support, but found a smile instead. Allowing the confusion to wash away, he brought his attention back to the reason for the meeting. "Yes, lets," he said as he found a seat, Jade sitting beside him.

Celeste sat where she had been and John found a seat next to all of them so he could see all their faces.

"Well," John said. "It's been a while since the last event-filled expedition, and we have learned a lot from that. As you know, Celeste has made a couple more trips to Centauri and we've extensively used the wormhole to ferry scientists through for further research on what you've uncovered there." He paused, making sure they understood him.

Get on with it, Ethan thought. He saw expectancy on Jade's, and Celeste's faces too.

John continued, "The scientists on Chariclo have made an intriguing discovery."

"What sort of discovery?" Ethan asked, leaning forward in his seat, his interest piqued.

John looked at him. "They have found another cave with skeletons in it, but that's not why everyone's scratching their heads. There's something even more mysterious there. They discovered another sealed room in the cave." Everyone leaned forward in their seats more, waiting for enlightenment. "One of the cave walls had an etching on it. I'll show it to you. This is highly classified for the time being, though." John pressed a button on the desk and a holographic image appeared above it showing the wall with the unusual etchings on it. The others jumped when they saw it.

Ethan stood and looked closer, tracing some illusory lines and dots with his fingers. He considered the image a while longer. "It looks like a map showing stars or something similar."

"That's what Professor Jakobson thought. He's the head of the archaeological expedition that discovered it. He played around with a star map of the sky as seen from Alpha Centauri. Not that it's that much different to what we see. There are slight differences though."

"Is the cave the same age as the other one?" Jade asked.

"Yes, it is."

"You'd have to view the sky as it was two million years ago then."

John smiled. "He did. You see those arrows and the star it points to?" The others nodded. "That's the location of Tau Ceti two million years ago."

Ethan looked at John. His mind exploded by the revelation. "Why would a map pointing to Tau Ceti be in a cave on Chariclo?"

"You tell me."

Ethan looked at Celeste and then Jade and back at John. "What's this got to do with us?"

"We want you to go there and find out why."

Ethan's eyes bulged, considering what it may mean for both Jade and himself. He didn't want to go through what they all did on Chariclo, with the unintended release of the virus they discovered there. He frowned, the creases of his forehead showing distinctly.

John saw Ethan's concern. "We will take even stricter precautions this time. We don't want what happened last time to happen again either. There was enough public backlash over that, once the news of the deaths leaked out."

"It was bound to happen eventually," Jade piped in philosophically. "It's actually good that it happened. We've learned so much from it, even though it's tragic that we had to suffer the deaths."

Ethan's eyes widened as he looked at Jade. How could she be so philosophical about it? She almost died. His reason to live almost died. He was distraught at what John might say next and looked at John again for him to continue.

John's eyebrows drew together, "We want you to lead the expedition again, Ethan, and Jade to support you. We know that you went through a lot last time and, believe me, I had a lot of soul searching to do before I agreed with the others to ask you. The others almost removed me from my position for being too emotionally involved. I can't guarantee that the same won't happen again. But then again, I can't guarantee that you won't get run over by a bus when you leave here either."

Jade looked at Ethan and back at John with pursed lips and blinking rapidly.

Celeste looked on with interest, taking in the seriousness of what was being asked with a natural expression. "I appreciate what it might mean to you Ethan. I have more respect for you than anyone I know. You went out on a limb and placed faith in me, when even I didn't think I could do what you were asking me to do."

Silence engulfed the room while everyone sat in their own thoughts, ruminating on the opportunity John presented.

Ethan stared into Jade's eyes. He couldn't go through what had happened on Chariclo again, but he also knew himself and how much he needed to be up there. He couldn't decide what to say, but realized he needed to talk to Jade in private. Turning to John, he said, "Can we have a few moments alone to discuss this?"

"Certainly. You can take as long as you like. I know it's a big decision for you. Come Celeste. Let's go get a coffee from the cafe," John said as he moved to leave the room.

"Sure," Celeste said. She stood and followed him out.

"Call me when you're ready," John said from the doorway before he closed the door behind him.

Ethan looked out towards the ocean sparkling in the near

distance. He saw waves lapping the beach and some adventurous children playing in the sand, some even splashing in the water. The calmness of the sea diametrically opposed to the turmoil going on in his head. He didn't want to turn to face Jade to discuss the issue, but knew he needed to. He just couldn't start the conversation.

"What are you thinking?" Jade asked eventually to break the silence. She too was looking out to the ocean outside.

Ethan sighed and looked down as he fumbled with his hands as a distraction, while he thought of what to say. He sighed again, "Watching you slowly dying on Chariclo was the worst time of my life. I have never experienced such emotion and pain. I didn't realize that a person could endure such pain. People talk about the excruciation of physical pain, but I now think physical pain is nothing compared to what I experienced there and yet..." Ethan turned to face Jade. He saw a tear slowing fall down her cheek.

Jade also turned. "And yet..." she asked, raising her brow as she wiped the tear away.

Ethan looked into Jade's eyes for a moment and then looked down and back up again, "And yet I can't get this bug out of me to see what's out there, not after doing the impossible by traveling faster than light, not after being the first to another planet outside our solar system. At the same time, I want to protect you and keep you safe. I can't have you coming with me."

Jade's mood changed instantly. "You're not going without me." Her forceful, powerful voice echoing around the room.

Ethan recoiled from her demand. He didn't know how to behave, how to tell her he couldn't have her there in danger, having to look over his shoulder with every move to make sure she was still safe. He pleaded. "You can't go. How can I protect you? What if the same thing happens? I can't go through what I went through before. It would kill me."

Jade jumped up from her chair, confronting Ethan and tapping her pointing finger on his chest. "Ethan Richards, if you think I'll sit here while you go out there risking yourself, you've got another thing coming. Do you think I don't have the same worry about you? Who's saying it's always me that gets sick, or injured and near death? Why do you think it's all right for you? You're being so selfish." She looked away and took a few steps, turning her back to him.

Ethan stood where he was, speechless. His heart twisted in agony, not just with the dilemma, but from seeing the vehemence of her rebuttal. He had never seen her so furious before. He didn't know what to do, what to say. "You know that's not true."

Jade twisted to give Ethan dagger eyes. "It is and you know it."

Ethan couldn't tolerate the penetrating stare twisting the blade of discord into him, so he looked away. They both stood in silence for several minutes, each not wanting to say anything for fear of escalating the argument, but each not wanting to give in either. It just struck him what his wedding vows meant. He could no longer just think about himself when deciding. He already knew he needed to share with the decisions in their lives, but he realized his carefree days were over, where he could do something on his own without really considering anyone else. They now had to decide together and live with that decision as one. Could he do that? He didn't know. Ethan finally realized they needed more time to discuss the request, he needed more time anyway. It seemed Jade had already decided. Could he, would he, sacrifice his dream of being among the stars for her? He didn't know. He didn't want to make such a choice, but he had to. "We need more time."

"I've made my decision."

He looked at her. "I need more time."

Jade's anger cooled slightly. "I can give you time to think about it, but will John?"

"We won't know unless we ask."

"Call him then."

Ethan gulped and pulled out his comm. "We're ready to talk."

Jade continued standing by the window while Ethan sat in a chair staring at the table, fiddling with his hands, trying to decide what to say.

John opened the door and stopped. Celeste almost bumped into the back of him. A flood of coldness poured out of the room. He warily continued entering the room and sat in a chair, Celeste doing likewise. "I take it that there's some disagreement?"

Jade turned to face him and Ethan, defiance and the hint of tears in her eyes.

"We need more time to discuss it," Ethan said, looking at the table.

John looked at Jade and Ethan in turn. "How much time?"

Ethan looked up at John. "Can you give us two days?" he pleaded.

"They can wait two days. Is there anything I need to clarify for you to make your decision?"

"No, this is between us."

"I'll wait for you to call me in two days then." Ethan saw John looking uncomfortable, as his eyes found it difficult to look at either of them, not knowing what to do now that the discussion was over, ending in such an inconclusive and unhappy manner. "Well, I think we'll leave you two to it then. Coming, Celeste?"

Celeste looked at Jade and Ethan. Ethan saw fright in her eyes as they blinked. It seemed she didn't know what she should do without their guiding hand. "Is there something I can do?"

Jade's expression softened. "No, it's all right. It's something we have to sort out ourselves. Thanks for asking. I think I need some shopping therapy. You want to come with me and Hugo?"

"Yes, I would."

"Let's go." Jade turned to Ethan, not sure what to do. Ethan started feeling hurt, not by her desertion, but by the fact she thought he would be hostile to her. He saw her decide and come over to him. She kissed him. "I'll see you later on. We can talk more then."

Ethan nodded. Jade and Celeste walked out, Ethan's eyes following Jade all the way until she disappeared from view.

John still stood in the room. "You OK?"

"Yeah, as I said, we need some time."

John left. Ethan felt isolated, as if they had boxed him into an enclosure he couldn't get out of. How could he reach for the stars and be at peace with Jade at the same time, protecting her? He knew she was a grown woman who could look after herself, but he couldn't help his protective instinct. Is this how a parent feels when they realize they have to let their child make their own way in the world? No. Ethan realized this was different. This was knowing how the two can be one being, but still permitting the other to make their own decisions within an envelope of love, and sacrificing for the sake of the other. He wasn't sure he was ready for such maturity. Did he have the strength of character for that yet? He sighed and left, walking out the door and going to the beach across the road, walking through the sand kicking slight puffs of it from time to time as he considered his morose thoughts, reaching no conclusion on what to do. He spent hours on the beach before returning home, having no energy for any work. Opening his tablet, he found a murder mystery novel he wanted to read and spent the rest of the day reading that.

Jade came home late afternoon. Her anger had abated, and she kissed him affectionately when she arrived, but they had little to say to each other. Neither wanted to continue the discussion, fearing it would end in the same standoff and animosity, not wanting the issue to come between them anymore that day. They had dinner and went to bed, the nervous tension of the day exhausting both of them.

5

PROPOSITION

Jade and Ethan woke up the next morning still uncomfortable with each other. Ethan knew they should talk, but he just couldn't drive himself to broach the topic. He didn't know what to say without getting into another argument, so they went about their morning chores and headed off to work as usual. Any productive work eluded Ethan though, as he sat at his desk feeling miserable and guilty. Was he being selfish? Was he wrong in wanting to protect Jade? He had to talk to someone. Picking up his comm, he contacted Hu.

"Hello, Ethan. I was not expecting a call from you. Is there anything wrong?"

"Hi Hugo, I was wondering if we could have lunch together."

"Sure. When and where?"

"Twelve. I'll send you the address."

"OK. See you then." He hung up.

Ethan knew he could talk honestly with Hu and maybe sort out the turmoil within him. Work still escaped him, but at least he felt a little better about things. Lunch time approached, so he set off for his rendezvous with Hu. He arrived slightly late, because of traffic, so Hu already sat at a booth in the cafe when he walked in. Hu looked up when he reached the booth.

"Hi Hugo. Glad you could come."

"I always help a friend, if I can. What seems to be the problem?"

"Let's order and we can talk then."

They looked at the menu and order what they wanted. Ethan looked at Hu afterwards, trying to find a way to start the conversation. "Jade and I have had an argument."

"Everyone has arguments."

"But I don't know what to do."

"Is this about your meeting with John yesterday? I thought Jade was a little quiet."

"Yeah, John asked us to go on another expedition. I want to go, but I don't want Jade to go. I don't want her to be in danger. She thinks I'm being selfish and unreasonable. Now I don't know how to talk to her about it."

Their lunch came, and they ate a little. Ethan saw Hu using the time to think.

"She has a point."

"Is it selfish to want to protect her?"

"Why do you want to protect her?"

"I don't want anything to happen to her of course."

"Is that the actual reason? Or are scared that you won't cope, if something happened to her? Are you afraid you will blame yourself if something happened? Every time my partner went away on one of his adventures, I worried so much that he wouldn't come back. I became ill with worry sometimes. And then he didn't come back, and they told me he was dead. I blamed myself for a long time. I thought, what if I had tried harder to stop him from going? What if I made him do something less dangerous? It didn't work. It just made me more miserable, because I knew it would have destroyed him, if I stopped him doing those things. That's why I didn't want to get into another relationship again. I didn't want the pain again. When John came along, I couldn't take the first step because of that. Then I realized I was only hurting myself. So I made the leap, and I haven't regretted it. Maybe something will happen. Maybe something will take him away from me. But I will be the better for having known him. I have grown because of him."

"What I am trying to say is, you can't protect people by preventing them from doing things. They will resent you for it. Jade is right. You are being selfish, but I understand why you are being selfish. I saw your pain on Chariclo. I related to that pain. That's why you need to let Jade go down the path she feels she must take. She wants to share your experiences together. Is that wrong? No. She loves you and I know you love her. Might something happen? Yes. You can't protect her by placing her in a padded cell, while you do something potentially dangerous. How would she feel if something happened to you? I know how she would feel. I didn't want to go do the things my partner wanted to do, and that was fine. But Jade wants to do this together. You need to take that risk, Ethan."

Ethan felt humbled by Hu's advice. He had no answer, no rebuttal, for what she said, because deep down he knew she was right. He chewed on his sandwich, thinking. "How do I talk about it with Jade?"

"Oh, grow up. You're a big man now," Hu said, a little too harshly.

Ethan went red with embarrassment from the reprimand. "You're a good friend."

"Thank you. You are a good friend too."

They talked more, as they ate, and left their separate ways to continue their day. Ethan arrived back at the office feeling better with himself. Hu had given him a perspective he would never have seen on his own or even with trying to discuss it with Jade. He just wasn't sure he could make the leap he needed to take. He called Jade.

"Hello Ethan."

"Hi. Do you want to go to Rubicon tonight?"

"... that sounds like a wonderful idea."

"Good, I'll make a reservation... and I'm sorry."

"Sorry for what?"

"Sorry for being me."

Jade laughed over the comm. "You are what I like, even if they're some parts I need to come to grips with."

"Well, anyway. I'll see you when I pick you up tonight."

Jade and Ethan arrived at Rubicon just after seven thirty. "Hello Leonard." Ethan said.

"Good evening, Ethan and Jade. It is good to see you both again. I have your table over by the window as usual." He led them to Ethan's favorite table.

They ordered the restaurant specialty, lasagna with a green salad to share and a bottle of red wine.

Leonard came over five minutes later with a bottle of wine in his hands, dust still on one side of it. He showed Ethan and Jade the bottle. "I know this isn't the bottle that you ordered, but I wish to offer you this one instead. The vintage is outstanding. I will only charge the same price as the bottle that you ordered. Consider it my wedding present to you."

"Why thank you," Jade said to him.

Leonard cleaned and opened the bottle, pouring a sample for Ethan and Jade to try.

They both took a sip. Ethan's eyes opened wide, "Wow, that is fantastic."

"I agree," Jade replied.

Leonard smiled. "You're welcome." He placed the bottle on the table and left.

Their meal came, and they ate. Ethan sat back as he completed his meal and picked up his glass to have another sip of the magnificent red. He felt sated, and it dulled his current troubles for the moment from the pleasure of the meal. He let the liquid linger in his mouth as the complex flavors penetrated his senses.

"You look like you're enjoying that," Jade said. They talked little throughout the meal with short retarded snippets of no real depth, because of the gulf between them created by their disagreement.

Ethan smiled. "There is only one other better than this."

Jade raised an eyebrow, "... being?"

"You."

Jade laughed. "Now you're trying to get on my good side. You know I love your compliments, but where is this leading?"

"Who knows," Ethan said with a mischievous grin. He felt himself relaxing slightly from the tension of the day.

The door to the restaurant opened to disturb the moment. A chill wind seemed to enter the restaurant, and Ethan looked up to see who it was. His mood instantly changed as he gritted his teeth when he saw the men as they came through the door.

"What is it?" Jade turned to see who Ethan looked at and why the person had soured his temper so. "Oh."

Loki Mason and Carson looked around and Carson pointed as Leonard came to do his duty. Ethan heard some muffled talking over the background din and music of the restaurant. Leonard stepped aside and allowed the two to continue with their business. They both casually walked over to Ethan and Jade.

"I am sorry to disturb you both, but I wish to have a word with you if I may," Loki said.

Ethan's temperature rose as he resented the presumptuousness of the man, "No, you may not disturb us, not now, not ever."

"Now let's be civil about this. I know we may not have met on the best of terms last time, but I wish to make amends, hopefully. I heard about your recent marriage. I congratulate you both. I wish to offer a small present for the occasion."

"You may not offer us anything, and I do not wish to talk to you."

Jade looked at Ethan, concerned, and reached out to place her hand on top of his to offer him support. "Let the man speak," she said, kindness in her eyes as she looked at him.

Ethan looked at Jade with anger momentarily and finally sighed. He couldn't refuse the look that Jade was giving him, and she knew it. "OK then," he said as he looked back up at Loki. "Have a seat and tell me what's so important that you have to disturb our dinner."

Loki grabbed a chair and sat across from Ethan and Jade. Carson stood to one side, a slight frown on his face. "May I?" Loki asked as he pointed to the bottle of wine sitting on the table.

"Feel free," Ethan replied sarcastically.

Loki picked up the bottle and looked at the label, "Very good choice, if I may say so. I have several dozen maturing in my cellar. I do not wish to deny you of the wine, but may I have a taste to see how this year has matured?"

"As I said, feel free." Ethan folded his arms.

Carson picked up a glass from an adjacent table and gave it to Loki, who poured a tasting quantity into it. He swirled the contents and sniffed the aroma before pouring the liquid into his mouth and running the wine over his taste buds with the movement of his cheeks before he swallowed. "That is exquisite."

"Say your piece and go," Ethan commanded.

Loki put the glass down and looked at Ethan with interest, "You are fired up, aren't you?"

"You had my friend murdered and then you tried to kill me and everyone on my ship."

"That is history. You must learn to move on. You will miss out on opportunities if you don't," Loki said, with a slight wave of his hand, although he studied Ethan's temperament intensely.

Ethan bit his tongue and waited for Loki to continue with whatever business he wanted to talk to him about. Jade sat, tense with one hand gripping Ethan's and the other gripping the table, looking at both Ethan and Loki.

"It's come to my attention that scientists on Chariclo have discovered a star map."

Ethan and Jade jumped in surprise. Ethan thought that piece of information was a secret. "How did you find that out?"

Loki chuckled. "I have my sources. Now that star map shows some connection with Tau Ceti."

Ethan sat stunned with his mouth open by the information Loki seemed to have gleaned.

"I see I am correct. Now, would it be too much of a leap to assume that you are about to undertake another expedition, this time to Tau Ceti?"

"Possibly...," Ethan replied. "What interest is that to you?"

"Extending the bounds of human knowledge always places one in a position to exploit opportunities, as they present themselves. This is what I wish to talk about. I understand that you dislike me personally, and that is fine by me. This is purely business. What I propose is for you to allow one of my people as a member of your team, so they can pass on information that may provide business opportunities, especially Xeno-tourism. There would be a financial recompense, of course."

Ethan's face grew redder as Loki revealed the scheme he was hatching. Jade squeezed her hand tighter to help him control himself. He slowly took several deep breaths before speaking, "This mission is not being financed by you, so you do not have any right to any information from it. I haven't committed to any mission yet anyway, but, if I were to go on it, I wouldn't want anyone from your organisation as a member of my team, especially after what happened the first time."

Loki looked put out as he leaned back in his chair, as if he was not used to being refused what he wanted. "I see." He thought for a moment. "I would provide some finance for the mission."

"That is nothing to do with me."

"I see."

"And, quite frankly, I would strongly object to any member being on the team backed by you with your interests, and not the interests of the expedition. The work is dangerous enough, as the last expedition proved, without conflict of interest issues arising about what needs to happen for the good of the expedition."

"The person would always have the interests of the mission at heart."

"No, they wouldn't. If it came down to a decision of whether to take the best interests of the team or the interests of your objectives, they would opt for your interests. That would be what they are being paid for, would they not?"

"I wouldn't instruct them to compromise anyone's safety or anything like that."

Ethan's eyes widened and sat back, "Like at Iapetus?"

"I may have been a little over-zealous then, but it all worked out for the best."

"Did it?" Ethan said, raising his voice. "You didn't get what you so desperately wanted to own, and I lost three people - murdered - by your daughter. One of them was my dearest friend. How did that work out for the best?"

Jade squeezed Ethan's hand slightly to make him aware of the volume of his voice, as others in the restaurant were looking in their direction. Ethan looked at her and gave a slight smile, calming down again. He looked back at Loki, waiting to see what he might still have up his sleeve.

"There may have been a better outcome but, as I said, that's in the past. As I see it, there are immense opportunities for the future, and I will be a part of it, one way or another. I may have to go there myself then."

Ethan laughed. "And how will you do that? Do you have a ftl ship tucked away somewhere?"

Loki thought for a moment. "You just may have given me an idea."

"What do you want to go there now for, anyway? It might be a gigantic waste of time and your money. Wouldn't you want to wait and see if there's anything worth exploiting first?"

"Sometimes you have to make your own luck and spend some money. There has to be something of significance there. The star map wouldn't point to it if there wasn't."

"It pointed to it two million years ago. Everything will have changed. Nothing might be there anymore."

"Let's find out."

"There is no way I'm taking you or anyone associated with you to Tau Ceti."

"Then you are going."

Ethan looked at Jade and back to Loki. "We haven't decided yet."

"Take one of my people with you. I'll give you whatever you want."

"You can't bribe me."

"I can see that there is no getting through to you, so I will leave you to the rest of your dinner." Loki glared his power at Ethan as he rose from his seat and prepared to leave. He tidied his coat and started walking off, but stopped after a step and turned back to Ethan. "I will get to Tau Ceti and I will get what I want. You will regret not taking up my offer." He turned again and walked out of the restaurant. Carson followed with no reaction to the encounter, although he turned his head to look at Ethan just before they left. He seemed to have a menacing smile on his face.

Ethan struggled to sit still in his chair. He looked at Jade, "Did that sound like a threat to you?"

Jade sat tense and upright, "I don't think so. He was just frustrated, I think."

Ethan saw she didn't really believe what she said, and he didn't either. He decided. "What do you want to do?"

"About what?"

"About going to Tau Ceti."

"I want to be where you are."

"Welcome aboard."

Jade smiled. "About time you came to your senses." She reached over and kissed him.

They stared into each other's eyes for some time after that, exchanging their emotions, connecting the two into the one that seemed so natural to Ethan, now that they had made up. They finally broke the mesmerizing instant and finished the wine.

"Are you going to get Celeste to pilot the ship?" Jade finally ask with a slight smirk.

"Gives me more time with you."

"That's not an answer."

Ethan laughed. "I'm sure we can share the duties. I think I'll still want the final say though. So yes, and no. She can pilot it, but I want to play with it too."

Jade burst into laughter at his almost childish response, as if they were discussing a toy Ethan had to share. "Just what I expected. But that's the man I married, and I love him." She reached over and squeezed Ethan's hand tenderly.

They rose and went home and to bed... and finally sleep.

Ethan called John the next day.

"Hi Ethan, have you decided then?"

"Yes, we have. We will both join the team."

"Good, I wasn't sure what I would do if you turned me down."

6

PREPARATIONS

Ethan busied himself in the mission office complex at JPL Laboratories in Pasadena, where his office sat amongst the multitude of others in the enormous complex of buildings. Jade had her office next door. He gave her a greater role in the expedition than previously, placing her in charge of the expedition planning and recruitment, a duty he detested, not that that was the reason he downloaded the responsibility. She was just better at it than he ever would be. He also made Celeste the Captain of *Destiny*, a responsibility she had already proved her competence in. She spent most of her time aboard *Destiny,* but was down on Earth to help him with the preparations. Ethan had contacted Marie, Max and Angelo for an expression of interest in resuming their responsibilities from the last time, and he was happy that they all agreed to join the team, although they hadn't arrived yet. They still needed to wrap up their existing responsibilities. John and Hu also occupied offices in the building as part of the preparations. Ethan wondered just how much the actual project required their near proximity. He didn't mind. They were both very dear and trusted friends.

Jade walked into Ethan's office, tablet in hand and a loving smile on her face. "Ready for the weekly meeting?" she asked.

Ethan looked up and marveled at Jade's radiant beauty. He thought her beautiful before, but marriage seemed to have added an extra shine to her features. "Almost, just wrapping up a few notes." He looked down again and spent a minute to complete his task before packing to leave, while Jade waited patiently. He rose, collected what he wanted and moved to her, kissing her lightly on the lips. "Missing you," he whispered afterwards, the touch of her lips on his sending a shock of pleasure through him.

Jade raised an eyebrow in surprised, but blushed with delight. "I'm only next door," she said teasingly.

"It's too far away."

Jade laughed. "We'd better go. What happened to keeping hands off at work?" she said, a mischievous look in her eyes as they sparkled.

Ethan sighed, "I couldn't resist, sorry." Jade sniggered, and he allowed her to lead the way out of the office, walking silently side by side down the hallway to the meeting room.

Hu and John already waited at the table in the conference room, which comfortably seated sixteen people. They huddled close together, murmuring.

"Not interrupting anything, I hope?" Ethan asked, a cheeky smile on his face as he entered the room.

Both Hu and John looked up innocently. "We have our minds on work occasionally," Hu riposted.

They all laughed.

"Did I miss something?" Celeste asked as she walked through the door and looked at the others.

They turned towards Celeste and burst into laughter again.

"No Celeste, nothing important," Ethan said.

Celeste smiled, a little confused, and sat down, setting her things on the table.

Ethan and Jade also sat.

The atmosphere in the room calmed to a more businesslike ambience as Ethan prepared to chair the meeting. "Well, let's get started then," Ethan said. "I'll let Jade give an update first."

Jade nodded. "On the recruitment side, both Max and Marie should be here next week. Angelo won't come on board this time until we are almost ready to depart, as everything needed in his area is still in place from the last voyage. I've been working through short-lists for the geologist, meteorologist and biologist and I am still to make a final selection. I want to give Marie a look through the list of biologists. She may know some people on the list and have a comment about them. At present it may take up to ten weeks to get everyone here. Any questions on that?"

Jade looked around the room.

"I'm glad Max is coming next week," Celeste said. "I want him to inspect the drives and organize any overhauls before we leave."

"Excellent idea," Ethan said. "We may need to speed things up on the personnel selection Jade, depending on progress in the other areas, but we'll look at that if it becomes an issue."

"Sure."

No one had any further comments or questions, so Jade continued. "Supplies for the trip are being requisitioned. I intend having a six-month stock of food and other consumables. We shouldn't be away longer than that. If we are, we'll have to bring them in through the wormhole." Jade flicked through her notes to see if there was anything else that she needed to report. "I intend having them here and loaded on *Destiny* in three or four weeks. That's it for me, I think."

"Any more questions for Jade?" Ethan asked. There weren't any. "Celeste, do you have anything new?"

"Not really. We've been on more practice runs in *Destiny*, but there have been no issues there. I have replaced a few personnel on the ship. Some existing crew wanted to change for various reasons. I've started investigating Tau Ceti, and any exoplanets identified in the system. They have identified four as orbiting the star, with two of them promising to be in the temperate zone. They have more mass than earth though, so I'm unsure what sort of gravitational strength they may have on the surface. Depends a little on their diameter and that is a little hard to tell from this distance."

"Have you worked out how long it will take to get there?" John asked.

"Unfortunately, at almost twelve light years away, about two months with *Destiny*."

Everyone groaned.

"What on Earth are we all going to do for two months?" Hu asked no one.

Ethan looked over at John and he looked even more upset. "You going to hold out for two months?"

John blushed. "I recall you having separation issues when Jade went to help on the moon."

"You didn't have to bring that up." Ethan looked down with a sheepish grin.

Celeste winced. "I could shorten it a little. I've tuned the ship up a bit and it can travel at almost 120c, if I push it to the limit. At least it will give us all time to get to know each other."

"You don't want to get to know me that well," Hu replied, fake daggers from her eyes.

"We need a faster means of travel," John said. "Maybe you should start looking at how to increase the output of the muon generator more, Ethan."

"Yeah. In my spare time. Let's get back on topic, shall we?"

"Well, that's all I have unless someone has a question," Celeste said.

Everyone shook their head so Ethan moved the meeting on to Hu. "Hugo, do you have an update on the wormhole portal we're taking with?"

"Yes, I do. It's fortunate we were already constructing another pair of portals. We intended replacing the existing ones for Chariclo with larger ones, but we will use these for Tau Ceti instead. Manufacture and trial assemble is progressing at present. The increased size of the aperture will allow *Destiny* to fit through this one. The timetable suggests that it will be ready for loading in six to eight weeks."

"What are you going to do at this end?" Celeste asked. "How will you synchronize any transfers from our end with ones from Chariclo?"

Hu shook her head. "It won't be an issue. We are building a separate portal at our end. We thought about it a lot and decided that it was simpler to do than having some kind of coding system, or other means of coordinating transfers. It wouldn't be acceptable to have two ships trying to arrive at the same time. *Destiny* can't fit through the Centauri portal, anyway."

"The timing seems in line with other things on our schedule then," Ethan commented. He pondered the revealed information for a moment, "John, do you have any comments?"

"No. It all seems to be coming together well. The military will have several landers standing by at this end waiting for you to establish the wormhole. We want a higher security level this time with more information flow in case something similar to Centauri happens."

"That sounds like a sensible move," Ethan said.

"Just something we discussed at length after the last expedition."

"Well, I think I'll rest more comfortably this time all the same. That seems to be it." Ethan paused for anyone to make any further comment, which they didn't. "Let's get back to it then."

Everyone packed up and rose to leave. Ethan and Jade walked back to their offices.

"Seems you've a bit to get through, if you're going to get these people selected," Ethan said. "Do you want a hand?"

Jade looked at him and sighed. "You must have been reading my mind."

Marie and Max arrived two weeks later, and the others welcomed them. They mentioned that they received celebrity status from their colleagues when they found out about their impending expedition. Marie had several of her staff begging her to include them. They got straight to work when they started, Max going up to *Destiny* to review the drives and power systems and Marie helping Jade select personnel, especially the biologist. Another four weeks passed before the new personnel came to the project for the first time and settled into their offices while still on Earth.

Ethan called a meeting to welcome the newcomers and looked around the room as he viewed the assembled people waiting patiently for him to speak. The familiar faces except Celeste were there; Jade, Hu, John, Marie, Angelo and Max, but three new faces now joined them. He prepared to greet them formally, although he had already met them. The meeting room buzzed with conversation, as small talk filled the air, and a general sense of nervous anticipation and excitement emanated from the recent arrivals to various degrees. Ethan allowed the chatter to continue a while longer, as he consulted Jade on an administrative matter. That decided, he raised his voice to the group, "Let's calm down and start our meeting shall we?" The others looked at Ethan and slowly complied until they all fell silent, waiting for Ethan to start proceedings.

Ethan slowly scanned the room before speaking, "This is the first meeting we are all together, except for Celeste, so I thought we would quickly introduce ourselves and familiarize us with the others in the group. So let's go around the table and make a brief introduction before we proceed. I'll start and we will go clockwise."

Ethan talked about himself for a minute, something he was unfamiliar in doing, and then Jade, Hu and John did the same. Ravi Dev, the geologist, sat next to John, so he spoke next in a soft deprecating voice, as if apologizing for having to talk about himself. "I grew up in India and lived a humble life. My parents sacrificed much for me. I have always been interested in geology and studied hard to get where I am. My parents are very proud of me. I knew Senna Jacobs well, and her death is a great loss to us all. I still have much to learn to have as much insight as her. My current activity before coming on this project included studying the interactions of the earth's core with the surface material, and how that might affect stability of the tectonic plates. I am very excited to study whatever we find in the Tau Ceti system. I only hope I meet your expectations." He bowed his head with humility.

John looked at Ethan, a questioning eyebrow raised.

"You don't give yourself enough credit, Ravi," Ethan said. "Your revelations have caused a lot of interest in the scientific community. I hope that you can continue your excellent work on this expedition."

A groan came from someone else in the room and Ethan looked around to find the source of the noise. It was one of the other new members, Pia Sanchez. She rolled her eyes in frustration at the deference circulating. Ethan fought back a smile. He had already read that she was fiery at times, and she wasn't disappointing with her subdued outburst. She saw Ethan looking at her and refrained from continuing her discord with the current atmosphere in the room.

"Let us continue," Ethan said.

Marie was next, and then another newcomer had his turn. Gerhardt Thiele spoke in a commanding voice and strong Germanic accent. "As you can tell, I am a proud German. I originate from the Black Forest region and educated in Munich university in biology and have progressed with substantial success. My primary field of interest is the interconnecting dependencies of organic species and the effect of environmental change on the balance. I have great importance in the field and am humbly proud of my achievement. I believe this to be the reason you have selected me for this mission and will be of great value to you all."

Ethan took another look at Pia. She almost gave a reaction, but refrained at the last minute, when she saw Ethan looking at her. A general air of disbelief hung in the room with Gerhardt's apparent arrogance. Ethan spoke, "I hope that you can provide what we need for us to achieve the results we want."

"I also hope that, Sir."

Gerhardt's deference momentarily caught Ethan off guard displayed, but recovered to gesture that the next person should continue, which was Max.

Pia's turn came next. She was an enigma to Ethan. She looked a placid, harmless sort of person, but a sense of fiery emotion lay hidden somewhere in her, waiting for something to spark it. A hint of it surfaced previously with Ravi and Gerhardt, but Ethan felt she could display much more, if something or someone set off the right chain reaction. Pia cleared her throat, "My name is Pia Sanchez. I was born in Barcelona, Spain and have specialized in meteorology, so I can contribute to the noble cause of managing our climate and stopping humanity from some of its stupidity." She stopped, face flushed with fervor, suddenly becoming self conscious, but continued, "... anyway, I am studying the effects of various environmental factors on our climate at the World Health Organization in Geneva, Switzerland. This is me... who I am."

The others in the group looked at Pia with interest and a couple had slight smiles on their faces as they took in the obvious passion she had for her work.

Angelo rounded up the introductions before Ethan took control of the meeting again. "I thank you all for volunteering to be on this expedition. I pray that it won't be as eventful as the last one. I'm sure that you have all updated yourselves on what happened. If you haven't, there is briefing material in your orientation folders. For the benefit of the recent arrivals, we are in the middle of preparations to ready the ship for departure. The date of departure is in four weeks and we have much to do before that. We all must ensure that we have everything that we need for our responsibilities on the expedition. Jade and I have pre-empted some of those needs based on what we took with last time but Ravi, Gerhardt and Pia, you need to check what we have placed on the lists and decide whether that is adequate for your needs."

The newcomers nodded, although Pia looked agitated about something.

Ethan saw her fidgeting, "What is it, Pia?"

She looked annoyed and there was a fire in her eyes, "No disrespect, but what do you know about what I need?"

Ethan jumped slightly in his chair at the challenge in her voice, "Well, we had a meteorologist on the last expedition who took certain pieces of equipment with. We have bought more of that equipment as it seems logical that we will need the same again."

"Yes, I know about David whatever his name is. He's a jackass. He knows nothing but forecasting."

Ethan started getting annoyed at Pia's attitude and looked directly at her, "That is why I asked for you to check what we have and to requisition whatever you consider is missing, but necessary."

"I will," Pia said, looking straight back at Ethan, but then left the discussion at that, lowering her head in silence.

The tense atmosphere that had surfaced in the room slowly dissipated back to a business level again. People asked and answered several other questions before the meeting broke up and everyone left except Ethan and Jade who sat looking at each other for a while.

"She's a fiery one," Ethan said.

Jade grinned in amusement. "She going to be too much for you?"

He huffed, "Not likely. You've taught me all the tricks you women play..."

"All the tricks women play..." Jade looked astonished at the comment.

Ethan blushed, "I didn't mean it like that."

"Well, what did you mean then?"

"Well, um... ah... oh, forget about it. I just meant that... well... I'm learning." Ethan looked down.

Seeing Ethan's embarrassment, Jade didn't torment him further, "Yes, you are and I appreciate it."

Ethan looked at Jade again, "Thanks. Still... she seems to get her heckles up easily."

Jade pursed her lips in thought, "Yes, but I'm sure she can control herself and stay professional."

"I hope you're right. I'm hungry. Let's go get something to eat."

"Let's."

They spent the next weeks completing arrangements for departure.

7

APEP AND GALENA

Apep rose from his bed early in the morning. He stretched and rubbed the sleep from his eyes. Looking over, he saw Galena still oblivious to the world and smiled. How life had changed for him once they had both opened up to each other. A frown momentarily touched his face, as he remembered his late wife of many years ago and the tragedy of her loss, both to him and the children. They had struggled through the grief the best they could, but life had somehow changed after that. If anything, he had grown closer to his children, but losing the intimacy and spark of love, that only two inseparable people could have, felt overpowering for a very long time. He had thrown himself into work afterward, work and caring for his children, until they grew up and started their own independent lives. Affection returned as he looked at Galena again. That spark had returned to him once they met and got to know each other. It felt different to the first time, but it was there and the closeness of enjoying it pleased him, also giving her so much that she had missed in her life. She told him often that she didn't realize a relationship, like she shared with him, could give her so much joy and happiness, even when things weren't going well. His thoughts turned back to the present and the responsibility of work, so he grudgingly went to the bathroom.

Darkness still held its tentacles on the day outside when he looked out the window. The days were lengthening, but a chill still lingered in the air from the winter they had just gone through. He completed his toiletry activities, got dressed and went to the kitchen to make breakfast before leaving for work. He thought about making some blini but decided to just have a kolbasa sandwich instead. He made some piping hot coffee too.

Noise emanated from the bedroom as he sipped his coffee and Galena emerged from the doorway moments later, sleep apparent in her sluggish steps and unkempt hair.

"Zolotse, why are you up?" Apep asked surprised.

"My warmth left me," Galena replied grumpily, scratching her hair as she shuffled to the table.

Apep chuckled. She always snuggled up to him at night, especially in last winter's cold. It was reassuring and comforting for him too, as he felt the warmth of her against him. "Come. Have a coffee with me before I leave."

Galena sat while Apep got up to get a cup and poured coffee into it. He brought it back and placed it in front of her. "Thanks."

"Nyeh zah shtoh." Apep sat down again. He spoke mainly English around Galena, but appreciated her taking the effort to understand some Russian.

Galena nodded in appreciation as she smelled the aroma of the coffee before taking a sip. She stopped and looked at him. "What are you doing today?"

"I hope today is big day for us. We finally conduct last test of hyper-drive. We hope to install in spaceship after test. See if can actually use to go anywhere."

Galena's eyes sparkled, "That's excellent. I hope it all goes well. I can still remember the excitement we felt when we first tested the warp bubble drive. You might impress Ethan and Hugo at last with another one of your big entrances."

Apep sighed in mocking exasperation, "Sweeping you into room on my arm is only entrance I ever want to make."

"Stop it, you're making me blush."

Apep finished his coffee and rose, taking his plate and cup to the sink. He came back to her, "I must go Zolotse, but I will see you tonight, yes?"

Galena giggled, "Yes you will." She leaned her head back so he could kiss her, which he did with just the right intimacy to have them both wanting more, but being able to part knowing that they will meet again later to decide what would come next. "See you tonight."

"Da." Apep walked out the door and to his vehicle to make the twenty-minute trip to the project offices at the secure compound near Serov in the Ural Mountains. As he had told Galena, the day was a big day for him and for Russia. It would herald, or not, Russia's place alongside America and China in faster than light space travel. Russia's approach had been the most ambitious, as their part in the three-pronged research into the technology. The coming day would prove whether they had spent their time and money wisely.

Apep felt envious of Ethan and Hu, being able to embark on journeys no one else in history had ever achieved. He was also pleased for them. They were both wonderful friends, and it was a great honor to him to have been a groomsman in Ethan and Jade's wedding. He chuckled to himself as he remembered being paired with Hu, the two troublemakers of the trio, and the schemes of mischief on the day they had discussed, much to Ethan's consternation.

He arrived at the facility and hurried the distance from the cold outside air in the carpark to the complex that housed his project, and other highly secretive activities that even he wasn't aware of. As strategic as his project was for Russia and humanity, it wasn't particularly secret, bearing the same level of cooperation as the American and Chinese projects had. They all had their little secrets, as anyone would, but the end results were overt, as agreed to by the respective governments at the time of embarking on the three-prong approach. Apep, and in turn, Russia, hoped that the results of the day's tests would make the hyper-drive the one of choice for long-distance space travel. It was the most ambitious project of the three and required the greatest concentration of power to achieve the breakthrough. It had its struggles early on, but, especially once the sabotage had ceased, it had progressed at an accelerating pace since.

After leaving his belongings in his office, he walked to the testing laboratory where the others on the team assembled, preparing for the hopefully last test. "Welcome to you all," Apep said cheerfully. "Let us make this a momentous day, yes?"

"Yes indeed," Alexi Stenanko, the chief engineer, agreed. "We can then both sleep better."

"Ah Alexi," Apep commiserated. "We have had our troubles along the way, yes, but imagine the leap forward we will achieve today."

Alexi looked tired and in need of time doing something other than working on the project. Apep felt for him. He had put his all into the work at the expense of time with his family and, at times, his health. His family had stayed with him, despite not seeing him for days on end sometimes, surprised Apep, and he appreciated it. He was concerned for Alexi, as he always was. He was a good man. "Alexi, a successful test today and I do not want to see you for a week, no arguments."

Alexi gave a wan smile of appreciation, "Thanks." He went off to start the test. The equipment sat in the middle of the laboratory on supports constructed to hold the drive and insulate it from the surroundings. The test was simple. Send the drive, with a mouse attached in a self-contained survival sphere, in a circular spacial loop and clock the time of travel. An odometer on the drive would tell them the distance it traveled. Divide the distance by time and they would know if they succeeded. The test would last the blink of an eye unless something went wrong. The drive would enter the fifth dimension, reappear some place else, confirm its surroundings with the monitoring equipment it carried, and return.

"OK. We are ready," Alexi said, nervous in anticipation.

Apep walked up to him, slapped him on the shoulder and said, "Let's do it."

Alexi flipped the switch to start the drive up. A rumbling noise began and rose in pitch and intensity until it almost deafened everyone. All but a memory and echo of the sound stopped for a moment and then returned before the drive powered down and the noise abated to silence again.

Apep didn't realize it, but he had been holding his breath, and let it out when Alexi confirmed that the drive had traveled faster than light, and the mouse still lived, and didn't seem to have noticed its pioneering achievement.

"How much faster?" Apep asked. "Is it what we had programmed into the test?"

Alexi sat at the tablet screen looking at the results that the drive had transferred to it. He performed a few calculations, a frown of concentration on his face. A smile appeared moments later as he looked at Apep, "Looks like I get my week off."

Everyone in the room cheered, and Apep slapped Alexi on the shoulder again in congratulations. Alexi rose and gave Apep a hug, tears in his eyes as the exhilaration of the success sank in. They both went around to the others and hugged each, acknowledging their efforts in bringing about the momentous event.

Apep quietened the group down. "This is a momentous occasion. We will all celebrate tonight in the hotel. I will pay. Enjoy your success, but remember your families too, who have suffered much for what we have done. If anyone wants a week off, put in the form and I will grant you the leave. I do not want anyone contacting the project under any circumstances until they return. Your families need you now, so give them as much as you have given this project."

Everyone cheered at the invite and the offer. Apep could see many exhausted faces in the room, although none would have admitted it, if he asked. People started filing out and tidying up, leaving Apep and Alexi alone thinking their own thoughts for a moment.

"Thank you," Apep finally said, looking at the drive, but directing his gratitude to Alexi.

"Thank you, Apep. I couldn't have lasted or taken the grueling punishment of the long hours without your support, and I know how much you have kept from me, from us, to shield us from your superior's demands and frustrations. Will you take time off too?"

"I did nothing, Alexi. I did what any good project manager would do. No, I will work through. Someone has to keep things running. But don't have pity for me. I take it easy, I think. Not blow any gasket."

Alexi smiled and chuckled at the remark, "Yes. Not blow gasket."

"Let's tidy things up and go celebrate."

They spent some time recording the results and packing things away. Apep went off to his office to inform his superiors of the success of the test. He spent the rest of the day approving leave and catching up on administrative matters, before joining the others at the hotel for the celebrations. He sent a message to Galena earlier not to wait up, as he would be late.

Apep stumbled into his house in the early hours of the morning, having had someone from the facility drive him home in his state of intoxication. He swayed into the bedroom and somehow undressed and slumped into bed.

"It was a successful test then?" Galena asked, waking up from the noise of his entrance.

"You could say that," Apep slurred before he started snoring.

Galena smiled as she shoved Apep to roll over, so he stopped his snoring, draped her arm over him and went back to sleep.

8

EXPLOSION

Hu spent her time reading on the shuttle back to the moon. She missed John more with every kilometer and minute that separated her from him. It was an odd feeling for her, one she hadn't felt for so long. She knew the feelings from before though, and that unnerved her. She didn't really believe that someone could replace the partner she had lost, but maybe John could, or at least provide a similar feeling of union of the soul. She sighed. Only time would tell. One thing that she knew was that her feelings for John were strong and getting stronger. Looking out of the porthole to change her thoughts, she saw the sun flaring through the heavily tinted glass, reducing the radiation to a safe level. The blue, brown, green and whiteness of the Earth also shone, still just visible in the bottom left corner of the porthole. The people on the Chinese moon base had advised her a few days before that the two portals for the Tau Ceti wormhole were almost ready for testing, so she had to return to the moon to lead the commissioning of them.

The shuttle docked at the base several hours later, and Hu disembarked, dashing to her quarters. She felt tired and sluggish though, a sign for her to perform an intense workout in the gym. Quickly changing in her quarters, she headed straight there and started her exercises, finishing with her usual kick boxing routine with the punching bag. Bending over in exhaustion after half an hour at the bag, she smiled with satisfaction at her effort. She thought she may have been a little more out of practice than what she was, since she hadn't kept up her exercise schedule as religiously as she usually did, while back on Earth. She smiled, *maybe other activities were a good substitute*. Wiping off the perspiration, she went to the change rooms and went through her tai chi routine before returning to her quarters to shower and change into working attire.

Half an hour later, she walked into the wormhole portal control centre set up on the moon. "How's everything going, Liang?" she said, seeing him at the console reviewing information on the screen in front of him.

Liang looked up. "We managed to drag you away for your lover then?" he said, a quirky smile on his face. He had been formal and reserved in his conversations with everyone at the start of the project, but Hu, and especially Jade, when she came to review the wormhole theory with him, had gotten him to loosen up a lot and not take everything so seriously.

"Ha! We should have let you stay the way you were. You're impudent to your superiors now."

They both chuckled before settling down to serious work. "We're just about ready to power up the first portal," Liang said.

"Had any problems?"

"No. The manufacture went without a hitch. We removed most of the bugs from the design during the production of the first two."

Hu sat at a spare console and brought up the screens for the portal Liang was commissioning. She reviewed the settings and energy levels Liang had brought the portal up to so far. She was impressed. It all seemed to go smoothly. Maybe she could get back to Earth sooner than she expected... Stopping in mid-thought, she realized what she was saying to herself. She had changed so much. Before her relationship with John, she would have buried herself in her work and not have let anything interrupt her. Now her priorities seemed to change slowly. She smiled. *For the better*. Removing her personal considerations from her mind again, she returned to the job at hand and started coming up to speed with Liang.

Twenty minutes later Liang said, "I think we are ready to place some power into the ring."

Hu checked the readings on her displays, "I agree. You want to power it up?"

"OK, then." Liang straightened himself at being given the honor. He initiated the start sequence and green lights came on the screen, as each step completed successfully. Lights came on at the portal and Hu felt a sense of anticipation as each ring segment glowed green on the screen one by one.

With two-thirds of the portal powered up, the next segment to come online seemed to delay initiation of its sequence, and the power level in the segment increased dangerously until it spiked. A flash of light emanated from the part, as an explosion released the pent-up energy. The portal sequence shut down. The excitement immediately left Hu, and the adrenaline drained away, as she studied the cause of the failure.

"That's disappointing," Hu said, reviewing the readouts on her screen to make sense of the mishap.

"Yes, I don't understand. Everything was double checked."

Liang looked worried, as if it was his fault when Hu looked at him. "Don't worry. The same thing happened to me at Alpha Centauri, when we first powered up the portal there. Although I would have thought the technicians would have especially checked those connections this time." Hu looked back to her screen before standing, "I'll go out and find out what damage there is and why this happened."

"I'll come with you."

"No, I need you here in case I want you to change some settings."

"OK, take a technician with you then."

"I will." Hu walked out of the control room and headed for a construction shuttle to take her to the portal. She organized a technician as she walked there, and they met when she arrived. The shuttle left with them on board and arrived at the portal thirty minutes later.

Suiting up, they entered the airlock with tools and a tablet that had the design stored on it. They closed the inside hatch, depressurized and opened the outside hatch, floating out into space. The hatch closed again. The portal rotated slowly close to where they floated, its outline reflecting light from the sun. They jetted over to it and attached their magnetic clamps, so they wouldn't accidentally get thrown out into space. Hu and the technician circled the portal with slow deliberate steps on the steel surface, inspecting it as they went, until they came to the damaged segment.

There was substantial destruction, but it looked mostly superficial to Hu on initial inspection. She pulled up the design for the segment on the tablet and checked the equipment for error or damage. The connections seemed to be as the design intended, so both Hu and the technician couldn't work out why the segment had malfunctioned. Hu finally decided to power up the segment again to see if that would shed any light on the problem. "Liang, are you there?" she asked over the comm unit.

"Receiving."

"Can you power up segment seventeen to minimum power? We can't see what the problem is. I hope that putting some power onto it will provide some information. Watch the power levels from your end too."

"You think that's wise? You saw what happened last time."

"It had a lot more power then. I don't intend placing that much power into it."

"OK then. Powering up now."

Seconds later Hu measured the electrical current flowing through the portal segment with the instrument she connected. She tested several other sites but found no anomalies. Frustration set in as she tried to work out the source of the problem. She paused for a moment to think. "Liang, can you set the power level to ten percent?"

"OK." Seconds later, "Ten percent."

Hu started testing again.

"Get out of there now," Liang shouted over the comm. "The power is spiking again."

Hu and the technician disconnected their magnetic tethers and tried to scramble away with their jet thrusters, but the portal exploded again. Hu and the technician rode the wave of radiation from the explosion. The force of the blast dislodging several parts that collided with both of them. Hu blacked out.

JOHN SAT IN ANOTHER MEETING, another one he wished he could avoid, but couldn't. He marveled at the inefficiency of so many meetings to get things done, but who was he to question the chain of command. He played with his pen, as he usually did when bored, and watched as an aide came into the room and circled around the table towards his side. His eyes followed the aide until he stood behind him and bent over to whisper, "Comm from the Chinese on the moon, Sir. They are asking for you." John raised his brow. He shrugged. It would at least let him get out of the meeting for a while. He bent over to his commanding officer and whispered his apologies, before standing and following the aide from the room.

"Office over there, Sir."

"Thanks," John said, as he went to the office. He entered and closed the door. Sitting at the desk, he pressed the 'Connect' button on the comm to make voice contact with the Chinese. "General John O'Conner here. How may I help you?"

"Jian here. I'm on visual if you want to change."

"Oh." John switch to visual and saw a worried Jian on the screen. He braced himself for something, but didn't know what.

"We have had an accident commissioning our portal today, I'm afraid. I... um... Hu has been injured. She had you on her emergency call list... at the top. You and Ethan. I will call him next."

John opened his mouth to speak, but nothing came out. He didn't know what to think, what to say. He didn't understand the turmoil inside of him. He had never experienced the particular feeling of dread before now. "How... bad is it?" he finally got out, his face turning white.

Jian looked down and then back at the screen, "I don't really know yet, except that it is very serious. We don't have comprehensive medical facilities here. We are emergency evacuating her and another back to Earth for treatment. I will send you the details of where she is when she gets back there. I had better go. I have more calls to make. It hasn't been a good day."

"Yes... sure. Thanks."

"I didn't realize you mean so much to her. Keep your spirits up. She is a fighter."

"Thanks."

The screen went blank, leaving John unable to move. He could feel his heart tearing apart in disbelief. His mind swirled with so many thoughts he couldn't keep track of what they all were. Why did he feel such devastation, such a sense of impending loss, such a need to be with Hu, as an iron filing is drawn to a magnet? His emotions were moving too fast for him. Sitting where he was, time went by for ten or fifteen minutes, he couldn't tell, before his personal comm buzzed. He took it from his pocket and saw Ethan's name on the display. Indecision about answering it crushed him, but he eventually took a large slow breath to release the built up tension. Pressing the button for visual, he said, "Hello Ethan. I guess you've heard."

"Yes. How are you feeling?"

"I don't really know. I'm lost. I can honestly say, that for the first time in my life, I don't know what to do."

"Go and see her, John."

"But..."

"But nothing, I'm coming with you as soon as we know where she is. Don't be an idiot. You know what you're feeling and you know why. Just admit it and move on. She needs you now."

"But..." Tears started dripping from John's face. "But what if I never see her again?"

"Let's hope that you do. She's strong. I don't know how serious her injuries are, but, if anyone can pull through, she can."

"Yes, you're right." Normal functioning returned to John, as his mind started planning what he needed to do. "I'll start making arrangements."

"Jian said that she should be back on Earth in three hours now, so we should know where she is in about five hours."

"Ok, I'll get us transport into China. Be ready to get picked up."

"I will."

"See you soon." John disconnected, but he still couldn't raise himself from the chair he sat in. His muscles eventually responded, but he felt like an old man who had to use all his strength to overcome the pain of standing up. He moved to go tell his commanding officer he needed to be relieved from duty.

THE TRAVEL ARRANGEMENTS had John and Ethan standing in the Shanghai hospital waiting for news of Hu twenty-four hours after Hu's arrival. She spent most of that time in the operating theater. Worry plastered John's face as he impatiently waited for news. He looked at Ethan and saw he wanted to help him. He patted Ethan's shoulder to let him know he was OK. John continued pacing the floor, waiting.

A doctor came toward them, momentarily looking at his notes. "Is one of you Mr. John O'Conner?"

"I am," John said.

"Ching Hu is in recovery in intensive care. She is very lucky to be alive. She has regained consciousness of sorts and is asking for you. She is in a somewhat delirious state, but the fact that she is calling for you is significant. It means that you are very important to her and her brain function is returning. I can let you see her for a moment."

John nodded. He looked at Ethan and saw he was anxious to see Hu too.

The doctor, looking at Ethan, said, "I'm sorry. I know you want to see her, but she is too weak to see more visitors at the moment."

Ethan nodded in disappointment. "I'll wait here," he said to John.

John followed the doctor into the intensive care area and went into Hu's room moments later. John silently entered and stood at the foot of the bed looking at the person who he now realized meant so much to him. Her face remained uncovered and looked uninjured, but the rest of her body looked badly mangled in the accident. Healing wraps covered every limb and significant areas of her body. He gasped in shock.

The noise disturbed Hu, and she stirred. Opening her eyes, she looked around and eventually saw John standing nearby, "You came." She said, her voice hoarse and weak. She tried to give a smile, but failed.

John smiled, "Yes, I came. Save your strength so you recover. Ethan is here too." He moved to the side of the bed and saw her left hand uncovered and apparently uninjured, so he held it gently in his and rubbed it softly, as he gave her a worried smile.

Hu watched him intensely. "I was so careless," she finally said.

"I don't know what happened and at the moment it doesn't matter. All I want is for you to recover."

Hu tried to nod, but grimaced in pain instead. "Say hello to Ethan." The energy seemed to drain away from her suddenly, as she slumped back in the bed.

John saw her exhaustion, "I'll go now. Rest. I will return tomorrow."

Hu coughed before she whispered, "You look OK in your civvies."

John laughed, "Yeah. Thanks for the compliment." She always said that when she teased him. He let go of her hand. "See you tomorrow." He turned to walk out, but turned back to her. Bending over, he gave her a tender kiss on her forehead. Hu's eyes opened momentarily, contentment and a slight smile appeared. He turned again and walked out, still worried for her.

John returned to the reception area and Ethan, who waited impatiently for some news. He asked, "How is she?"

"Not good. She's beat up quite a lot, but she's strong and fit. She'll pull through."

Ethan could see John's worry, "You think?"

John looked away, "I don't know. But I know what I truly feel about her now."

9

AT LAST

Apep stood watching on the video monitor, as the technicians worked on the last of the connections for the Hyper-drive, transferred from the test centre to the specially built ship for the project. He felt proud of the achievement, despite the enormous time taken for the Russians to get to that stage. "How are things looking?" he asked Alexi, who stood next to one technician.

"Good. We're almost ready to commission the drive. A few hours and we might be ready to test it out and go somewhere."

"I hope so. It will be such an achievement, don't you think?"

"Yes, it will. Maybe I'll get to spend some proper time with my family again."

Apep chuckled. Alexi had worked like a draught horse, more so than anyone, to make the hyper-drive work. "You will deserve it. I'll see what I can do to make sure it happens. A week isn't enough."

"Thanks. How is your friend doing?"

"Hu?"

"Yes."

"Mending. She will take a long time to heal from what others tell me. Tragic. I hope she recovers quickly. She is strong."

"That's good. I had better see how things are going." Alexi went off to another area of the ship.

Apep went back to his office and did some paperwork, which never seemed to have an end to it. He put down his stylus after two hours and rubbed his eyes, as he turned to look out of the window while he thought. His spirits warmed as he realized his fortunate circumstances. The Russian project finally showed results after so much heartache. He remembered times when he felt like giving up and telling his superiors likewise, but when he looked at all the people working so hard towards the goal, he relented and had to appease his superiors a while longer. The faith they placed in the team was finally paying off. His thoughts changed direction as the image of Galena entered his mind. He sighed in wonder. Apep thought he would never find another woman like his late wife again, but he did. Galena was nothing like her, but that was what attracted him to her, and his children instantly warmed to her too, which he appreciated immensely. He straightened slightly. Maybe he still had that infamous Chernakov charm, as his late wife always used to say. It attracted Hu completely differently, with hilarious results at times. His thoughts drifted to Hu's accident and he willed her to recover as he sat at his desk. He so dearly wanted to see her again and see the mischievous eyes he remembered so well.

A knock on the door brought him out of his reverie. "Comrade Chernakov. The ship is ready for the test," an aide said.

Apep jumped in his chair and looked around semi-dazed for a second before the present returned. "Oh... OK... I'll be there in a moment."

The aide disappeared and Apep tidied his desk, to make sure he securely locked away the confidential correspondence on it, before he rose and followed the aide to the control centre in an adjacent building of the project base.

He entered the control centre and frowned as the people there came to attention, one or two of them saying, 'Welcome Comrade Chernakov'. He thought he had drummed the formalities out of them over the years. Maybe the significance of the occasion brought the habit back to them. He nodded and walked to the chair designated for him.

"Ready for departure," Alexi said over the audio comm system from the ship.

"Go with my blessing," Apep said, "and come back in one piece. You still have a lot of living to do, and a family to support."

"Yes Comrade," came over the speaker, and the tone of the words suggested a chuckle behind them. "Take us out, Captain."

Apep saw the ship move from the parking position at the Russian docking facility in Earth orbit. It ambled at first as it distanced itself from the bustle of space in the area. Once in open territory Apep heard, "Engaging Hyper-drive." The ship disappeared from their screens. The plan intended the ship to travel ten light years distant from Earth, take a recording of the view of space from there and return, scheduled to take half an hour. They needed most of the time to record where they traveled to. The view would be like that from Earth, but different enough to prove that the ship had traveled there. Unfortunately, the ship was incommunicado whist in Hyperspace, until they could develop a technology to provide it, and any transmission from their destination would take the normal flat spacetime interval to travel back to Earth, making the ship blind to anyone there. Any mishap would take maybe ten years to confirm on the assumption that the ship had traveled ten light years, and not ten thousand.

Apep rose from his chair and paced the floor while he waited, the tempo in the steps increasing as the time neared for the ship's return. The allocated half hour ticked over and Apep stopped his pacing, eyes glued to the screen, waiting for any sign of a ship in one piece. The ship reappeared about thirty-seconds after the scheduled time, and Apep gave a relieved sigh at seeing it.

"*Gagarin*, reentering spacetime and returning to dock," Alexis said, with an excited smile.

"Welcome back. I'll be waiting for the de-brief," Apep said, a smile on his face too. "At last we have the result we aimed for." A buzz of success reverberated throughout the control centre as they all clapped and hugged each other.

Apep booked himself on a plane to Shanghai the next day, his duties on the project either completed or delegated for the week. He anxiously wanted to see Hu. Reports showed that her recovery proceeded well, but he wanted to see for himself and give her any moral support that he could. He entered the hospital at ten the next morning and found his way to the ward Hu recuperated in. Being visiting hours, he gained entry with an empathic smile from the nurses on duty as he passed them. "Where is Ching Hu?" he asked at the nurse's station.

The attending nurse looked at her notes, "She should be in the repatriation lounge. She has just completed her physiotherapy for the day. It is the third door on the right."

"Thank you," Apep replied with an enticing smile, which the nurse took an instant liking to. He chuckled to himself, *I've still got the charm.*

He walked the distance and turned into the room. Several people sat there, one or two looking at the holovision and a couple reading. He saw Hu instantly, but she faced away from him. He walked a little closer and then whispered, "Hugo." The body froze at the sound of his voice. It seemed to want to turn, but couldn't. Apep rounded the chair, and he faced her, a sentimental smile on his face, "Partner in crime."

A slight smile appeared on what looked like a very tormented face. "Apep," Hu whispered.

He saw a vacant chair next to her and gestured to it, "May I?"

Hu nodded.

He sat and looked at Hu again, studying her for a moment. "You look troubled."

Hu looked down to compose her emotions and then back at Apep, "Look at me. I am broken. All because of my foolishness, my belief I was indestructible."

Apep felt deeply for her and the situation she faced. He sighed. "We all break eventually. Look at me. I am no longer a good advertisement for the human species. My joints are aching, I no longer move like I used to, and I'm certainly not a paragon of physical shape. Some have more acute challenges in that respect, when something unexpected happens." He reached across to place his hand on hers and pointed to his heart with his other hand, "But it is what is in here that is important. The human spirit. That is what grows in beauty as we grow, and nothing can take that spirit away from us, unless we allow it to be trampled on and discarded."

Tears rolled down Hu's face as she looked into the sincerity of Apep's eyes, "You bastard." She wiped the tears away with her free hand and smiled a smile almost like Apep remembered. "You are incorrigible."

Apep smile too, "I know. Anyway, I still need someone to assist me in waking the world up now and then with our little schemes. Galena just doesn't have that spritely mischief."

Hu laughed.

A nurse stood nearby watching the interchange between the two and smiled when Hu laughed. "At last," she said.

HU RECOVERED her determination after Apep's talk to her. She had sunk into a pit of despair that no one seemed to be able to bring her out of. Not even John, who visited her as often as he could get time off away from his duties. She could see his frustration and confusion, but could do nothing to allay his sorrow for her and, because of her, himself. She had almost told him to stay away but couldn't. She sensed that she needed his support and, if she rejected that, she would sink even deeper into her depression. She smiled as she recalled Apep's talk again. Only he could say what he said and make it into almost a game that she just had to play with him. Only it wasn't a game. It was serious. It was life. And Apep knew it, and he knew what spark Hu needed to rekindle the flame that she had lost.

Her body perspired heavily as she concluded her daily physiotherapy routine, now with determination. She panted as the therapist came over, "That was quite a workout. The best I've seen from you so far. I'm impressed."

"It's amazing what a gentle kick up the butt can do to get someone refocused," Hu replied, as she reached for a towel to wipe her face.

"Keep it up, but don't overdo it just yet. You need to regain your strength gradually."

"I won't," Hu agreed, as she considered the effort she had just put in, and made a mental note of it. The therapist walked away with a departing nod.

Hu wanted to get back to her room and shower promptly, ready for John's impending arrival that day. He hadn't been since her talk with Apep, and she wanted to surprise him with her change in attitude. She wanted to look as special as she could for him too.

John came into her room several hours later, a frown of unhappiness on his face, and stopped mid-stride. The change in Hu was obvious as she looked at him with an enchanting smile, the first genuine smile he had seen from her since the accident. The frown instantly vanished, "Am I in the right room?"

"Yes you are," Hu replied. "Do you like what you see?"

"I... you... I don't know what to say... yes, yes, I like what I see, but..."

"What changed?"

John nodded as he sat down in the only available chair in the room. Hu sat in the other one, a pair of loose-fitting pants and top elegantly covering her body in style and almost a sense of sensuality. The nurses had helped her get the clothes over the preceding days.

"I had a visit from Apep since you saw me last, and he told me the facts of life, as only Apep can. He reminded me of what is important."

"Well, I owe Apep."

"We both do."

John rose from his seat again and bent over Hu, kissing her gently on the cheek first, and then on the mouth with a little more firmness before he broke off and sat again.

"I would ask you how you are, but it's obvious. Welcome back. I missed you." He looked away momentarily, the hint of a tear in his eyes.

"I am a long way from what I was, but I know where I want to be now, and it is refreshing to have the demon possessing my soul out of me."

"Good." John looked at her. "I thought I had lost you. We had grown close before your accident, and every visit has been harder and harder to make, as I saw you become more distant from me each time. I... was about to give up. The only things that kept me coming to see you were my feelings for you and my hope that you would snap out of your depression."

"John," Hu said. "I know where I have been, and I know that I didn't realize the toll on the people around me especially on the ones that matter. It has been rough. It is not an excuse. This is over. I am back." Hu looked away momentarily while she thought about what she was about to say. Turning back to him, she said, "I love you."

A radiant smile broke on John's face, "I love you too. I only realized how much when I received the call about your accident."

They both looked at each other for what seemed like an eternity until a knock on the door portal broke the spell.

"Is this private conversation or can anyone come in?" Apep asked, beaming with a wide smile.

Hu and John looked at each other momentarily and Hu said, "It was private, but we might make an exception for a special friend."

Apep straightened himself at the compliment with a twinkle of mischief in his eyes, "I should hope so. There is still much work we must do, Hugo. You cannot get out of it with this pretence of incapacity."

John looked on in disbelief at the supposed insensitivity of the remark, but Hu burst out laughing, "Oh Apep. What am I going to do with you? You always make me want to strangle you and hug you at the same time."

Apep stood where he was, indecisive and fidgeting about what to do next, "Well... I could use that hug. I return to Russia today and just wanted to say goodbye before I left."

Hu smiled radiantly, "Come here, you big bear."

Apep moved over to Hu and they hugged with strength, a tear trickling down Hu's cheek. Hu pulled away, but still held him, "Thank you so much. You have always known me and known how to get me out of the moods I get myself into. You are a great friend, and I am lucky to have you. Look after yourself and I hope to see you soon. Say hello to Galena."

Apep acted affronted, "What? No more strutting with you, making trouble wherever we go?"

Hu and John laughed. "Never say never," Hu said.

"Yes. Never. I hope you recover quickly, but now I must go."

"Goodbye," Hu said.

"Say hello to Galena from me too," John added.

Apep nodded and left.

"He is an incredible person," John said to Hu.

"Yes, he is," Hu said, gazing out the doorway that had contained Apep moments earlier.

John stayed another week before he had to return to his duties in America.

Hu made amazing progress physically in her recovery in that time. Her mental state also returned to its steely strength. She was sad when John had to leave, sadder than she had felt in a long time. She made it her goal to go to America when she was fit enough to travel.

Sitting in the recreational area of the rehabilitation section of the hospital two weeks later, continuing her recuperation, she looked up from her reading, surprised, but quickly smiled. "Jian, what are you doing here?" She saw his tentative approach.

Jian walked towards her and stood in front of her. "I thought it about time I visited you." He leaned over and kissed her on the cheek, something Chinese rarely did, but Hu appreciated it. He also gave her a bouquet of roses, the scent filling the room with its pleasant sweetness.

"Oh Jian, they are beautiful. Is this a peace offering?" Jian went red, unable to answer her. Hu suddenly realized he blamed himself for her injuries. "It's OK. I don't blame you. If anyone's to blame it's me. Come sit with me." Hu pointed to the adjacent chair next to her.

Obeying Hu, Jian sat. "It is difficult being responsible and I should have seen you sooner. I have been fearful to come and guilty for what happened."

Hu placed the flowers on the small table next to her. "Well, you're here now. It's difficult to get time away, I know. I appreciate what you have done for John. It would have been much more difficult for him visiting me without your approval."

"The least I could do. You look like you mend well?"

"Yes. I had a visit from a friendly Russian to kick my butt, and I've been improving ever since."

Jian smiled. "I heard about that."

"How?" Hu asked, surprised.

"I receive reports on your progress. I understand you had many issues early on."

"Yes, I was in a dark place until he came along. Anyway, that's enough about me. How is the project going? Did Liang find out the problem with the portal?"

"They fit a wrong capacitor to that segment, an old smaller one by mistake. Liang has commissioned the portal successfully. I came straight here after that. They are busy disassembling it at present."

"That's good. I always knew Liang could commission it. He just needs pushing sometimes."

They sat in silence for a moment, each in their own thoughts. "When will they discharge you?"

"Soon, I hope. I still want to go with."

Jian frowned. "Is that a good idea? You will still be recovering."

"I just need to be fit enough to join them when *Destiny* comes to pick up the portal. I will have two months to get my fitness back fully. Besides, I'll die of boredom, if I have to sit around here much longer.

There are only so many books someone can read and doing nothing else."

Jian chuckled and shook his head. "You always couldn't sit still for more than five minutes. Won't someone miss you though?"

Hu went red. "We'll be able to communicate once we establish the wormhole."

"Oh." Jian nodded.

Hu leaned over and hit him lightly on the shoulder. "Don't tease me."

They both laughed. They sat and talked and laughed for some time. Jian got some coffee and brought it back, continuing the conversation where they left off. Time passed quickly, and Jian finally had to leave.

"Thank you so much for coming to see me. It means a lot to me."

"That's OK. You mean a lot to me. I hope to see you back on the moon then. I know you won't let much impede your plans. I will say hello to the others."

"Give Liang a special hello. I hope he isn't blaming himself."

"He did originally, but I counseled him about it. He's happy it was nothing he did that caused the accident, and he now knows the cause."

Jian left. Hu watched him leave, pleased he had come. She saw his tension being released as they talked together, his bottled-up guilt draining away. She saw him another couple of times before he returned to the moon.

Another two weeks lapsed before the hospital released her and she could start thinking about a future other than recovery from her injuries. She was determined to make the most of it.

10

SCHEMES

Loki sat in his luxurious leather chair in his office, swiveling it from side to side as he held his one-of-a-kind gold embossed fountain pen, caressing its smoothness with his fingers. Things looked grim, and he needed a plan to counter whoever attacked his empire. He realized at the time that the fallout from his disastrous Iapetus episode would hurt his business in the short-term, but he hadn't counted on someone trying to take it over. It sniffed too much like his manipulations when he removed his father from the business, and he didn't like it. The other board members would die to see the last of him, but he wasn't going anywhere without a fight. It bothered him though that whoever attacked him seemed to be well informed, and knew exactly what to break to have the maximum impact on his business's cash flow.

He thought back to his meeting with Ethan at the restaurant and gritted his teeth. He would get to Tau Ceti somehow and take what he wanted when he got there. Ethan would not have the glory Loki deserved. Loki's comm buzzed. "Yes, Eleanor?"

"Carson is here. He wants to see you, if you have the time."

"Send him in."

Carson walked into his office, looking to see where to sit. Loki had a chair in front of his desk and a sofa along the wall next to the door. A drinks cabinet and bookshelf lined one wall and a large window behind Loki displayed the beach view outside. Seeming to change his mind about sitting, he walked to the window and looked out. The mid-afternoon sun shone onto the pure white sand of the beach nearby, white-tipped waves gently cascading along the shoreline. Several of Loki's 'harem' frolicked on the beach and in the water, getting the sunlight necessary to tan their slender, curvaceous bodies. Too far away to see properly, they ran around naked to make sure the sun reached every part of those bodies. He turned to Loki. "I've pooled the information from my contacts. The Americans are almost ready for their mission to Tau Ceti. It will be the same team as the Alpha Centauri expedition. Ethan Richards is leading it and the other members... the ones still alive... have joined him. There are three fresh recruits. Pity. It could have been an opportunity to place one of our own on the team. From my information, they are leaving in a few weeks."

Loki gritted his teeth as he realized another opportunity slipped through his fingers because of Ethan Bloody Richards, a fire of hatred kindling in his eyes. "Have you checked out the backgrounds of the recruits?"

"Yes. Nothing to use as leverage with any of them, I'm afraid."

"Hmm... no such thing as nothing, but we can't do much now." Loki sat in thought for a few moments. "Can you find out anything about Ethan's past?"

Carson looked at Loki, brow raised in surprise, "Well, he reunited with his siblings, a brother and sister, who he hasn't seen for many years, apparently."

"Siblings?"

"Yes."

"I see." A germ of an idea started forming in Loki's head, but he left it at that for the moment. "Have you chased up on any potential at this Chariclo place?"

"There is a lot of resistance to any private enterprise getting involved. Part of it is the risk of infection from the virus that the orig-

inal team encountered, but they don't want to 'disturb the virgin environment' either, so they say. I'm sure that we can talk them around in
time. Touring the caves the archeologists are uncovering would
create a lot of interest. We just have to take care of infection by the
virus."

"Virus you say?"

"Yes. Ethan's team discovered a virus that killed half a dozen
people, I think. You must have read about it at the time? My understanding is that it infected Ethan's wife, but they developed a vaccine
just in time and saved her, and some others."

"So, if anyone comes down with the virus, an antidote is available
to cure them?"

"Presumably. They would have had to vaccinate the people
working there."

"What else do you know?"

"The Russians are progressing with their hyper-drive project. My
sources tell me they conducted a successful test the other day."

The information piqued Loki's interest. "That's the drive that can
travel almost anywhere in an instant, is it?"

"Yeah, it might make the other technologies obsolete, although
people tell me it uses a sizeable amount of energy, so it's probably
most economic for long voyages. The wormholes are probably
preferred, but you need to get to the other location and place a portal
there in the first place for them to work."

"Have they put it in a ship yet?"

"What? The hyper-drive?"

"Yeah."

"Not sure."

Another plan started germinating in Loki's mind. He might get to
Tau Ceti after all, if he could somehow get the Russians to take him
there.

Loki sat in silence for some time, thinking. "We need to work on
the environmental tourist angle at Chariclo. I would think that would
satisfy any concerns with any other incentive we may need to
provide."

"I agree. I've been working on that angle and started our agents lobbying for permits based on that. It will be a long haul though, based on progress so far."

"Keep at it. Let me know if you need some heavier persuasion or other resources to get a foothold there. This smells like a great opportunity." Carson's pre-emptive thinking pleased Loki immensely. His development progressed well since Loki found him on the down and out. He proved an excellent replacement for Jezebel, in the short-term, anyway. "Maybe... we should locate this brother and sister of Ethan's."

Carson looked at Loki in alarm. Loki knew his opinion of the antics out at Iapetus. "What do you want with them?"

"Nothing at present, but they may prove useful at some stage."

"I'll get someone to look into it," Carson said reluctantly.

Loki stood and looked out of the window with Carson. "A sight for sore eyes, aren't they?" he said, watching the nymphs playing on the beach.

"They add a certain flavor to the day."

Loki laughed. "You don't have to be that cautious around me, especially with them."

"I just like to show some respect."

"For them or me?"

"I'll let you decide," Carson said with an enigmatic smile.

Loki sighed and looked at Carson. "You hear any whispers about who might be attacking me to gain control of the company?"

"No, that's above my pay grade."

"It's not really, the position you're in now. You need to start thinking more strategically. Help you with your business skills. It's not just running the business, you have to fend off the jackals circling it too, waiting for their chance to attack. You need to identify the parasites and work out how to keep them at bay, or better still, have them fight amongst each other. You need to know your enemies."

"Keep your friends close and your enemies closer?"

"Something like that."

"Well, I haven't heard any whispers around my area. Most of the board members and shareholders just complement me on the success of the tourism portfolio at present. As you know, it's generating a great revenue stream now."

"Well, can you sniff around a bit? See if you can find out anything."

"OK. Is that all?"

"For now."

Carson walked out, leaving Loki to admire the view. The sight stirred a thought, until he realized he had to catch up on the asteroid mining operations performance, before returning to America in the evening. He sighed at the inconvenience of the responsibilities, but the empire kept him alive. It was his child, his legacy that people would remember for all time, once he made himself the most powerful man on Earth.

He went back to his desk and sat down. Booting up his tablet, he opened up the latest production report for the asteroid mining operations. There had been whispers of slippages in product delivery to the smelting units and he needed to get on top of the truth of the matter or confront the manager of the mines. His frown of concentration developed into concern as he delved deeper into the report. Something wasn't right. There were far too many shutdowns and machinery failures. What was going on out there? He needed first-hand knowledge to find out. Not only were the figures worrying, but the worst of it was being glossed over and hidden. He knew from experience that he needed to review the operations himself to get to the root of the matter. It didn't look good for Virgil, the manager of the operations, if his suspicion turned out to be true. Pity. He liked Virgil. There was enough questionable data in the reports for him to warrant his personal attention. He pressed the button on his desk comm, "Eleanor, can you link up a phone call to Virgil please... and can you get me a coffee."

"Will do."

A steaming mug of coffee came moments later as Loki continued working through the report while he waited for the call. Eleanor advised him of the connection half an hour later. Loki pressed the button on the comm. "What the hell is going on out there?" Loki blasted at a cowering Virgil sitting in his office at the other end.

Virgil licked his dry lips as a drop of perspiration ran down his face, his wide eyes unable to find an immediate answer. "I've been trying to find out," he finally whispered frantically.

"Well, why didn't you tell me you thought something was amiss?" Loki's voice reduced in its menacing tone slightly.

Virgil shifted in his seat, squirming for a comfortable position that he couldn't find. "You would have blasted me, sir. You always say, 'Don't come to me with issues, come with answers.' I don't have an answer yet."

Loki glared at Virgil across the link to reinforce the seriousness of his situation, but the intensity softened as Loki pondered what exactly was going on. He sighed in resignation, "What do you know?"

Letting out a large breath and physically relaxing slightly, Virgil gathered his thoughts. "It's strange. There have been unexplained machine breakdowns, and lodes have suddenly deteriorated as if someone else has removed the ore, but, when you look at the deposit, it has been undisturbed. The only explanation for it is that someone has been falsifying the exploration reports, but who and why?"

Loki drilled his eyes into Virgil's, eager to detect any hint of deception, but found none. A seed of doubt germinated, as he realized there was something else that he knew nothing about, and that troubled him. He rubbed his chin with his hand in thought before looking back at Virgil. "What do you intend doing to find out?"

"I've been painstakingly reviewing the personnel files of all our senior management and delving into their past, to see if anything crops up that could hint at disloyalty to this business. So far I've come up blank. Everyone checks out. Now I'm wondering if it's someone from outside of my business unit hacking into our records and altering them. But that would take some extraordinary skills, and why?"

The prospect of someone outside the business interfering with it increasingly worried Loki, "But that doesn't explain the equipment breakdowns."

"No, it doesn't. I've been discretely investigating that too, but there's no pattern to what breaks down and the frequency of it, except it's always at the most critical times in the production schedule."

"You might need some outside support to sort this out." Loki was happy that at least he still had a competent manager running the business unit who was thinking. He seemed to be doing everything in his power to understand the problem, but the intrigue may be beyond his resources to solve. "I'll have Carson pay you a visit and between both of you, you can map out a course of action to get a resolution. I only hope that this is an isolated occurrence and isn't spreading to other parts of the business. Thank you for being frank with me. I was set on replacing you, as you know is my habit with underperforming employees, but I can see you've been doing what I would have done."

"Thanks boss." Virgil relaxed in his seat, seeing he had satisfied Loki for the time being.

"Keep me posted," Loki said and broke the link. He leaned back in his chair, realizing that his problems were escalating. He felt sure the issues at the asteroid mines and the wrestling for control of the business were related, but how? He sighed. He needed a game-changer somewhere. Maybe his embryonic plans for Ethan and Tau Ceti would provide the answer.

11

TO TAU CETI

Ethan waited to board the Lander for the spaceship *Destiny*, keen to get back into space again. Jade stood next to him, watching him, bemused, as she watched him pace the floor of the boarding area of the Lander.

"We won't get there any faster with you pacing around like that." Jade said, a smile on her face.

Ethan looked at her, feeling as sheepish as his smile, "I know. I'm just eager to get things going. We've waited long enough."

Jade hugged him, "I know. I'm eager to get going too."

The announcement to board finally arrived, and they both went up the steps to the Lander and inside, seating themselves either side of the aisle. Ethan sighed. The tension he had while he waited left him and he finally relaxed.

Gerhardt walked in moments later, purpose reflected in the way he strode. He looked at Ethan, "We travel together."

"Yes, welcome aboard," Ethan said, a little amused at the obvious.

"Thank you." Gerhardt looked at Jade and gave a greeting too.

"Does this trip take long?" Gerhardt asked Ethan, ignoring Jade completely, which Ethan could see vexed her, as she pulled an annoyed face at him. He just managed to keep a straight face.

"You haven't been up to the ship yet?"

"No, I have not had the need. It makes me a little nervous, to be honest. Living in such a compact space with just a thin wall between us and nothing."

"What's the actual difference between that and the thin layer of air that keeps us alive on Earth?"

"There is less chance of something hitting it and punching a hole in it."

"I can assure you that we have adequate protection to prevent that, but any large boulders would give us some concern."

"I hope you are right." Gerhardt continued down the aisle and sat in one of the back seats.

Ethan looked at Jade, who raised her brow in a 'what the...?' expression. He just shrugged. Ethan knew that the rest of the team had already boarded *Destiny*. He would have too, but he and Jade had last-minute discussions with John about updated security matters. He was glad that they would finally be on their way.

The journey to the ship lasted an hour and the Lander casually settled on the floor of the Lander bay, the hatch opening moments later for them to disembark.

Celeste stood in the reception area to greet them as they stepped out, her usual cheerful smile welcoming them aboard, "Hope your transit was comfortable," she said to Ethan and Jade, Gerhardt having rushed off to the elevator with no social recourse.

"I hope he knows where he is going," Ethan said to Celeste, nodding his head towards Gerhardt.

Celeste shrugged. "He will ask if he needs help. I know a little about how he thinks, I guess, being the same heritage."

"Your personalities are slightly different though."

"Yes."

"Have you been looking after my ship then?"

Celeste raised an eyebrow, "Your ship...?"

Jade sniggered, "Are we going to have a little tussle about who owns what then?"

"Of course not," Ethan said, a little put out. "Is she ready to go?"

"Everything is functioning and ready to go to the moon to pick up the portal."

"We'll get settled and I'll be in the control centre shortly then. We can be on our way."

"Of course," Celeste said with a bemused smile.

Jade rolled her eyes, "Let's go get settled in then."

They all walked off to the elevator and the accommodation level. Ethan and Jade got out, leaving Celeste in the elevator. He turned and nodded to her, before the doors closed to take her to the control center for departure.

Ethan walked into the control center half an hour later, looking around at the activity before going over to the command chair, where Celeste sat working through departure procedures. Others in the control centre remained busy with their assigned tasks. Celeste looked up as Ethan approached, "Want your chair back?"

"No, no. Looks like you're doing fine."

Celeste gave a smirk, "Good. You would have to fight for it, if you said yes."

"Whatever happened to that shy astronomer I plucked out of obscurity?"

"You saw more potential in her."

"Touché, what's the status?" Ethan asked as he sat in the seat alongside of her.

"Ten minutes to departure."

"Good, have the Chinese contacted you about the portal?"

"Yes, it is ready, and they said that there will also be a passenger."

"Really? They say who."

"No."

"Well, let's hope the person is constructive to the operation."

"Yeah," Celeste said, her concentration elsewhere as new data came up on her screen. She pressed the button next to her, "Prepare for departure. Lock down all hatches. We depart on green." The overhead screen flickered a display of ship status information on it with lights progressively changing from red to green.

"All green to go," Someone said behind Ethan.

"Disengage," Celeste said.

An exterior view came up on the screen, and Ethan saw and felt the ship judder and then slowly drift sideways away from the docking facility. Celeste pushed power into the EM Drive, and the ship slowly moved forward under its own energy, gathering speed by the second. She eased off on the power two minutes later and allowed the ship to coast through the departure lane from the dock. Once outside of the restricted zone, Celeste brought the drives up to full throttle and the ship started powering away from Earth, changing course until the moon was in the front view screen. She relaxed back into her seat once she confirmed the course.

"I'm impressed," Ethan said with pride, not only in Celeste, but with himself for having such confidence in her.

Celeste looked across at Ethan and blushed. "Thanks."

"Aggressive on the acceleration?"

"You aren't the only one that wants to get started."

"Yeah," Ethan said. "It's been a while. Any more thoughts on what we may find when we get there?"

"Not really. The major problem is that Tau Ceti has a large debris disk orbiting the star. Asteroids could have bombarded the planets too much for life to have developed on them."

"Let's hope that's not the case."

"Yes."

"How long to the moon?"

"Six hours."

Ethan raised his brow, "That's fast."

Celeste smiled, "We've made a few alterations while you were away enjoying your time of bliss."

"Ha, don't let all this power get to your head," Ethan said as he looked at her.

"I won't," Celeste replied, looking him in the eyes, not bothered by his remark. "There's nothing to do here for a while. May as well check the rest of the ship out. See you soon." She stood and left the command centre.

Ethan stayed for a while longer, enjoying the view on the screen, and marveling on how mature Celeste had become. He wondered how she would get along with Gerhardt. They seemed opposite personalities. He didn't think they had met yet. She had been on the ship, and too busy to take part in the bonding activities that Ethan had organized in the lead up to the expedition. He eventually rose from his seat and left too.

The team congregated in the ship's lounge three hours later. Ethan and Jade hosted the gathering. Marie, Angelo and Max sat talking with each other. Ravi and Pia joined moments later, said hello and got a drink before sitting with the group. Gerhardt did the same and Celeste arrived ten minutes later. She came over, "Hi, I'm Celeste if anyone doesn't know me."

Most just nodded their greeting to her as they had met before, but Gerhardt stood with a formal erect stance, "It is a pleasure to meet someone else from the fatherland. I am Gerhardt, the biologist."

Celeste extended a hand, "I know. I've studied your file. I need to know about everyone who's on my... the ship." Celeste glanced at Ethan with the hint of a smile.

Gerhardt raised a brow, "I hope that all is in order."

Celeste barely held back a laugh, "Yes, all is in order."

"May I get you a drink then?"

"That is kind. I'll have a lemonade."

"Are you sure that you are German?"

Celeste laughed, "Yes I am sure, but I have to fly the ship. You want me to get us to our destination in one piece."

Gerhardt smiled at the reasoning, "Of course. Lemonade it is." He left to get Celeste's drink while she found a seat to move into the circle of the group.

"You look young for such responsibility," Pia said.

Celeste bristled, becoming tense, "I had an excellent teacher."

Pia saw the defensive barriers go up, "I am sorry. It didn't come out the way I intended. Your competence is apparent."

"That's OK," Celeste said, relaxing once again.

Gerhardt came back with Celeste's drink and the group talked and socialized for an hour before breaking up, some for bed and others for duties, as the arrival at the moon neared.

Ethan hung around, to be on hand if any issues arose with the loading of the portal. "I'll see you later on," he said to Jade as he gave her a quick affectionate kiss.

"OK, don't be away too long," Jade said as she departed with a wink.

Ethan just shook his head as he watched Jade go, while walking off with Celeste to the command centre.

The loading of the portal components went smoothly and Ethan and Celeste talked about minor topics, while waiting in the reception area for the mysterious Chinese delegate to emerge from the shuttle that had just landed in the *Destiny's* Landing bay. Ethan looked over to the shuttle with frequent regularity to see who it could be. He wondered why the Chinese didn't say who it was. The hatch of the shuttle opened and Hu hobbled out moments later, still weak in her recovery from her injuries.

"Hugo!" Ethan and Celeste said at the same time.

Hu slowly descended the short stairs from the shuttle and hobbled to her waiting audience. She stopped and smiled, "Yes, it's me. I wanted to surprise you and deliberately told Jian not to tell you who would join you. I see it worked."

Both Ethan and Celeste beamed. "It's a surprise all right," Ethan said. "The last I heard you were still recuperating."

"Convinced everyone I was well enough to come with, considering that it will take two months to get to Tau Ceti. Angelo can cater to any medical needs I may have."

"Welcome aboard then," Celeste said.

Hu looked at Celeste and then at Ethan, "Who is in charge here?" she said, raising a brow.

Ethan laughed, "I'm still in charge, although Celeste is responsible for the ship."

"Good to know. Make sure he doesn't boss you around."

"I won't. Well, let's get you to your quarters then, and I'm sure there're others eager to welcome you, once they know who we've picked up," Celeste said.

Ethan creased has brow, "How's John taking the separation?"

Hu laughed, "He is not happy. I believe he has made a reservation on the first shuttle through the portal." She sobered, "And I will miss him too."

Ethan placed an arm around her shoulder and squeezed her, "I understand."

Hu looked at him, eyes widened, "Thank you."

They walked to the elevator, once Hu and Celeste had organized someone to unload Hu's belongings from the shuttle.

Hu asked, as the elevator rose to the accommodation level, "And do you have someone in your life yet, Celeste?"

Celeste blushed with slight embarrassment, "I've been too busy flying *Destiny* for Ethan. I don't think I would tell you if I did though."

Hu smiled, "Good answer."

Celeste got Hu settled in. The next day, the other team member who knew her, eagerly sought her out to say hello, once word got around. Ethan introduced her to the unknown members of the team without incident, unlike the previous time, although the meeting with Gerhardt and Pia was a little strained.

12

BOREDOM AND CHAOS

"I'm bored," Pia said, looking out of the porthole she sat near. The transfer to ftl had been flawless over a month ago.

"Well, you're the meteorologist. Why don't you do something about the atmosphere in here then?" Max responded as he read a book and lounged with his leg over the arm of a beige cushioned chair. They were in one of the relaxation areas spread out over the accommodation level of the ship.

Pia gave Max a dirty look, but eventually laughed.

Max looked up, "What?"

"That was funny."

"What?"

"What you said."

"What did I say?"

"You said that... ooh, you know very well what you said."

Max gave an impish smile, but said nothing. He went back to reading his book.

"Well?"

Max looked up again, "Well, what?"

"Aren't you bored?"

Max put the bookmark in his book and placed it on the table next to the chair, as he thought about what Pia said. "I don't really get bored."

"Why not?"

Max frowned. "I've lived a fairly secluded life over the years when I was running my department. With everyone else gone from my life, I settled down to just being with myself and not much else. I just got used to it, I guess."

"That's boring."

"Maybe."

Pia said nothing for a while. "What changed?"

"What do you mean?" Max asked. He hadn't gone back to reading, but sat, eyes staring at the floor as he kept thinking, in the meantime.

"What changed? Why did you join this team?"

"Ethan gave me an offer I couldn't refuse," Max said, trying to avoid the question.

"No, he didn't. You could have refused. You could have stayed in your cozy non-eventful lifestyle, but you didn't. Something changed."

Max looked out of the same porthole that Pia had been looking out of. After several seconds, he said, "No, I couldn't. Not after he explained to me what had been missing in my life, and how I was my own worst enemy in not trying to find it."

Pia crossed her legs on the seat and faced Max. "That sounds weird."

"Probably is. I had let myself atrophy at CERN. I wasn't doing any of the things I had gone into physics to do. Ethan pointed out to me what I'd been missing. The responsibility of looking after reactors to keep people alive and the thought of discovery again..." Max looked away, feeling uncomfortable. He mumbled, "I'm probably boring you."

"I would have stopped you, if you were boring me. I know what you mean about Ethan. He seems a bit of a straight person at first, almost naïve, but, when you look at his eyes, there seems to be something there that says 'I know exactly what you need'. It's hard to explain."

"He hasn't had it easy either."

"What do you mean?"

"How much have you looked into the last expedition?"

"Not much really. I know they... you... found that virus, and it killed several of your team before they found a cure for it. That's about it."

"Well, Jade had the virus too. She almost died. They got the anti-vaccine to her just in time. I wasn't privy to many of the conversations, but I talked to Celeste a little about it afterwards. She said that he was beside himself. He was like a madman with distress. I can understand, I suppose. It wouldn't be easy watching the person you love dying in front of you. And that's just the half of it. On their first voyage, when they first went ftl, someone murdered his best friend. I wasn't there, but I'm told it cut him deeply. He caught the culprit and also saved the ship, when someone started firing at it, so they could get to the Astatine deposit on Iapetus first to claim it for themselves. I'm told he stared the person down as he did it."

"Oh. I didn't know." Pia looked down, pensive in thought at the revelation. "He's a strong man."

"He can surprise you, that's for sure."

They both fell silent.

"I'm still bored," Pia said eventually.

"Ha... So how can I ease that boredom?"

Pia blushed and adjusted her seating position, but then stood, "That's OK. I think I'll..."

The ship rocked uncontrollably, which threw Pia across the room and into the wall causing to her to scream. Max just grabbed hold of his seat, bolted to the floor, in time to prevent him suffering the same fate.

"What the...?" Max said. He looked at Pia, who lay slumped on the floor, "Are you OK?"

～

～

~

CELESTE RAN into the control centre with Ethan three steps behind, both ready to grab something at an instant's notice, as several shocks had lurched the ship since the first one. Alarms blared and lights flashed as Celeste slid to a stop in front of the command chair. "Status," she shouted.

"One of the muon ring position field generators has failed. The ring is losing its position. The warp bubble is becoming unstable. We're in danger of destroying the ring," the person in charge shouted back at her, so she could hear him over the rest of the noise.

Another tremor rocked the ship. Celeste and Ethan grabbed the first things they saw and held on as the reverberations subsided. She strapped herself into the command chair and brought up the warp drive screen, immediately decelerating the ship and taking it out of ftl. Shutting the drive down, she brought up the EM-drive to at least keep them moving forward. She wiped a bead of sweat from her face, and a stray lock of hair out of the way before she turned to Ethan, "How the hell can that happen?"

"It should be impossible. Not only do the generators that hold the ring in place have backups, the drive should have tripped and taken us out of ftl immediately."

Jade and Hu entered the command centre, Hu hobbling still. "What's happening?" Jade asked.

Ethan looked at her, "I don't know. One of the ring positioning generators failed, which allowed the ring to come loose. We're lucky we didn't lose it completely. We're even luckier that we didn't destroy the ship."

Jade looked around, "Some people are injured."

Celeste responded immediately, her voice calm and commanding as she pressed the comm button, "Medical to the command centre and check on all personnel on board for injuries." She looked around, seeing the others look at her with astonishment, "What?"

"How can you be so calm?" Ethan asked.

"People are injured. It's my responsibility to make sure we take care of them."

Ethan shook his head.

Hu laughed. "Bet you didn't realize that when you took her under your wing."

"No, I didn't." He smiled in admiration at Celeste for a moment, before his thoughts veered towards other needs. "We need to find out what caused this. We need Max."

Celeste gestured to the communications officer to find Max.

Max came on the PA moments later. "Max here."

"Max. We need you to come to the command centre," Celeste said.

"I can't. Pia's badly hurt. I can't leave her. Not until medical gets here."

"OK, do what you need to. Then go down to the generator level. We need you to help us down there when you can get away."

"Will do."

"We need to go to the generator level to see what's happened to the magnetic clamp generators." Celeste rose and started walking towards the door. "Are you coming?" a slight smirk on her face.

"Right behind you," Ethan said, as he hurried to keep up.

Jade and Hu looked at each other in amusement.

Celeste and Ethan arrived at the generator level two minutes later, both out of breath from running.

"Maybe it wasn't necessary to go so fast," Ethan gasped between breathes.

"Maybe."

They both started walking through the generator level, examining the generators one by one. They all seemed to be running smoothly.

"That's strange," Celeste said. "I thought one would be damaged or something maybe worse."

"Yeah, let's get to a terminal, and see if we can locate exactly which clamp failed. Maybe we can trace the problem back from that."

They both moved to a terminal nearby and Ethan started interrogating the control system.

Max turned up five minutes later, walking at a brisk pace. "Found anything yet?" he asked when he reached them.

"Nothing," Ethan replied, shaking his head. "Something should have turned up."

"Mind if I look?"

"Be my guest," Ethan said, as he stood away from the terminal for Max to access.

Max typed instructions and examined the display before coming out with, "That's strange."

"What is?" Celeste asked, moving closer to Max so she could see the screen display.

Max leaned back away from the screen, "This might interest you too, Ethan."

Ethan moved closer to the screen so he could also see what Max had found.

"See these parameters," Max said. "They are all wrong. Not hugely wrong, but enough to cause one of the muon ring clamps to disengage. That shouldn't happen. There should be a hard-wired interlock that trips the drive if that even looks like happening. It didn't kick in."

"So you're saying that something has changed these parameters," Ethan said.

Max nodded. "Yes."

"Recently?"

"Yes."

"How do you know?"

"It's my job to know. I know each parameter by heart and these are not what they should be."

Ethan moved away from the screen to think. He looked at Celeste, who stood frowning. He turned back to Max, "But they aren't that far out. Just enough to cause serious stability issues and disconnect the clamp."

"Yes."

"That means that we either have a gremlin who just won the

lottery, or a saboteur with a bit of knowledge of this system, and knew exactly what needed changing, and by how much."

Max thought for a moment, "That seems a good allegation, but we need to go to the hard-wired circuit breaker cabinet to confirm it. It's over on the far side." Max stood and walked across the ship with Ethan and Celeste following.

When they arrived, Max opened a small cabinet and pulled out three sets of long-sleeved thick rubber gloves. "Here put these on. There's some high voltage equipment behind the doors I'm about to open. I don't want you to get zapped."

Ethan and Celeste obeyed and put the gloves on their hands. Max did likewise and donned a rubber apron as well before he opened the doors of the large cabinet next to the small one. Max jumped back as the doors opened. A thick cable collapsed onto the floor with a loud thump.

Ethan and Celeste gasped.

"What the...?" Max said.

Ethan moved forward, once he had recovered from the initial shock, and examined the cabinet contents. "Look Max. That cable's been cut from there," Ethan pointed to a sawn-off cable end matching the end lying on the floor, "and there's been a jumper cable placed across these two terminals. What does that mean?"

Max shook his head. "It means two things. One, someone bridged out the interlock to shut down the drive, as I suspected, and two, the person who did this knew exactly what he or she was doing. They had to have intimate knowledge of the circuitry of this ship, and how to protect themselves from electrocution. This is all high voltage equipment. Any small mistake, or brush against the wrong thing with your hand, would fry you to a crisp in an instant."

Ethan frowned in frustration. *Why do these things keep happening to me and my ship?* He thought. He paced for a moment. "We have to find this person. I can't keep having these people infiltrate my ship doing these things and get away with it. There are too many people's lives at stake."

Celeste raised an eyebrow when Ethan mentioned 'my ship,' but asked, "How do we do that?"

"I don't know. What I can't understand is what the person was hoping to achieve. Destroy of the ship? They would have died too."

"I don't think it would have caused the ship to explode, although there could have been greater and more severe damage than what we may have sustained. I haven't heard of any hull breaches or major damage," Max said.

"Then what?" Celeste asked. "What is the point? Does this person want to delay us? To what end? Is someone coming with another ship who wants to get there first? They don't know what we'll find. It's not as if this will be the first extraterrestrial system we've visited either."

"I don't know," Ethan replied. "But it seems someone doesn't want us to get there in a hurry. How hard is this to fix Max?" Ethan's thoughts returned momentarily to Loki's words weeks ago in the restaurant. *Why would he do this? He can't get to Tu Ceti, or can he?*

"Couple of days at the most. We need to shut down a few systems so the technicians can work on this safely. I can change the parameters back to their correct settings anytime, and we should be on our way again, if there isn't any mechanical damage outside."

"OK, we need to get someone to check that," Ethan said. "In the meantime, we keep what we've seen here between us and no-one else, not even Jade. I trust her with my life, and I don't normally keep secrets from her, but I don't want something to slip that might tip the culprit off. Agreed?"

Both Max and Celeste nodded.

"OK, Celeste. Can you organize a maintenance detail to inspect the damage outside, and you get some technicians to fix this, Max?"

They both nodded.

"Let's get to it then."

～

～

∾

A CALL CAME into Celeste two hours later from the maintenance crew sent to inspect the Warp Bubble ring. "I think we need someone with more expertize out here," one of them said.

"What do you mean?" Celeste asked.

"There's been a lot of damage and we're not sure what to do."

"Oh, OK. I will let you know." Celeste disconnected and thought for a moment before she contacted Ethan. Ethan answered moments later. "Ethan?"

"Ethan here, Celeste."

"Can you go out and join the maintenance team to inspect the damage to the ring? It's apparently more than what we were expecting, and they're not sure what to do."

"... OK. I can do that. I need a good spacewalk, anyway."

Celeste sat drumming her fingers, waiting for news of the situation. Max reported in the interim from his end and informed her he had started repairs to the drive system. She waited for an update report from Ethan, who had joined the maintenance crew at the ring. Her hand went to the comm several times to call him, but paused before making the call. *He'll contact me when he has something to report.* The waiting was killing her, though.

The call from Ethan eventually came in, "Bad news I'm afraid."

"What is it?"

"We can't fix the ring. Not with what we have on board, anyway."

"But that leaves us stranded."

"I know. I'm coming back to the ship. Can you call a meeting of the team, including Hugo?"

"I will. You seem to have a plan."

"Maybe, see you soon." The comm went dead.

∾

∾

≈

Two hours later, the conference room buzzed, as the team members sat talking to each other, speculating about the purpose of the meeting. Celeste sat in silence, her brow drawn together with her hands clasped tight.

Ethan walked into the room, followed closely by Jade and Hu. They sat, Ethan next to Celeste with Jade on his other side and Hu next to her. He looked at Celeste and gave her a knowing smile of '*I've been in your place, but don't worry*'. He composed himself and called the others to silence.

"I'm sure the rumor machine's been working overtime, and you're all aware of, or suspect, what has happened. To make sure you have the facts, I will tell you what I know to be the truth. One of the magnetic generators for the warp ring failed, which allowed the ring to move. The failure damaged the ring in the process and we don't have the parts to fix it."

"How could this happen?" Gerhardt asked. "I would have thought backup systems would have been in place for such a valuable part of the drive system."

Ethan looked at Celeste and Max, unsure of what to say. Max butted in. "There are backup systems but, for reasons we are not sure of yet, they failed to engage properly to prevent the damage."

Ethan acknowledged Max's response with a slight smile. "Anyway, whatever the cause, it doesn't help us in our current predicament."

"No, it does not," Gerhardt said.

"How are Pia and the other casualties, Angelo?"

"No serious injuries," Angelo replied. "Pia suffered a concussion and a serious sprain of her ankle. She'll be sore for a while."

"Glad things aren't worse. We are stranded until we can work out a way around the problem, or a way to get word back to Earth. We've been traveling for over a month so we are about six light years away. Normal communication would take six years to get to Earth and six to get back. We'll be long dead by then. Any suggestions?" Ethan looked at Hu once he finished speaking.

Hu looked at Ethan, blinking rapidly as her eyes fought to hold back tears. She jumped a little when he looked directly at her. Her face changed to a concentrating stare and her eyes moved from side to side for a few moments and she smiled, "Well, the obvious solution would be to construct the wormhole portal. We will get word back and even fly back and forth with parts and whatever else we need."

Everyone nodded, several sighing at the same time.

"Will it be able to generate a wormhole, since it isn't in the place we intended it to be?" Max asked. "I'm not sure of the physics of wormhole generation with distance."

"Good question," Hu replied. "That is not a problem. It may have been a problem if we were further away than our intended location, as distance influences the power required, but we are closer."

"Good," Ethan said. "That seems to be the quickest way out of our current dilemma. How long till you have the portal assembled and ready?"

"About a week, maybe a little longer."

"Let's do that then. In the meantime, it might be an idea for Jade, Max and myself to get together, and Hugo, if she has time, to see if there are any other possibilities for the Warp Bubble drive. It may not be of use this time, but it may be something that can we can implement if the problem happens again, especially if we don't happen to be carrying a portal with us."

Everyone nodded.

"Let's get to it then." Ethan said, and the others, except for Jade, stood and left the meeting room.

"What didn't you tell us?" Jade asked Ethan when they were alone.

Ethan had difficulty looking Jade in the eye and sat flustered, wondering how to respond to the question, until he finally sighed. "We think it was sabotage. I didn't want the word to get out and alert whoever it was."

"You don't even trust me?"

"No, of course I do. It's just better, the fewer people that know the better, that's all."

"I'll leave you off this time," Jade said, a smirk on her face and a twinkle in her eyes.

"I'd better make it up to you then," Ethan replied, grabbing hold of her hand and leading her off to their cabin.

13

TAU CETI

Hu had the portal assembly completed well ahead of her estimated time, beginning testing five days after she started. She felt pleased by how well it all fitted together with no mishaps, unlike the last time. She sat in the command centre working through power up sequences when Ethan walked in.

"How's everything going?" Ethan asked.

Hu looked up from her testing, "Good. With any luck, we should be able to power the portal up by the end of the day and see if we can produce a hole."

"Will the others be ready at the other end?"

"They won't be expecting us, but they will monitor their end. They will notice my message when I send it through."

"Good. I want to get on the way again as soon as I can." Ethan's mood mellowed from the business manner, "You may even get some time with John."

Hu looked at Ethan a little annoyed, because he seemed to read her mind, but went along with his humor, "Maybe. It depends if I have the time."

"Yeah right."

Hu laughed, "Yes. That was my thought too."

"I'm sure he'll be eager to see you too, when he hears we're in trouble."

"He had better be."

"Need a hand with anything?" Ethan asked, getting back to business.

"No, I just have to work through this myself."

"Well, keep me updated then."

"I will."

Ethan walked out to let Hu get on with her work, and she continued her tasks. She was ready to power up the portal six hours later. She called Ethan with the news, and he returned to her side to watch the event. Jade and Celeste also came to watch.

Hu started the power up sequence and power fed into each section of the ring's circuit. Green lights glowed on the portal, as each ring segment went to ready status. "We are ready," Hu said. All the segments of the portal showed green lights, and the controls displayed the startup completed.

"Let's do it then," Ethan said.

Hu pressed the power on button on her tablet and gradually raised the energy level. A micro hole broke through at thirty percent power level. "We are connected," Hu said, smiling. "I will send the message." She opened the file she prepared beforehand and sent it through the wormhole on the communication link she established. "Now we wait. A reply will depend on how attentive they are at the moon station."

"Let's hope they're alert then. I'm getting sick of this waiting, everyone is."

A reply came an hour later with a time to attempt a full wormhole aperture. Hu acknowledged their response and shut down the wormhole at her end.

The time to open the wormhole arrived and Hu powered up the portal again, increasing the power until the wormhole opened fully and stabilized. She smiled with satisfaction at the smoothness of the operation. A message came through that a shuttle would travel through a few minutes later. *That's unusual. Wonder why they are sending a shuttle without finding out what's happened first. I'll just have to wait and see.*

Ethan walked in. "Is the wormhole open?"

"Yes it is, and a shuttle is coming through in about ten minutes."

"Really? They are panicky."

Ten minutes went by and a shuttle emerged from the wormhole portal, decelerating quickly before matching speed with *Destiny* and turning to head for the Lander Bay.

"Better meet them," Ethan said.

"Yes, we should," Hu responded.

They both headed for the door of the command centre and to the Lander Bay, reaching it as the shuttle maneuvered for landing. Hu wondered who had flown through and fantasized about it being John, but shook her head in dismay at the direction of her thoughts. The door opened, and moments later a man emerged. Hu's jaw dropped. It was John. She stood fixed to the floor and couldn't move.

Ethan looked at her and smiled. "You going to go greet him or not?"

"But... how... why is he here?"

"Maybe he was worried?"

Hu looked at Ethan nonplussed, but finally got control of her senses and body. She smiled, "Of course I will greet him." She turned and started running in her healing gait to John, who had already descended from the steps of the shuttle. He looked at Hu and smiled. They met with open arms for each other, Hu almost knocking both of them over with her inertia. They hugged and held one another for a while, looked into each other's eyes with smiles that they couldn't erase.

Ethan walked over to them in the meantime and coughed, "This is rather public. Do you want to go somewhere private for a while?"

Hu and John turned to him and reddened in embarrassment, but continued to smile. John eventually sobered to the reason for his presence, apart from Hu, "What's the situation?"

Hu disentangled from him and looked on, waiting for Ethan to answer.

"Good to see you too," Ethan said with a smirk. "We're stranded at the moment. But a few more minutes won't change anything. Maybe you would like to go to a cabin and freshen up and I'll organize a debriefing in an hour?" He beckoned a security person over, who had been standing nearby, ready to intervene if any trouble arose. "Can you please organize for someone to assign a cabin for General O'Conner?"

"Yes, Sir," he said. "Sir, if you will follow me," He directed to John.

"Lead the way." John looked at Ethan, eyebrow raised, but shrugged. Hu walked only two steps behind him as they left.

～

～

～

ETHAN CHUCKLED AS HE WATCHED, wondering if he and Jade behaved the same way in the same stage of their relationship. He gave a subdued laugh as he pondered the way Hu followed John. He didn't think she would have followed anyone like that, but he wondered whether John would have done the same if the roles were reversed, and decided that he probably would have, as he followed them to the elevators to the upper levels.

An hour later the expedition team assembled in the conference room with John, who had freshened up. Ethan didn't put too much thought into Hu's slightly disheveled clothing, as he couldn't blame her. He was just pleased that the relationship seemed to be as strong as it appeared. He looked at Jade and winked. She sniggered softly, but left anything she thought unsaid.

Ethan called the meeting to order. "As you all can see, we have established a wormhole back to earth and we have an emissary come through to help. We're all pleased to see General O'Conner, some more than others."

Both John and Hu reddened slightly.

Ethan decided not to put them through any more embarrassment. "However, as I said before General, we are stranded. One of our warp bubble ring lock generators failed, and the ring dislodged, causing damage to the ring that we can't repair with the spares on board, thus the reason for assembling the wormhole portal. We need parts from Earth to get us going again."

"Sounds like the portal lifeline has become invaluable yet again," John said. "Thanks to the Chinese." He looked at Hu and nodded in appreciation, his eyes lingering a little longer than necessary. He dragged them away, "The shuttle, and whatever facilities you need back on Earth, are at your disposal to get things going again. How did the generator fail?"

"We're unsure at this stage," Ethan lied, "but we're investigating."

Jade looked at Ethan with interest, but said nothing.

"Max, can you get together with me in fifteen minutes and we will put together a list of parts and equipment we need to fix the ring? I want you to go back to Earth with the General and collect them and then return."

Both Hu and John looked at Ethan, John ready to protest his speedy departure from them.

Ethan held his hand up to John, "I know you have things to catch up on, but I need you for the time-being, to make things back on Earth happen for Max as quickly as possible." Ethan smirked slightly, "And by sending you, I know that it will happen without delay, so you can get back to us as soon as possible."

John shook his head, but said nothing in retort, succumbing to the direction, "As you wish. I only ask that you take your time in coming up with your list."

The people in the meeting laughed, Hu with slight embarrassment, which she let John know by elbowing him moderately in the ribs.

"Are there any other questions?" Ethan asked when the humor settle down.

The others shook their heads.

"Let's get to it then."

Everyone vacated the room except Ethan, Jade, Max, John and Hu.

Ethan looked at John for a moment, considering what to say, "I lied back there. We know what happened to the generator. Someone sabotaged it."

John nodded, "I see. Any leads?"

"No, not yet. We're still looking into it, but as quietly as possible."

John smiled as he remembered something, "I have news from Earth. The Russians have finally made a spaceship journey with their hyper-drive. If they can prove it reliable, it may put us all out of business, ever the Chinese."

"Apep must be smiling," Ethan said.

"He is overdue for it," Hu responded. "They have worked hard for so long."

"Maybe he'll make a grand entrance on Ceti while we are there," Ethan said, as he winked at Hu. He momentarily wondered if that was the reason for the sabotage.

"Ha! If anyone can, he will."

"Well, now that we know where we stand, maybe you can let Max and me get to our shopping list."

The others nodded and left, John and Hu making sure they were close to each other as they disappeared out the door.

Ethan and Max worked through the list of parts and equipment needed for the ring repair and, once they received them from Earth and the parts installed, the ring powered up fully functional again.

"Not bad," Celeste said when she saw all the lights for the ring functions turn green on the command screen. She turned and nodded to Ethan.

"What were you expecting?" Ethan replied.

"I don't know. I just thought it would take longer than this."

"Well, let's test it and we can get on our way again."

"What about the wormhole portal?"

"Oh, almost forgot. We had better take that with us."

Destiny continued its journey five days later, with an extra member of the team.

PEOPLE ON *DESTINY* continued going stir crazy with nothing to do. Ethan sighed in recognition of the problem as he walked towards the command centre. *There must be a faster way of doing this*, he thought. *At least the wormholes will make return visits fast and efficient.* The doors to the command centre opened, and he walked through, surveying the surrounds as he did so. People manned the workstations, busy with their designated tasks. Celeste sat in the command chair, one leg straddled over an arm rest while she worked through the status screens for the ship. She didn't notice Ethan's entrance until he stood almost in front of her. She whirled her leg from the armrest and sat up straight, her face reddening as she did so. Ethan chuckled. "Don't feel too embarrassed. I would probably do the same after all this time."

"Everything's just so boring. I almost wish something else would happen to break the monotony." She packed away the screen and looked back at him. "Anyway, we're approaching the interesting end of the journey now. I'm just starting to get some useful images of Tau Ceti and its system."

Ethan noticed her enthusiasm returning. He could appreciate it. Her engagement increased in the same way that his would be, if he got an intriguing engineering issue. "How far are we away now?"

"About another day before going sub-light again. We'll be able to assess objects of interest with more detail after that. We're starting to see the large debris disk, though. We may need to stay outside of the solar plane as we pass it, so we don't collide with any of the larger bodies. Fortunately, we're approaching at about thirty degrees to the disk."

"Any large planets?"

"No, there aren't any gaseous super giants like home. A bit of a worry, actually. They moderate the possibility of debris heading into the inner system and colliding with the planets there. It'll be interesting how the inner planets have coped with so much debris about."

"Let's hope they've coped well enough."

"Yes."

"Well, nothing much more I can do until my shift. I'll see you in another four hours to take over." Ethan turned and walked out, heading for the gym to burn some pent-up energy.

Half an hour later he entered the gym and saw Hu there hammering a punching bag, like it had just tried to assault her. He smiled. He could see her fitness and fluency of motion returning to the level she was renowned for.

"What?" Hu said when she saw him watching, stopping and breathing heavily to regain her breath.

"Nothing, it's good to see you working out like you used to, that's all."

She smiled, "Thanks. I needed to blow off some steam."

Ethan cocked an eyebrow, "Any reason?"

Hu looked at him. She sighed. Sitting on a nearby bench, she said, "It is John. He seems distant. Not sure of himself or what he wants."

Ethan stared at her for a moment, contemplating what she had said and how to reply. "He isn't what you're used to in a relationship?"

Hu looked away and shook her head. "No, last time we talked about everything, even when it was a problem with the other person."

Ethan took Hu's hand in his. "There is nothing wrong with you or your relationship. John is just different. He's in uncharted waters for a start, but I don't think he will even open up completely about everything. That's who he is, and his training doesn't help either, having to keep top level secrets, as he does. I assure you, you mean more to him than anything, and I think deep down you know that. Maybe you just need to adapt a little."

Hu stared at Ethan, "Maybe. I know he cares. It is just..."

"And you care too. Maybe that's the problem. You don't want to get hurt like you did last time?"

A tear fell from Hu's left eye, "No, I do not." She thought for a moment. "Yes, I care... maybe more than I want to admit to myself."

"If you want my advice, relax. Enjoy what you have and take it from there." Ethan started laughing.

"What is so funny?"

"Here I am telling you about relationships."

Hu giggled. "Yes, that is funny. I have taught you well."

"You have."

"You want a little boxing?"

Ethan raised an eyebrow. "You want to beat me to a pulp?"

"Not on my life, Jade would murder me. You came here for a workout and I have not finished yet."

"Yeah, OK. That'd be good."

Ethan came back into the quarters he shared with Jade, hot and sweaty.

"You look like you had a good workout."

"Boxing match with Hu." He rubbed his shoulder, trying to relieve a punishing punch Hu had inflicted on him. "Anyway, do I get a hug?"

Jade backed away, "Not until you've had a shower, you don't."

"Please!"

"In the bathroom, I'll hug you when you get out."

"Really?"

Jade rolled her eyes, "Just a hug."

Ethan shrugged in defeat, mumbling under his breath, as he obeyed and walked to the bathroom to freshen up.

The next day, everyone came into the command centre to witness the transfer to sub-light speed, and maybe find out something about the star system they had entered. Celeste sat in the command chair, being on shift, but Ethan sat next to her watching the view of the outside on the screen in front of him. Celeste looked over to him as if wondering whether he wanted to check up on her, but looked back to her screen. The time came and Celeste reduced the warp drive power to the minimum setting. The ship slowed and re-entered sub-light speed with a flash of light from the warp bubble that encased them, as all the accumulated photons and particles escaped. The surrounding space clarified as normal visual inputs started again.

Celeste magnified the view of the inner system, and people pointed out objects they saw. Four enormous spheres became visible with the magnification.

"What are they?" Pia asked. She had fully recovered from her injuries a week after they resumed their journey.

"They are planets. The two outer planets interest us, the inner one in particular. People have long speculated that it is just inside the temperate zone for the system. From what I can see at the moment, it looks promising, especially since it seems to have a green tinge to it."

"That would be promising. You'd better get busy and think of a name for it then," Ethan said. Celeste had named Chiron and Chariclo, the habitable planets orbiting Alpha Centauri.

"Will do," Celeste replied with raised eyebrows and a smirk.

"How long till we get close enough to start our work?" Pia asked again.

"Another couple of days, I'm afraid. We went sub-light a fair way out because we weren't sure about the dispersion of the debris zone outside of the system plane."

Everyone groaned.

"That means we have two more days to exercise," Ethan said.

Everyone groaned again as they disappeared out the doors of the command centre.

Two days later the two planets of interest loomed in front of them, overwhelming the screen, the inner one now definitely displaying signs of an ecosystem on the planet. The outer one did not seem as promising. It looked cold and barren with little signs of life, or that there ever had been life on it, very similar to Mars. The atmosphere on the ship transformed, as they anticipated the discoveries they may make in the near future.

Ethan called a meeting and everyone in the expedition team sat at the conference table. "Have you thought of any names yet Celeste?"

"Only for the planet of interest, I call it Caerus because it signifies an opportunity to me."

"Hmm, excellent choice again," Ethan replied. The others nodded.

"Now, we need to set up the wormhole portal first. So. Hugo, where do you want it?"

"The experience from Alpha Centauri suggests that we can have it relatively close to the planet — Caerus — without causing space-time disturbances, so I think about one hundred thousand kilometers should be fine. That means that transfers will be quick, if they prove necessary."

"That sounds good," Ethan said. "How long will it take to assemble? The same as last time?"

"No, it should only take four days once we get all the modules out into space. We made a few modifications with this one to make the assembly easier and, hopefully, foolproof."

"Good, we'll do that then. In the meantime, we'll start exploring the planet from close orbit like last time. Pia, are you ready to drop your probes?"

"Yes, I have Marie's biological units ready too. We just need to get there."

"Good, Celeste, what about astronomical data?"

"Already collected and analyzing. There doesn't seem to be any unstable activities with the star, and the magnetic fields are ideal to protect Caerus from radiation activity."

"I must agree," Pia added. "The general atmosphere seems very protective of whatever is below regarding cosmic rays."

"OK, anything else?"

"When can we get down there and do some real exploring?" Ravi asked.

"Be patient. We learned from last time that it's wise not to rush things too quickly," Ethan replied, looking at Jade in particular.

There were no further questions, so Ethan closed the meeting and let everyone go do what they needed to. Jade stayed.

"Do you think you're ready?" she asked.

Ethan sighed. "I don't think I'll ever be. I don't want us to go through what happened last time, but being an explorer is a risky business. If I'm not prepared to take the risk, then I shouldn't be on this expedition, as you have also had to decide. I just want to make sure things are safe this time around."

"Yes, I have." Jade reached out and held Ethan's hand. "We'll be fine. We have each other."

Ethan smiled, "Yes, we have each other."

∿

∿

∿

THE LANDER SHOT out of *Destiny's* Lander Bay two days later, as the wormhole portal assembly feverishly started, the circular aperture taking form as the segments connected with each other. Pia, Ravi, Marie and Jade formed the team on the Lander for the first reconnaissance of Caerus. Pia and Ravi looked out of the portholes, watching the planet grow larger and pointing to things they saw, making comments. The others sat in silence, contemplating their thoughts. Jade mused about the recurring circumstance in particular, thinking about the crew members they had lost from the last expedition. She knew the futility of dwelling on it, but couldn't help feeling sad that they were not around to continue the adventure with the rest of them.

It took three hours to cover the distance to the planet, as they settled into a five hundred kilometer orbit around the equatorial zone. Ravi set up his scanning equipment and produced a map, as they completed a full orbit of Caerus. He gave the view screen to Pia, who marked the locations she wanted to send the probes to. The Lander pilot soon worked out the release points in orbit with Ravi's help, and the crew settled into the routine of loading the probes into the launch tube and launching them on the pilot's signal. They released all six probes, and those aboard sat patiently while Pia worked on uploading data from them, once they started broadcasting the information back to the receiving tablet. Marie, in particular, was fidgety to get visual feeds showing any vegetation, or possible animal life on the planet.

"We're starting to get something back," Marie said, as she looked at the pictures displayed on her tablet.

"Bring it up on the Lander screen," Jade said, enthusiastic for all to see.

Marie worked on the tablet, and an image appeared on the screen. Silence engulfed the cabin as they all looked at the images the small microbiological rover transmitted back to the ship.

"Look," Ravi said. "The vegetation looks similar to Earth's."

"It does," Marie agreed. "Completely different to what we discovered at Centauri."

The probe transmitting the images they viewed had landed in a tropical part of the planet. There were lush trees towering overhead and green long bladed grasses in view, almost as if they were back on Earth.

The small roving vehicle moved over the surface in jerking fashion as it hit the micro bumps and gullies of the terrain. It stopped moving when it sensed motion coming from a direction out of the camera's field of view. The camera turned and brought into focus an image that had all aboard mesmerized. A bird, maybe ten centimeters tall, was hopping towards the camera lens, jerking its head from side to side as it went, trying to make sense of the strange object in front of it. It had green and red feather coloring along its body and brilliant blue for wings. The feathers around the eyes and beak were black.

"I don't believe it," Jade said. "How can something so similar to a bird be on this planet? Surely evolution on the two planets can't have occurred in such an equivalent manner."

"It seems somewhat unlikely," Marie agreed. "But there it is."

"Gerhardt will have a field day explaining this one," Pia added, a sardonic smile on her face.

"Well, are we finished for today?" Jade asked.

"All the probes are transmitting back," Pia said.

"My rovers are all active too," Marie added.

"Let's get back then," Jade said. She went to the cockpit and advised the pilot to take them back to *Destiny.*

Ethan called a meeting of the team the next day and they all slowly assembled in the conference room attached to the command centre. Ethan and Jade were first. Marie, Angelo and Max filed in not long after, Hu and John walked in next and Ravi, Gerhardt and Pia brought up the rear.

Ethan called the meeting to order, "The reconnoissance mission has been very successful, judging by the visual footage streaming back to us."

The others nodded.

"The vegetation and animal life is explosively fascinating," Gerhardt said. "This is going to re-write all the textbooks on evolution. It will take years to develop an adequate theory on how life can be so similar on two distinct planets, separated by such substantial distances."

"There may be a very logical explanation in the end, when you gather further information," Ethan suggested.

"Maybe..." Gerhardt's attention wondered off into his own personal thoughts momentarily, as if he was already contemplating potential theories.

"Is there anything else to report on the planet so far?"

"I can tell you then the planet is about one point three times the size of the Earth, a little smaller than astronomical observations from home. Its gravity is one point two times that of earth, slightly heavy but adaptable. The atmospheric pressure is one hundred and four kilopascals. The big negative though is the oxygen, it's only fifteen-point four percent. We won't be able to breathe it without the oxygen enhancers. Good thing we brought them with," Celeste said.

"That is most extraordinary then. How did life develop so similarly with very different oxygen levels, and how do the native species on this planet survive on such low oxygen? Very fascinating," Gerhardt interjected.

The group smiled at his inquisitive postulations.

"Be that as it may," Ethan said, "it seems we will find out, eventually. Anything else?"

Pia had a frown on her face the entire meeting. She eventually raised her voice. "I've been studying the visual information we took while we orbited the planet to get some insight into the meteorology of the place. I would like to share an image I came across and see what you think of it. I'm at a loss to explain what it is." She took her tablet out and adjusted the settings until the image she wanted to display came on the screen in the conference room.

"I see nothing out of the ordinary," Max said.

"Let me magnify it." Pia circled an area of the image. "Keep your eyes on this as I enlarge it." She zoomed in on the particular region until it started to pixelate and zoomed out slightly before letting the image settle. "Can you see something out of place there?"

Ethan looked closely. He gulped, as ideas of what he thought it might be came into his head. He said, "That doesn't look natural."

A buzz of confusion echoed through the room, as they took in the comment, and started coming to the same conclusion.

"What is it then?" John asked.

"A very good question," Hu agreed, as she leaned forward towards the image.

14

GRUBEXL

G rubexl walked through the forest next to his residence, looking for berries and other fruit to collect for his sustenance. Each day seemed like a repeat of the previous one, and there had been so many of them. His bitterness grew with each day. His loneliness felt overbearing as he waited for his civilisation to forgive him and have him back, but he knew they had very long memories, as did he. He had been right in what he did, even if the others didn't think so. Having filled his basket, he walked back to the compound where he lived. Several buildings stood in a roughly rectangular arrangement, one building being his residence, the others containing equipment and other things needed for his activities, and in the middle of it all stood a stela, obsidian black, the physical focus of his hate. He went to his residence and packed the gathered food away, returning to the outside again. The compound lay surrounded by forest and sloped up at one end, allowing him to see above the treelike towards the east, south and west. He had constructed a seat in that position for him to sit on as he contemplated from time to time. He headed for the seat to calm his thoughts.

The sun stood directly overhead. One of the two moons hung in the sky just to the south of west, the other already below the horizon.

The verdant vegetation swayed gently in the breeze as the chirp of birds came to his ears. He closed his eyes to let the sweet music of the birds better absorb into him, allowing the rhythm to synchronize with his soul. Opening his eyes again, he saw the contrail of a craft in the sky in the distance. His heart leaped as he wondered what it might mean. He hadn't seen such a thing for a very long time. When he thought about it, he realized it must have been at least two million Earth years since he had experienced such a sight. At one point two metres in height, his appearance resembled human makeup — two arms, two legs and visual and auditory senses in the head. His skin tended towards the reddish-brown part of the visible spectrum, and he had no hair. Sexual organs were also similar, as some of his species had taken advantage of. His longevity attributed to his cells' ability to regenerate, without mutation or clipping of any gene segments, as needed.

He got by in his solitary existence, delving into various projects on the planet. Astronomy was a favorite, but had been fruitless in its results. He had found no other life forms it the area of space he occupied until a few days ago. A flash momentarily brightened the night sky and an extra glow appeared above the planet a few days later. He knew it wasn't a star. It could maintain its own position, but moved against the background stars as the planet rotated. Hurrying back down from his perch, he rushed to his observatory to see if he could get a visual image of the object. Adjusting the telescope to the general position the object flew towards, he changed the focus and magnification until he just saw the speck of the craft disappear into the space beyond. He now knew that a spaceship had traveled to the planet.

This may be his chance to escape his prison finally, if only he could attract the beings' attention. He presumed that the unnatural form of his shelter would pique their curiosity, and they would come to investigate, eventually. He needed to learn patience. He went back inside his shelter and did just that.

15

CAERUS

The Lander plunged through the atmosphere, the occupants as excited with the prospect of stepping on an alien planet as the first time on Chariclo. They peered out of the view ports in anticipation. Ethan had kept the team off the planet for what seemed like weeks, but was actually less than a fortnight, while everyone checked for habitability and any hint of microscopic organisms that could harm humans. Their frustration with him grew by the day and his with them, but he would not budge until he convinced himself it was safe to descend to the planet. Even then, they had to go through the same strict routine of fully self-contained environmental suits while they explored the area. Some were sympathetic to Ethan's dictatorial requirements, some like Marie and Jade who had almost died on Chariclo. Ethan's extreme caution dismayed the newer members of the team. They reluctantly complied with Ethan's instructions, all the same. Ethan, Marie, Gerhardt and Pia were the fortunate ones now descending to the planet.

"What are you thinking?" Ethan asked Pia.

Pia disrupted her looking out the view port to look at him, eyes wide, "It is just so incredible that we are here, in another star system, descending to another planet."

"Amazing, isn't it? Unfortunately, some beauty has a tendency of creeping up behind you and biting you when you least expect it."

"You are exaggerating, surely," Gerhardt said, as he overheard the conversation and joined in.

"I'm not. We had a real fright on Chariclo. A fright that turned tragic. I don't want that to happen again."

"Well, Let's see what is down there. Then we can decide what might bite and what will not."

"Yeah, let's see."

Pia and Gerhardt went back to peering out of the view ports as the planet came closer by the second. They entered the lower atmosphere and cloud formations buffeted the Lander as it prepared for landing. The Lander hovered over a suitable landing site half an hour later and slowly descended to the ground, a slight jolt reverberating through it when it made contact. The full weight of the vessel bore down on the soil moments later as the engines powered down.

"Suits on," Ethan instructed, as he moved to the change room.

Everyone had their environmental suits on half an hour later, ready to disembark and start exploring outside. They also placed their oxygen enhancers in their noses so they could breathe the filtered outside air without having to don breathing apparatus. Ethan thought enhancers were very useful technology, and he wished he had the option to use them at Alpha Centauri so they could have gone to Chiron to explore the surface of that planet.

Ethan stepped through the airlock first and onto the native soil at the bottom of the steps from the hatch. It reminded him of the previous time, and the awe and wonder of the moment felt the same, as he looked at the panorama of a new world, like an explorer stepping onto the shores of a new shoreline on Earth for the first-time centuries ago. He thought he would never get bored with the sensation. He moved away from the Lander, so that the next person could come down, which was Marie. She stepped out and down the steps, looking around too.

"Amazing, isn't it," she said as she took in the view.

"Yes, it is. I don't understand how it could look so much like earth though."

"Well, that's one thing that we are here to find out, I suppose."

"Yeah."

"What if we find pathogens that are compatible with us?"

"That depends on what they are and how they interact. I suspect that, if we find one here, we will find many. That may not be bad depending on what their DNA structures are. They might infect us, but not in a lethal manner, like on Chariclo. Their structure may be such that we can fight them with our existing immune system, which would make them basically harmless. We just have to see what eventuates."

Ethan stared at Marie, deciphering what she had said, "Yeah, we have to see."

Pia stepped out next, followed several minutes later by Gerhardt. They all wandered away from the Lander, taking in their surroundings, but kept within one hundred metres of it.

Ethan drew close to Pia. She looked around and gazed at the trees nearby and the sky. "Amazing," she said.

"It is," Ethan agreed.

"Look, look... a bird," Pia said, pointing to an object in the sky.

Ethan saw her mouth gape wide open through the transparent visor of her suit. He looked to where she pointed and was equally astounded. "Gerhardt," he shouted. Gerhardt looked over to see what the commotion was. "Look up there."

Gerhardt looked in the direction and stood still as the creature flapped its wings across the sky and out of view. He walked over to Ethan and Pia, "That was magnificent. This will take a long time to investigate. It is going to re-write the theories we have on evolution. It looked identical in physiology to avians on Earth."

"Yes it did," Ethan responded.

Marie walked over, hearing Gerhardt's comment. "It may not be as coincidental as we think. Maybe certain species types are just better adapting to our type of environment."

Marie wondered off towards the tree line. The tropical climate produced trees resembling species typical in that environment. She jumped, as a cacophony of shrieks started from high in the trees with an instantaneous riot of movement, her hand reaching for the laser pistol she had strapped to her waist. What seemed like hundreds of simian type creatures expressed their displeasure at Marie's intrusion into their territory, as they retreated further into the jungle and safety. Marie stood still and took in the spectacle, as her hand relaxed its grip on the pistol. The creatures had bright green snouts and orange and yellow posteriors. They became camouflaged again as they disappeared into the depths of the jungle. The others looked over towards Marie as they heard the noise.

They all returned to the vicinity of the Lander once they had satisfied their curiosity of their surroundings.

"Let's get the gear out of the hatches and set up camp," Ethan said.

They spent the next three hours doing that, feeling exhausted afterwards, the drain exasperated by having to conduct the activity in the environmental suits. Ethan thought the oxygen enhancers worked surprisingly well, although he noticed that he had to stop and rest more often than he considered he would have at a normal oxygen level. He presumed it wasn't because of a lack of fitness, since the others seemed to have the same difficulty. Looking around, he saw that the assembled equipment started looking like a work facility, Marie already busy setting up her instruments for the test work she needed to do.

Looking up to the sky, Ethan saw cumulonimbus clouds starting to form towards the horizon, suggesting a storm sometime later in the day. Not unusual for the climate, he thought, if it replicated the climate on Earth. A mountain range hid most of the western view. It looked reachable for exploration once they settled into a routine.

"That's about all we can do for now," Marie said, as she walked over to Ethan.

"You don't want to do any testing before we go?" Ethan asked.

"No, we've had a busy day so far. I'd rather get back to the ship and have a good rest. Get a fresh start in the morning."

"That sounds like a good idea." Ethan stood thinking for a moment. "That unusual structure we saw, is it far from here?"

"I don't know. We can ask Pia."

Finding Pia busy recording a few climatic observations, they both walked over to her.

"Pia, that strange structure you showed us. Is it anywhere nearby?" Ethan asked.

Pia stopped what she was doing and thought. "It's not too far away, I think. Just give me a minute." Pia walked over to one of the trestle tables they had set up and retrieved her tablet. Turning it on, she flicked through the images she captured of the planet and found the location of the structure. "Yes, it's just a thousand kilometers northwest," she said, as she walked back to Ethan and Marie. "We could fly over it and take a closer look as we return to the ship."

"Good, we'll do that. Let's get things secured and we can leave for the day," Ethan replied.

They all went to work strapping everything down and secure against storms or any potentially inquisitive animals that may venture into the camp, wondering whether any of the unknown things were edible. They were ready to leave an hour later and entered the Lander through the decontamination chamber to remove any unwanted material or life forms from their suits. Getting settled inside the Lander, Ethan talked to the pilot about their route as Pia showed them where to fly over. Several minutes later, the pilot powered the Lander up and they started their trip back, traveling about five hundred metres above the ground in a northwest direction. The pilot kept the Lander at a leisurely speed to give the others an excellent view of the landscape below, so it took about two hours before they approached the site of interest.

"Target approaching," the pilot advised.

Ethan and the others looked out of the window in the general direction where they expected seeing the formation. The canopy of the trees disguised most of the site as they approached until it gave way to cleared ground, giving an unimpeded view of the area. Ethan opened his mouth to speak, but nothing came out. Obvious buildings stood below them with tracks crisscrossing the area, presumably made by animals or another creature they could not see. There were several other structures, geometrically arranged, on the site, but one stood out, ever from the top aspect view that they had, a thin tall stela that looked obsidian black. Nothing seemed to move below.

"You want another flyby?" the pilot asked.

"You get a recording?" Ethan asked Pia, finally recovering from the trance he found himself in.

"Yeah."

"No, let's get back to the ship."

The Lander banked sharply and oriented almost vertical as it propelled out of the Caerus atmosphere.

TWO EYES PEERED out of the doorway, looking at the object in the sky, as it flew over and then disappeared. A calculating smile appeared on Grubexl's face.

16

FRESH AIR

Several weeks passed, exploring and analyzing the biology of the planet, while they had the environmental suits on. The team started complaining, but Ethan stayed adamant of the need for it until he had definitive confirmation, from Marie in particular, that it was safe to continue without protection. He did not want another incident like Chariclo. The others tried to understand, but it was clumsy and difficult work when that had to use the suits. Ethan finally assembled the team in the conference room on *Destiny* to decide on whether they could finally get rid of the suits.

Ethan walked into the room at nine thirty in the morning GMT, his thoughts momentarily on the cuddle Jade and he had enjoyed earlier, before having to get up. The pleasure quickly evaporated as his mind refocused on the matter at hand. Hu, John, Marie and Celeste already sat there, discussing news sent through to them via the wormhole that morning, which they had assembled and activated within a week of arriving at the planet. They received regular updates on current affairs back on Earth, transmitted through to them, to help keep the crew informed and occupied when not on duty with their various tasks. "Good morning," Ethan said, as he rounded the table to his usual seat at the head.

"Good morning," the others responded, breaking from their discussion.

Gerhardt and Ravi entered moments later and sat, followed in quick succession by Jade, Angelo, Pia and Max. Ethan was glad that the team was no larger, as the current number just fit into the room. They all greeted each other.

"Can I have your attention, please?" Ethan said, bringing the meeting to order. The others slowly became silence. "There is only one topic on the agenda this morning. That is whether we have enough information to decide on removing the environmental suits when on the planet."

A buzz of excitement circulated the room at the prospect.

"About time," Gerhardt said. "We would have removed them weeks ago, if it were up to me."

"Well, it wasn't up to you," Ethan retorted. "Experience has taught the rest of us a valuable lesson on Chariclo. I do not want a repeat."

"Only making a comment," Gerhardt grumbled.

"Anyway, maybe you can provide some analysis of the general biology of the planet for us, before we move on to Marie's assessment."

Gerhardt straightened his posture in the chair before starting his exposition. "As several of you may have observed, the general flora and fauna are uncannily similar to that on Earth. How this can be, is mere conjecture and hypothesis but the explanation will keep a myriad of scientist busy on PHD's for many years, I think." Several people in the room sniggered at the comment. "The cell structure and physiology of the species observed so far, show complete compatibility with that of Earth based biology. It seems to have the same DNA and chromosomal based building blocks as ours. The possibility of interbreeding would be very interesting. The evidence would suggest that we could successfully digest the various plants and animals as a food source, once tested for toxicity."

"Has the lower oxygen level in the atmosphere affected the physiology?" Angelo asked.

"A good question," Gerhardt said. "Yes, it has. The animals have much larger lungs for their body mass than their Earthly counterparts. The plants are much the same as Earth as they breathe in carbon dioxide, which is higher here than on Earth, even with the effects of the recent climate change crisis earlier this century. You could say that the plants are belching out oxygen as quickly as they can absorb it. It wouldn't surprise me if the atmosphere is increasing its concentration of oxygen. Not sure if Ravi can determine this from geological sampling."

"That is a good point. I will make a note to include it in my list of research topics," Ravi said, as he jotted a note on his datapad.

"To sum up my current observations, I would say that there is nothing inherently hostile to us biologically. Marie will provide a comprehensive assessment on the pathological level."

"Thank you, Gerhardt," Ethan said. "Any questions for Gerhardt...?"

"I have one," Jade said. "Are there any carnivorous animals we need to watch out for, that would pose a threat to us?"

"My depth of observation has not included a large enough area to answer that question comprehensively," Gerhardt replied. "However, I have seen nothing that would be of danger to us yet, although there are carnivorous species present."

"Any more...?" Ethan asked after a pause. He continued after another pause, "OK then. Marie, can you want to provide your assessment?"

"Certainly," Marie started. "I am astounded by the similarity of the pathology of this place with Earth. The structure and makeup of the bacteria and other micro-organisms are almost identical, so much so it is just impossible for this to be a mere coincidence. I will be happy for someone to prove it otherwise. It's as if someone has transported the organic matter from one planet to the other, but that is for someone else to work out."

"Does that mean that we are at high risk of infection, like on Chariclo?" Celeste asked.

"On the contrary, it means that, since most of the micro-organisms are so similar, we are likely to be immune to them already from our exposure on Earth. As I hope you understand, I cannot one hundred percent guarantee that any of the ones here won't affect us. However, we can easily treat any adverse reactions to any of them that cause problems."

"Why wasn't that the case last time?" Jade asked, her eyebrows drawing close together.

"That was a distinctly different problem. That virus was a genetically engineered virus specifically developed to cause a modification to the chromosomal structure. The micro-organisms observed are nothing like that. They just cause infections similar to that on Earth."

"Is there any sign that other areas of the planet would contain anything different to what you have observed?" John asked both Marie and Gerhardt.

Gerhardt shook his head.

"Micro-organisms spread over the entire planet, given time. We have collected samples from three climatic areas with the same conclusion for each area," Marie responded.

"I see."

"That is about all that I have to say," Marie concluded.

"Does anyone have a question for Marie?" Ethan asked.

"Not a question, but an observation," John said. "I think we should take a step back and check whenever we see an enclosed space like that on Chariclo, just to be certain it doesn't pose a threat."

"Good suggestion," Ethan said. "Anything else?"

Silence filled the room and everyone leaned in to the table and looked at Ethan with bright expectant eyes.

"If not, then Marie and Gerhardt, what is your assessment? Can we throw away the suits?"

"Marie and I have discussed this and I will leave her to answer you, as it is more a question for her than me. I agree with what she is to say," Gerhardt said.

"Even though there will never be a one hundred percent guarantee, I see no reason to continue wearing the suits, based on the evidence we have before us," Marie concluded.

People burst into smiles and started talking about what it would be like to walk the planet without the restriction of the suits for the first time.

Ethan sat contemplating the information provided by Gerhardt and Marie, trying to decide. He looked at Jade, and the fear and torment of Chariclo crossed his thoughts. It was an irrational thought considering the assessment Marie had made, but it kept playing on his mind. He finally looked at John to see if he had anything to say, but he just raised his brow, showing that the decision was Ethan's, and he would support it. Ethan sighed. "I suppose we can test and analyze forever and still not come up with a foolproof answer, but at the end of the day we have to come to an informed judgement, eventually. So, given the evidence before us, unless anyone has an objection, I have decided that we can take the suits off."

The group cheered.

"So we have concluded that business. If there is nothing else..."

Celeste raised her hand with a sheepish smile on her face.

"Yes, Celeste?"

"Do you think I can go down to the planet this time?"

Ethan laughed. "Yes, I'm sure we can arrange at least one visit, unless you don't trust me to run away with the ship while you're down there."

"You wouldn't?" Celeste questioned, mouth open and eyebrow raised. Everyone laughed. Realizing the joke, she quipped, "I'll put a lock on the controls before I go." She smirked as she stood to leave.

Ethan shook his head. "The meeting is over," he said, as he stood.

An expedition of people descended to the planet the next day, minus the environmental suits comprising Ravi, Marie, Gerhardt and Ethan. Ethan was adamant that Jade stay on the ship until he confirmed the safety of the environment. Jade mentioned the illogical thinking to him, it was all right for him to be in danger but not her, but he stood his ground. She relented.

They landed without incident and the hatch opened, this time to the scent and aroma of fresh air.

17

THE DRONE

Now free from the restriction of the environmental suits, and all the difficulties they entailed, Ethan and the others could conduct a more deliberate exploration of the planet Caerus. They ferried a personnel buggy, accommodation modules and equipment down to the surface with the Landers and set up camp with other supplies. They quickly adapted to the restricting irritation of the oxygen enhancers in their nostrils as they concentrated on their delegated tasks.

"How is the setup of the camp coming along?" Ethan asked Marie, whom he placed in charge.

"Good, we will have all the personnel accommodation, amenities and workstations ready by tomorrow night. A skeleton group can remain tonight, with what we've constructed so far," Marie replied.

"I need to get back to *Destiny*, so who'll stay down here overnight?"

"I, Gerhardt and Pia have volunteered. Ravi wants to return to put together another consignment of equipment for tomorrow."

Ethan rubbed his chin. "An interesting trio of people. You must let me know how you get on."

Marie laughed. "I'm sure we'll be able to remain civil for one night. Gerhardt can be a little insensitive in how he says things sometimes, but he's harmless, and I think Pia knows that."

"But can Pia control herself?"

"I'm sure she can."

With the supplies and equipment safely moved to their corresponding locations in the camp, Ethan and Ravi said goodbye to the others, and boarded the Lander to return to the ship in orbit.

They had located the camp in a suitable clearing next to a river that wove a gentle u-shaped bend around it. Judging by the footprints and other evidence, animals frequently came to the stream for a drink. *We'll scare them off*, Marie thought with a little remorse at the intrusion to the animal life. Shouting coming from the other side of the camp, out of eyesight from where she stood, interrupted her thoughts. She rolled her eyes as she heard the altercation she knew she needed to resolve.

"What do you mean, I know nothing about ecology?" Pia shouted at Gerhardt. "I studied that topic extensively in my course curriculum. What don't I know? Come on, tell me."

Gerhardt, despite being stubborn, some would say typically Germanely stubborn, tried placating Pia, not wanting conflict over such a trivial matter, "All I said was the ecological system here isn't as simple as you may think. I apologize if you took it as me questioning your intellect in the matter. Most people have a basic understanding of ecological systems."

"Oh, now you think my understanding is no better than the common knowledge," Pia retorted.

Gerhardt cringed and sighed, "That's not what I meant either."

"What's going on?" Marie said, as she walked towards them at a rapid pace.

"He's insulting my intelligence," Pia stated.

Gerhardt pleaded with Marie to help him, "We were having a discussion about the ecological systems of the planet and somehow Pia misunderstood what I was saying. I hold Pia in high regard intellectually."

Marie looked at both of them Gerhardt with a confused expression, and Pia fuming for a fight to the bitter end. "Let's calm down, shall we... please? I don't want to spend tonight trying to stop you two from killing each other."

"Well, he should apologize."

Marie looked at Gerhardt, an eyebrow raised, suggesting he should comply for the sake of peace.

Gerhardt stood straight, in defiance, as if inferring that he didn't apologize to anyone, but he saw Marie's firm stance and sighed, his shoulders slumping at the same time. "I apologize if I upset you with what I said. I didn't mean it and what I meant came out wrong."

"That's better," Pia said.

"And Pia, don't you think you may have over-reacted a little?"

Pia turned to Marie, fire in her eyes with no intention of apologizing. Marie stared back in parental forbearance, making Pia uneasy after a while. The fire finally quenched, and she lowered her head as if in childlike repentance, "I apologize," she mumbled.

"What was that?" Marie asked, almost laughing at the insanity of the situation, her seeming need to be a parent chastising a child.

Pia looked up, stubbornly resisting for a moment, but then said, "I apologize for my behavior."

Marie sighed in relief. "Now can we think about getting dinner ready and a good night's sleep."

The three settled down for the night without further incident. It almost became convivial, surprising Marie as she thought the three most fiery personalities had congregated together with no moderating influence to tide things over, if needed. Marie looked out of the window of the mess cabin as dusk set in. Her eyes bulged. "Come look at this," she told the others.

Pia and Gerhardt came and looked out the window, curious about what Marie wanted them to see. "Wow," Pia said. They looked at deer-like creatures prancing to the water line of the river, furtively scanning the treelike of the forest area for any sign of predators. Some bent to drink from the water as others kept vigil and then swapped after the first ones had their fill. Other smaller creatures were also there. Monkeys, rabbits and birds, all quenching their thirst before darkness took over the landscape. Something suddenly scared the animals away and moments later two large carnivores slinked up to the river to have their fill of water, feline in appearance, not bothering to monitor the area for any danger. One cat looked over to the structures along the opposite shore to them, sensing something had changed, but it quickly lost interest, as it decided that it posed no threat. They too left after a while. Gerhardt virtually drooled with excitement at the unexpected spectacle so close to them.

After cleaning up the dishes, they walked outside into the open air and the illuminated area of the camp, as they wandered over to their sleeping quarters. "Look," Gerhardt said, as he pointed up. "Two moons."

The others looked and stared in wonder at the sight, amazed at their fortune of being the first humans to gaze up at the moons. They all went to bed after that.

THEY WOKE the next morning to a hazy orange-red sunrise, as the humidity hung in the stagnant air. They all started perspiring, even before the sun rose twenty degrees above the horizon. They had breakfast and prepared to start their exploratory activities for the day. The Lander came into the site about ten in the morning and Ethan, Ravi, Hu and Max leaped out of the hatch once it opened.

"Welcome back," Marie said to Ethan as she approached him.

"How'd the first night go?"

"I almost thought I'd have to bring you back to collect a dead body at one stage, but I got Pia and Gerhardt to resolve their differences without bloodshed."

Ethan chuckled. "So I had some cause for concern."

"I'm sure they would have come to their senses before it came to that. Anyway, they seem happy enough now."

Ethan walked over to Pia as she prepared to launch a weather balloon for data collection. "How are things going?"

Pia paused from what she was doing and looked at Ethan, a hand rising to her face to tuck a strand of hair back behind her ear, "Good. I'll have this balloon airborne in a moment. The sensors will send back a lot of data about the atmosphere to plug into the climate models I have."

"It'll be very enlightening, if they're anything like David's were."

"These are much better than his."

Ethan raised an eyebrow at the uninhibited boast.

"Well, they are," Pia said, sensing Ethan's scepticism.

"I'm not judging your assessment. Just a little surprised that you voiced it in such a way, that's all."

Pia shrugged, "I rarely hold back my opinions."

"Anyway, do you want to come with Hu and me to explore a bit in the all-terrain when you've finished here?"

Pia's eyes lit up. "Sure, you should have been here last night. All sorts of animals came out."

"I heard some claws came out in the camp last night too," Ethan said with an ironic smile.

Pia blushed, "We may've been a little overenthusiastic."

Ethan let a hearty laugh escape his lips. "Let's get this launched and get on our way."

Pia completed the last of the tasks to prepare the balloon and launched it half an hour later. They both watched it fly up into the sky until they couldn't see it anymore. She checked that the measurements were being transmitted back to the receiver and properly recorded, as Ethan went to the all-terrain vehicle, preparing it for departure. "I'm ready," Pia said, once she walked over to Ethan and Hu, as they talked to each other to fill in the time.

"I'll just tell Marie and we'll be on our way." Ethan had a brief discussion with Marie, before returning and hopping into the vehicle in the driver's seat. Pia got in the other side, and Hu occupied the passenger seat behind Pia. They drove off out of the camp.

The cabin rocked from side to side as they hugged close to the river traveling downstream from the campsite. A sandy bank provided a good pathway to travel on at the start, but they had to venture into the forest when the river dipped into a gorged area, etched out of the soil and rock over the eons. It seemed to cut deeper and deeper as they went further downstream, although they had to veer quite a distance from the watercourse sometimes to find a suitable path to follow. A sharp rise loomed ahead two hours later. Ethan drove up almost to the top of the rise and stopped. Rocks prevented them from continuing further.

"Let's go see what's on the other side," Ethan said.

They all hopped out of the vehicle and threaded their way through the rocks until the top of the rise appeared in front of them. They walked to the summit and stood, astonished by the panorama in front of them. The sea spread out in all forward directions to the horizon. They stood at the top of a very tall cliff face that plunged down to the beach below, waves crashing into the precipice as they carried their rhythmic motion ashore. Water burst away from the escarpment, halfway up, as the river plunged out as a waterfall into the sea, spray from the clash spewing up a rainbow of scintillating color.

"It's beautiful," Pia said, her eyes sparkling like diamonds.

"Yes, it is," Ethan agreed. "Looks like the river has gouged a ravine through the landscape over the millennia to get to the sea."

"Breathtaking," Hu said.

They all stood motionless, taking in the scene before them, not wishing to break the spell. After a while Hu asked, "What's that?" as she pointed towards a speck hovering in the air.

"Don't know," Ethan said. "Let me get the binoculars." He walked back to the vehicle and found the instrument in a bag in the back. He went back and brought the binoculars to his eyes, adjusting the focus as he did so. Pointing them in the direction Hu showed, he studied the air above the seascape intensely. His rhythmic side-to-side movement stopped in mid-sweep as he spotted something in the air. Sharpening the focus, he gasped. Taking the binoculars away from his eyes, he looked at the others, "It's a drone, or something very similar." His brow creased as he realized what it meant.

"I take it, it's not one of ours," Hu said. Ethan shook his head.

"Can I look?" Pia asked.

Ethan handed the binoculars to her. She raised them to her eyes and homed in on the object Ethan had found, studying it for some time. "It must have an anti-gravity propulsion system," she said as she maintained her watch. "I can't see anything that look like rotors or anything else."

Ethan looked at Hu, "Looks like something from Earth though."

Pia watched it as it slowly rotated. Two legs started projecting from the bottom of the drone, bringing a furrow to Pia's brow. Missiles fired. Moments later, the ground suddenly groaned and shook below them. "Run," Pia shouted at the others, as she turned to obey her own order. The cliff face directly underneath them started slumping, sending rock and soil out into the sea below, collapsing the part of the cliff they stood on, the three finding themselves in the air. They followed the disappearing ground into the abyss below.

The avalanche didn't fall as far as Ethan expected. He felt the ground solidify below him moments after being suspended in midair, a far shorter time that if they had fallen all the way to the sea below. He coughed and splutter the dust from his lungs as it rose from the debris. He lay flat on his back and he slowly rubbed the grit away from around his eyes before he opened them, trying to sense the rest of his body at the same time to find out if he felt any injuries he may have sustained. He couldn't feel anything serious. Opening his eyes, the dust settled around him as he looked around. His arms moved all right, as did his legs when he tried sitting up. It seemed he was intact and not injured, which amazed him considering what had just happened. The soil and rock had settled into a sloping scree that jutted out into the water, where it finally settled. He sat on top of the scree, but everything felt very unstable. Bits of rock rolling down the slope, as he dislodged them when he made any movement. The circumstances behind why he was there, and who were with him, suddenly came back into sharp focus. "Hugo... Pia," he shouted as he looked around for them.

Hu lay half buried in the rubble with her upper torso above the ground about five metres below him. She lay silent and motionless. He couldn't locate Pia for a time as he frantically looked for her. He finally spotted part of her arm sticking out of rocks and soil on the far side of the scree and about fifteen metres below, with not much else showing. He decided she was his priority, but moved to Hu to check whether she was still alive. Half crawling, half sliding on the loose rubble, he crept to her. She breathed regularly, and he silently thanked any god out there. He felt she would survive, despite the gash on her temple. She was unconscious.

He crawled past Hu and made his way to Pia. When he got to her, he saw that her head was only half buried, but the rest of her body lay hidden below the surface. Ethan dug around her face to free it completely and placed his fingers on her neck. He breathed a sigh of relief when he found a pulse and he also saw that she too breathed, but shallowly. He continued removing dirt and rocks from her face and cleared any particles from around her mouth, nose and eyes. Ethan continued removing debris from on top of Pia to expose as much of her as he could, so he could decide how badly injured she was.

Hu started moaning as Ethan dug the soil from around Pia. He looked up and saw her moving. Panic momentarily gripped him as he saw her slipping down the slope while she started wriggling herself to consciousness. "Stay still," he shouted back at her. Hu heard and understood him, as she instantly stopped moving.

She opened her eyes about half a minute later and looked around. "What happened?"

Ethan stopped what he was doing and thought about what had happened. He suddenly realized the obvious. He looked at Hu, "Part of the cliff collapsed. I suspect that drone had something to do with it."

"Oh."

"Are you hurt? I think you have a concussion. But do you have any other injuries?"

Hu tried moving her limbs, "Ouch." She lay motionless again. "Something is wrong with my left ankle. I think nothing else hurts too much. I have a splitting headache. Where are you? Where's Pia?"

"We're about ten metres below you. I'm trying to dig Pia out. I think she's badly hurt." He continued digging, developing a slight ledge from the dirt under him as he did so, making his position a little more stable.

"I am coming over," Hu said about three minutes later.

"Be careful, the ground's very unstable."

Hu turned over, wincing in pain from her ankle, and moved to a crawling position. She saw Ethan and started moving to him, keeping her pace slow to minimize any slippage. She arrived where Ethan still dug at the ground around Pia a few minutes later. "Hi," she said, as Ethan stopped and looked at her and immediately started giggling.

"What's so funny?"

"I am sorry. Your face is all covered in dust except for two circles around your eyes. I could not help it. I maybe look the same."

Ethan looked at Hu with a weird expression. "You can't hurt too badly then." He continued digging.

"She looks bad." Hu stated, starting to help Ethan with the digging.

Most of Pia's body finally became exposed from the effort and they saw that her buried left arm positioned at an unnatural angle, and her right lower leg, the bones bent almost at right angles halfway down.

"That doesn't look good," Ethan said.

"No." Hu moved closer to examine the leg. "At least the skin is unbroken."

"There's nothing to splint it with. What about her arm?"

"I think it is just dislocated at the shoulder. It concerns me she is unconscious though, and her breathing is so shallow. I hope she does not have internal bleeding." Hu looked around. "What are we going to do?"

What to do only entered Ethan's mind when Hu mentioned it. His concentration had been too intent on helping Hu and Pia until then. "I'll get hold of Marie to get some help."

"I lost my communicator and by the looks of it, Pia's is crushed." Pia's communicator lay next to her body, dented and bent beyond repair.

Ethan reached for his and found only air where it should have been. "I've lost mine too, great." He took a large breath and breathed out slowly, hoping to conjure a miracle from somewhere by doing it.

"The others won't start worrying until it gets dark."

"No, they won't. We have a bit of a problem, don't we?"

Hu looked out to where the drone had been. "Can you see that thing anymore?"

Ethan looked. After several seconds he said, "No, it must have left."

Hu lay on her back in the rubble. She started laughing moments later.

"What's so funny now?"

"We have to laugh, don't we? It is a strange predicament we find ourselves in. I wonder what Apep would think of it."

Ethan smiled, as he appreciated the ironic humor. He looked at Pia, "Not sure what we can do to make Pia more comfortable."

Hu looked over, "We should at least straighten her leg out, I think." She got up and moved over to Pia. Ethan did likewise and between them they moved her broken leg so it sat as straight as it could, given the circumstances. Pia moaned slightly as they moved the leg, but didn't wake. They also brought her arm around to sit at her side.

"Guess all we can do is wait. We can't climb back up," Ethan said.

"At least the weather is warm. We do not need rain though. It will be tomorrow before someone will start looking."

"Marie knows the general direction we went."

They both settled down on the scree, made themselves as comfortable as possible and waited, hoping Pia would last the night.

18

SEARCH AND RESCUE

Marie scanned the forested area where Ethan and the others had departed from the camp, as the sun started setting in the western sky, her brow creased. She tried raising each of them with their communicator system.

"I can't hear anything," Gerhardt said as he walked over to her.

"No, and I can't raise them on the communicator either. What could have happened?"

"I don't know. They probably stopped to look at something and time passed too quickly for them."

"Maybe, but Ethan at least would have called in that they may be late. You know how cautious he is. I don't like it."

"There isn't much we can do until morning, is there?"

"I suppose not. The Lander has returned to *Destiny*, so we can't do a quick sweep of the area, and we don't have another vehicle equipped with lights to follow them either."

"We might just have to wait till morning and go look for them on the hover bikes if they haven't returned yet or called in."

Marie rubbed her chin, "You may be right, but I don't like it. I think I'll call *Destiny* and get a Lander down here first thing in the morning."

"Surely it's not that serious yet."

"Better safe than sorrow. That's what I always live by in the micro-biological research facility I work in."

Gerhardt sighed. "We'd better go tell Ravi and Max then."

They walked back into the camp where Ravi catalogued the rocks he collected during the day and Max busied himself preparing food for dinner.

Max looked up as he saw the two walking toward him. "What's up?"

"The others haven't returned yet. I'm getting worried," Marie said.

"Ethan hasn't called in?"

"No, and I can't raise any of them on their communicators."

"Oh, that's not like Ethan or Hugo."

"No, it's not."

Noticing the conversation nearby, Ravi walked over to the others. "What is happening?" he asked.

"We can't get in contact with Ethan and the others," Marie responded.

"It is too late to search for them now."

"We know. I think I'll contact *Destiny* though." Marie walked over to the office area of the camp and went inside, sitting down at the desk that the ship communication system sat on. She sighed as she thought about what she wanted to say. She didn't want to alarm the people on the ship unnecessarily. Looking at the equipment, she knew it would not call the ship on its own, so she contacted the ship's command centre.

A crew member came online a few seconds later, "*Destiny* here."

"Can you get hold of Celeste please and get her to call me back?"

"Will do." The communicator went dead.

Marie sat patiently for the return call. A few minutes went by before the system sounded a call being received. Marie connected on visual and sat waiting to get a response. A picture came on the screen at her end. Celeste sat in front of the communicator on the ship. Marie saw Jade and John behind her, worried frowns painting their faces.

"Hi Marie," Celeste started. "What can I do for you?"

"I'm probably worrying about nothing, but Ethan, Pia and Hugo went off in the vehicle this morning and they haven't come back yet."

"What?" Jade shouted from behind Celeste. "Where did they go?"

Celeste, remaining calm, asked, "Do you know where they went?"

"Down river. Ethan said they would follow it to see where it went."

"I presume that you have tried to call them."

"Yes, I don't get any response."

Jade crossed her arms, the stress and panic showing on her face as she fidgeted about.

"It's too late for us to go look for them before nightfall," Marie continued. "Can you send a Lander down in the morning at first light, about six our time here according to our reckoning, that's fifteen hundred hours GMT. I'm probably overreacting. They'll probably turn up soon with sheepish grins on their faces when they realize the commotion they've caused."

"I can do that," Celeste said. "You don't want it to come down now?"

"No, as I said, I'm probably overreacting, and there isn't much it can do in the dark."

"OK. The Lander will come in the morning," Celeste looked at Jade and John, "with two passengers, I presume."

Jade and John both nodded as the communication disconnected.

Marie sat where she was for a few moments more. There really was nothing more that she could do until sunrise. She didn't like the fact that she couldn't get in touch with any of the missing and she didn't really think she was worrying about nothing. She knew in her gut that something bad had happened. Deciding to put the thoughts of what could have happened out of her head, she sighed and went back outside, walking over to the others in the mess cabin. "Celeste is sending a Lander down first thing tomorrow morning," she told them.

"Dinner is served," Max said as he dished out the food. The

aroma of lamb stew filling the air gave all a hint of what they were to eat.

They ate the meal, talked about the day apart from the missing team members, and went off to bed with the others still missing.

Marie rose well before dawn, dressed and walked to the mess cabin to fix breakfast for herself. Max was already eating when she walked in. "Morning."

"Morning," Max replied. "I couldn't sleep so I got up early."

"I thought I should be ready for the Lander." Marie prepared breakfast and sat next to Max. When she finished the meal, she put the bowl in the washer and prepared a mug of piping hot coffee. She walked to the window with the steam rising from the mug and saw the first hint of dawn as she looked out, sipping her coffee. A few small animals ventured to the river for a drink and the herbivores stood eating on grass, ever on the lookout for predators lurking in the trees nearby. They suddenly stopped eating and looked up, as if they heard a noise, and immediately rushed off into the forest's protection. After several seconds, Marie said, "Lander's here," as she heard it approach. She took a gulp of coffee and put the cup on the bench nearby before walking out of the cabin with Max. They both walked over to the landing area and waited. Ravi came and stood next to Max shortly afterwards, greeting the others as he did so.

The shape of the Lander appeared in the dimly lit dawn sky above them and grew in size as it descended to the ground. The landing struts emerged from the body locking in position and the craft landed moments later, the hatch opening shortly afterwards. Jade and John emerged immediately after the hatch opened and paced down the steps quickly, eager to hear of any news of the missing. The pilot came as well several minutes later.

Marie saw they both had black rings around their eyes from lack of sleep and updated them immediately, "No news I'm afraid."

"Do you have anything that you can tell us?" John asked.

"Only what I told you last night. Our best bet is to go looking for them. It shouldn't be long before we find something. They can't have gone too far through this terrain."

"OK, let's get moving then," Jade said.

Marie looked at Max and Ravi, "You two stay here. We may need you to come with some supplies once we locate the others. You'll be able to use the hover scooters. I'll direct the pilot."

"OK," Max said. Ravi nodded.

Marie looked to the pilot. "We'll follow the river down that way. I'll sit in the cockpit with you."

The pilot nodded and all of them, apart from Max and Ravi, went back to the Lander, the pilot taking off about five minutes later with the daylight present for the day. He rose into the air about one hundred metres, well above the tree line, and slowly followed the river downstream. Marie looked out of the front to see if there was any sign of the vehicle or the missing people. Jade and John stood behind her, trying to poke their head over her shoulder so they could see, but the confines of the cockpit prevented them from seeing much. They both eventually resigned themselves to letting Marie do the searching.

"I can see the sea coming up ahead," the pilot said about half an hour later.

"Well, they can't have gone any further than that. I hope that they stopped instead of following the coastline," Marie said.

The pilot slowed down further as they approached a cliff edge, Marie busy looking down into the forest, hoping to see any sign of Ethan and the others.

"There," Marie said as she pointed to the all-terrain Ethan had used, "There's the vehicle. I can't see anybody though." The pilot hovered the Lander just above the tree line and next to where the vehicle stood, allowing Marie a view of the immediate area. Marie thought about what Ethan might have done. She thought about what she would do. "Let's go to the coast and have a look there. I reckon I would have gone for a look at the sea if I was Ethan." The pilot slowly drifted to the coast. "There seems to have been a slippage of rock over there," Marie said pointing slightly to the left. The Lander changed direction and crossed the coastline just right of the avalanche. Two people waved their arms at them. Marie smiled. "We found them," she said back to Jade and John.

The pilot, not wanting to get too close to the cliff, looked for a place to set down. Seeing a small clearing on a rise nearby, he veered the Lander over to it and landed.

Marie came out of the cockpit. "We'll need some ropes," she told the others.

John went to one of the equipment storage lockers in the rear of the Lander and rummaged through the contents until he found two thick ropes they could use for the rescue. He grabbed them and a kit bag to put them in, and two harnesses. The hatch opened and Jade, John and Marie piled out, hurrying to the spot where they saw the two people. John dropped the bag as they approached the cliff and they all lay front down to peer over the edge.

"Hello," Marie shouted down.

Ethan and Hu looked up. "Glad you came so quickly," Ethan said, looking glad to see Jade.

"Are you all right?"

"I'm OK. Hugo has a sprained ankle and a concussion, but Pia's badly injured. She's been unconscious since our fall and has a broken leg at least."

"OK, how did this happen?"

"A drone caused it."

"What do you mean? Where would a drone come from?"

"Your guess is as good as mine at the moment."

"Stick tight and we'll discuss how to get you all up from there." Marie and the others crawled back away from the cliff face before standing up. "So, how do we get them up from there?"

John scratched his chin. "Ethan and Hugo shouldn't be too difficult. Ethan should be able to climb and Hugo might too. Pia is a bit of a problem though."

"There's a stretcher in the Lander," Jade said.

"Yeah, but we can't get it up from over the cliff unless we build an outrigger."

"Can we use the Lander? Winch her up through the hatch," Jade asked.

"Maybe." John nodded, thinking about the feasibility. "We should discuss it with the pilot."

"I can do that," Jade volunteered. "You two can get the others up."

"Let's see if they need anything first before you go back to the Lander."

They moved back to the cliff.

Marie remained spokesperson, "Hey, Ethan."

"Yeah."

"We'll see if we can get Pia winched up on a stretcher with the Lander, but we'll set up a rope for you and Hugo to come up."

"You'll need someone down here to put Pia on the stretcher and secure her. I'll stay here."

Hu looked at Ethan. "That probably needs two people. I will stay too until we get Pia safe."

Ethan nodded. "We're both staying to make it easier."

"OK. We'll discuss what we can do with the pilot and get back to you. Do you need anything in the meantime?"

"Some water and an energy bar would be nice. We had some in the All-terrain."

"We'll get some down to you. Hold tight."

"We're not going anywhere."

Ethan and Hu disappeared from Marie's view as she crawled away from the cliff face.

"Let's get back to the pilot," John said.

They all walked back to the Lander, and after a lengthy discussion with the pilot, they worked out the best way to get Pia up with a stretcher stored in the first aid equipment on the craft. They found some food and water, and a spare communicator, and Jade took them all back to the others while John and Marie set up the equipment for the rescue.

Jade placed the supplies in a bag, making sure that she protected the communicator well against damage, and tied it to a lighter rope. She poked her head over the side of the cliff, "I'll throw a bag down to you with water and food in it. It's attached to a rope. Hope I get it close to you."

Ethan shouted up, a smirk on his face, "Hope you don't hit us."

Jade poked her tongue out, "At least you still have your sense of humor." She moved back from the edge and lined up the missile, throwing it out over the cliff with her full effort. The package arced down and disappeared from sight, the rope uncoiling as the projectile fell. She glanced back over the cliff and saw that the package had landed much further down the slope than where Ethan and the others were, but the rope was within reach, so Ethan grabbed it and pulled the supplies to him. He looked up when Hu held the bag, giving Jade the thumbs up.

"Be back soon." Jade went back to the Lander. When she reached the others, Marie and John had rigged up a makeshift outrigger and tackle with a winch to pull the stretcher and the others up with. She looked around, "Looks like we're all set."

"Yeah, all ready to go," John said.

The Lander took off again with the hatch open and crept to the cliff face above where Ethan and the others were. John strapped into a harness and anchored himself so he couldn't fall out. He gave directions to Marie to position the craft in the right place, who relayed them to the pilot. Halting the Lander, John lowered the stretcher and two harnesses down while the pilot hovered in position, the occasional wind gust pushing him out of place from time to time. John advised which direction to reposition to as needed.

Ethan grabbed the gear when it reached him, and he and Hu put the harnesses on first. They temporarily hooked to the rope, so they didn't accidentally slip and fall further down the slope with no means to get back up again. They placed the stretcher next to Pia and moved her onto it, careful to minimize any movement of her broken leg in particular. They strapped her securely onto the stretcher. Ethan called Marie on the communicator when they were ready, and John started winching Pia up. John pulled the stretcher into the Lander when it reached him and undid the rope. Jade and Marie carried the stretcher to a safe place. John lowered the rope again. After a slight argument about who should go up first, Hu hooked her harness onto the rope and John pulled her up. She swung into the hatch and hobbled inside. John moved over to her and gave her a hug before lowering the rope again for Ethan. Ethan swung into the Lander five minutes later. Jade move over to him and hugged him, happy that he was safe. The pilot moved the Lander over to the clearing and descended to the ground.

"We need to get Pia up to Angelo," Ethan said. "She's in a bad way."

"Let's get the outrigger moved, so we can shut the hatch," John said, starting to disassemble it.

"Hugo needs checking out too."

"I'm fine."

"You're getting checked out," John ordered, agreeing with Ethan's assessment.

Hu rolled her eyes, but didn't argue.

"I should go back to the camp," Marie said. "We can put a splint on Pia's leg before you go."

"I think we need to get her to Angelo as soon as we can. The splint can wait," Ethan said.

Marie nodded, "I'll go back in the vehicle then."

They secured Pia for the ride, and the pilot ascended to *Destiny* shortly later. Medical personnel stood waiting for them when they arrived, the pilot having called ahead about Pia's condition. Angelo stood in front, poised to get into action as soon as he had access, medical bag in hand. The hatch opened, and he rushed in, going directly to Pia. Ethan told him as much as he knew about Pia's condition as Angelo scanned her body.

"She has serious internal injuries," Angelo said after looking at the results. "She needs immediate surgery." He went to the hatch and waved the other medical staff in, instructing them to take Pia to the medical bay immediately and prepare her for surgery. They sprang into action, lifted the stretcher and rushed her into the elevator.

Ethan shook his head. "I knew it was serious."

"Well, you got her here as soon as you could. That's all we can ask for. Are you OK?"

"I'm fine. Hugo has a sprained ankle, and she got concussed."

"I'll get a junior to look at her. Looks like you could use some rest."

"Get little sleep on the side of a pile of gravel threatening to slide you into the ocean. I'll be Ok."

"Better go." Angelo rushed off.

"You go up to medical too," John said to Hu. Hu reluctantly complied.

John and Jade came closer to Ethan. "What's with the story about the drone?" John asked, intrigued by the earlier comment.

"I don't really know." Ethan scratched at his day-old beard growth. "We were looking out at the ocean and saw it hovering out there. Pia studied it the most. From what I can tell by what she said, it didn't have the usual means of propulsion and the missiles it fired at us didn't either. I've seen nothing like it. It was off target, fortunately, unless it deliberately shot underneath us. Anyway, they caused that part of the cliff to crumble and fall into the sea. We were lucky that the water wasn't deep there, or we would have plunged into it, never to be seen again."

John looked down as he pondered the description. "So, we are not alone, or someone's grabbed hold of technology they shouldn't have."

"What do you mean by that?"

"You're describing a technology the military has been working on, but I don't know why it would be here. Do you think the drone will return?"

"I don't know. Why wouldn't it? The question we need to consider is, 'How do we protect ourselves if it does?'"

19

CONTACT

Ethan sat in the ship's lounge relaxing the day after being rescued from the side of the cliff, after having had a good night's sleep. He had been to see Angelo for an update on Pia before going there. Angelo informed him that Pia should recover completely, although it had been touch and go during the surgery. Jade, Hu, John and Celeste sat with him, each holding a cup of coffee and waiting for Ethan to say something.

"I really don't know what to do now," Ethan finally said. "Do we pull out of here all together, or do we just take more precautions? If we take more precautions, what should they be against such a device that can sneak up on us without warning?" He sat slumped in the chair, staring at nothing.

"Pulling out is a little drastic." John raised a brow at Ethan.

"You know I have *Destiny* continuously monitoring the campsite and the expanse of area around it," Celeste said. "I went back and looked at the logs for when the incident occurred and our radar picked up the thing when it attacked you. I should have thought of it earlier."

"What good will that do now?" Jade asked.

"We can have someone monitor the radar full time and alert us if they spot it again."

Ethan shook his head. "It will have been and gone before you get the chance to tell anyone on the planet. It traveled fast. Could you tell where it went afterwards?"

"It traveled along the coast and disappeared off the edge of the radar screen. You're right, it does travel fast."

"Do you think it came from the buildings we spotted?" Hu asked, frowning.

"It seemed to go in a different direction, but it could be possible, maybe. We're assuming it's not of human origin. John seems to think it could be one of our toys."

"It sounds like one of our developments and would be a little more believable than being of extra-terrestrial origin, but how did it get here? It would have had to come with you in *Destiny*. That means there's a saboteur, or worse, with us again."

"Fits in with the ring damage." Ethan nodded.

"Maybe we should go to the buildings and explore what they are," Hu continued. "It might give us some answers."

Ethan sighed. "We should at least investigate what it is while we're here. I hate puzzles, and I hate unsolved ones more."

"Let's do that then." John sat up straight, ready to rise from his seat.

Hu looked at the others. "Who'll go?"

"Ethan's staying here." Jade tensed and looked at Ethan.

Ethan started to respond, but thought better of it, when he saw how pointless it would be to try overriding her demand. "OK, looks like I have no choice." The others sniggered. "You wanted to go down to the planet Celeste. You want to tell us what's there?"

Celeste's eyes sparkled with excitement, "You bet."

"Jade and I can go with you," John suggested.

"I want to go too," Hu said.

John almost said she couldn't because of her sprained ankle, but realized that it wouldn't stop her.

"I'm stuck up here by myself then."

"Angelo's here to keep you company. We won't be gone that long."
Jade patted his hand and feigned sympathy.

"Some comfort you are." Ethan pouted, not enjoying being
teased.

"Is there a landing site there?" John looked at the others.

"Not that I remember, but there is a rise nearby I think might
have a large enough space for the Lander." Celeste sat in concentration.

"Well, let's get organized then." John rose from his chair.

The others, apart from Ethan, copied the move and left, Jade
giving Ethan a kiss before disappearing.

AFTER PACKING the things they needed, the Lander with John, Jade,
Hu and Celeste on board, left the bowels of *Destiny*, heading for the
planet an hour later.

They neared the site of the buildings. John piloted the Lander
and Hu sat in the copilot's seat. He slowed up and hovered two
hundred metres above the ground. Several structures dotted the site
of about one hundred metres by sixty metres in size. Boughs of trees
overhung the edges, as the forest tried to re-establish its dominance
over the unnatural entities in its domain. Considering the probable
time that the buildings had been there, it surprised them that the
forest hadn't taken back its territory long ago. No movement caught
anyone's eye as they hovered in the air.

"What do you think?" Hu asked John.

"Looks quiet enough down there. No one's shot at us yet. There
aren't any drones displayed on the radar. Let's land and go look. What

do you others think?" John looked around through the open cockpit door.

Both Jade and Celeste nodded, excitedly looking out of a window in the Lander.

"Let's find a place to land then."

John moved the Lander and searched for the clearing they had identified. He found the rise in the landscape that the trees mysteriously remained uninterested in occupying, and hovered over the area, slowly descending to the ground moments later. A slight vibration went through the Lander as the landing struts cushioned the load of the ship about a minute afterward. John wound down the drive and shut down the control systems.

Jade opened the hatch and descended the small set of steps when they extended out. She looked around. The serenity of the forest greeted her as in the other locations. Birds twitted in the trees, and the earthy smell of decaying leaves drifted past her.

Celeste followed a brief time later, her wide-eyed stare taking in the majesty of the exotic planet for the first time. "This is amazing."

Jade looked around at her. A smile crept to her lips as she saw Celeste's childlike mesmerism. Celeste's short and petite stature added to the effect. "Yes, it sure is. Are you glad you came down?"

"I would've come before this, if I'd known it was so incredible. Just imagine, we are the first humans on this planet... ever."

Jade laughed as she turned again to look at the surrounding landscape.

Hu and John came out, John holding some laser pistols in their holsters. "I think we should all carry one of these, just in case."

"That sounds like a good idea." Jade took one and wrapped the holster belt around her waist.

The others did likewise, and they all checked their weapon's status. John closed the hatch of the Lander, to prevent any intruders from the animal kingdom getting too inquisitive, while they were away.

"Let's have a look then." John started walking toward the buildings and into the forest. The others followed him, in single file, as he led them in amongst the trees.

The walk took an hour with the pace they could manage through the undergrowth. They eventually broke through the last of the bushes, the buildings they had seen from the air standing in front of them. They stopped, completely frozen. In front of the nearest building stood a hominid being, with what they took to be a smile on its face.

Celeste broke from the spell first. "Hello. Are you sentient? Can you talk? I take it you do not know our language." She stepped a few steps closer.

The being blinked, a puzzled expression on its face before saying, "Welcome," in perfect English.

Celeste jumped. "Um, wow, I'm not sure how you know English, but thanks."

"I have a translator. The language is not one in the repertoire, but it is similar to one. It took the translator time to tell the difference and modify its methodologies. Are you the leader?"

Celeste looked around at the others. They stood looking at her in amazement. She looked back, "Not really. There isn't really a leader in the group. Although John here," she pointed to John, "is probably the senior person if we had to look for direction. Our mission leader is on our ship. My name is Celeste. What is your name?"

"Grubexl."

"Nice to meet you, Grubexl. I have already introduced John. This is Jade and Hu." Celeste pointed at the two. She suddenly became shy as Grubexl continued to stare at her, blinking with lashless eyelids. "I have probably talked too much. I should let the others say something."

"You are doing fine," Hu broke in. "Please continue."

Seeing that the others agreed, she thought for the direction she should take in the conversation with Grubexl. "How long have you been here?"

"Well, I'm not sure what period you consider a revolution of a planet around its sun. Where are you from?"

"We are from a planet called Earth that is twelve light years away from here. That may not give you any information, since you still do not know how long a year is, if you don't know what our concept of time is. One year is the time it takes for Earth to make one rotation around our sun."

Grubexl nodded and smiled slightly, as he understood Celeste's dilemma in describing her concept of time intervals. "Does this planet revolve around a sun that I believe is called Sol?"

"Yes." Celeste raised her voice in surprise.

"I know of this planet and what you call a year. I have been on this planet for many of your years."

"How many?"

"That is a topic for another time. Please let me show you around. That is why you came, is it not?"

Celeste giggled, "Yes, it is. We saw this place from the air when we mapped the planet. It doesn't fit in with everything else."

"Come."

Looking around at the others, she shrugged her shoulders and led the others as Grubexl seemed happy to give an inspection tour. They came to within a metre of Grubexl as they walked. He had a slightly slouched gait, as if he was old and found walking difficult. He was short, even shorter than Celeste, at about one-hundred and forty centimeters. He appeared to be wearing overalls; the cloth comprising the fabric unlike anything they had seen before. He had no hair exposed on his body. Celeste drew up alongside of Grubexl and the others walked behind them.

Grubexl led them to the first building entrance. "This is my living quarters. It is spartan, but adequate for what I need." He entered the doorway and waved for them to follow him.

The team were reluctant to enter the building. Celeste touched the wall on the outside. It felt smooth and made from something that resembled plastic, but Celeste had the feeling that it was something other than plastic, or a superior form of plastic. She overcame her fear and caution and entered, just fitting through the doorway without ducking to clear the lintel. The others had to crouch to prevent hitting it with their heads. The interior was well lit with lighting alien to her. It was diffuse all over the ceiling with no apparent single source of light or group of lights, making an even illumination throughout the room. She stood in a room that had some kind of food preparation in the far end. It was four metres by six metres and looked to be spacious for one person. She looked back at the others, who still stood just outside the doorway, and gestured that they should come in. They complied and looked around with interest. Some luxuriously cushioned lounge type seats and a less cushioned chair were in the room and a table. "I take it, this is your living area. It looks comfortable."

"Yes, I spend little time here, except to have my meals and read a little. I sleep through there." Grubexl pointed with his right thumb.

Celeste peered into the next room, but felt embarrassed to investigate the private area any further, even though Grubexl appeared to be comfortable about it. She saw a cot type bed but nothing else from where she stood. The entire place looked well looked after and clean. "Let's have a look at the other buildings," she suggested.

"Very well." Grubexl led the way out again and over to another building was about ten metres by twenty meters and two metres to the eaves. The door was again low at one-hundred and sixty centimeters high. They all entered. "This is my workshop, laboratory and observatory."

Celeste walked around the expanse, as did the others, and looked at the equipment scattered over benches, or fixed to stands secured to the floor. She saw an opening in the roof at the far end with a telescope pointing out of the gap. "You observe the sky?" She pointed to the telescope.

"A little hobby of mine, to while away the time. I like to see any changes that might occur."

"Did you see us coming?"

"Only when you were close enough to provide a good reflection from the star. The telescope is not powerful, although I can conduct daylight observations and during the nighttime hours."

"May I?" Celeste asked.

"Certainly."

Celeste walked over and inspected the instrument. It was almost identical to optical telescopes that humans have used for hundreds of years. She looked into the eyepiece but saw little. Pulling back to find the focusing adjustment, she placed her eye back and turned the knob until she saw through the lenses of the telescope with a sharp image. She saw stars as if she looked during the darkest moonless night on Earth. "This is incredible. How do you filter out the background light?"

"Various filters in the light path remove what it does not require. You seem interested. Are you a stargazer?"

"Yes, I am. We call it astronomy. I have made it my profession."

"I see. You must know the sky well then. Do you have maps?"

"We do. I don't have any with me at present. We also look at sources other than visible light emissions with other types of telescopes."

"That is interesting. I'd like to have one of these other types, but I only have the equipment that you see here. I'd very much like to see your maps."

"I can bring one back with me when I return. Would you be able to point out where you came from?"

"I doubt it. My home is very far away."

Celeste thought for a moment. "How did you get here? I don't see any spaceship."

Grubexl studied Celeste again with his disconcerting lidless eyes before answering. "Come." He led them back outside. They followed Grubexl towards the edge of the settlement and to a rectangular slab of obsidian, approximately two metres high and one-hundred and twenty centimeters wide. When they were close enough, they saw that it was only two or three centimeters deep. "I came through this."

The other's eyes bulged. "Through that?" they all asked at once, unable to take the revelation in. It seemed too incredible. Celeste walked up to it and touched the front, sliding a finger slowly over the face. It felt smooth as silk, even though it had been there a long time. It had no sign of erosion on it at all. She slowly circled it, inspecting it for any interruption to its smoothness, but apart from the edges and corners, every face looked completely smooth. She just realized that it reflected nothing as she completed her inspection. It was opaque. She looked at Grubexl. "How does it work?"

Something seemed to make Grubexl change his mind about the discussion on the stela, some twinkle momentarily passing across his eyes. "Perhaps another time."

Finally getting the courage to say something, Hu interrupted. "Why is it we seem to have a very similar shape as you?"

Grubexl looked at Hu. "We can discuss that at another time too. I must continue with my work now, if you don't mind."

"Oh, I hope that you excuse our interruption."

"It was a pleasure to receive visitors after such a long time. Please come again at your convenience."

"We will," Celeste said. "I will bring a map with me. We thank you for your time."

"Can I ask one last question?" John asked.

"Of course."

"Do you have any flying drones that you use for reconnoissance?"

Grubexl's lidless eyes opened wider at the mention of drones. "I must get back to my work. Have a pleasant day." He wandered off before the team could say anything else, leaving them looking at each other a little perplexed.

"Let's get back to the Lander," Jade finally said.

They left the area and started the walk back. When John was certain that they were out of earshot, he said, "I get the distinct impression there is something he's not telling us."

"How do you know it is male?" Celeste asked.

"I was just going by the deep voice, but you're right, I don't know. I'll treat it as male all the same. You continue to amaze me, Celeste."

Celeste raised her brow. "Why?"

"How you opened up the conversation, anyone would have thought you were starting a conversation with another person on Earth."

Shrugging her shoulder, she said, "I was inquisitive, I suppose."

They fell silent. "You're right. He seemed to button up as soon as I asked him how that slab worked."

"Yes, he did," Hu said. "At least he has invited us back. He may be more talkative next time."

"I think we need to be careful," Jade said. "There's something about him I don't fully trust."

They continued their long walk back to the Lander and flew back to *Destiny* a quick time later.

20

ACTIVATION

Ethan called a meeting with the members of the team on board *Destiny* with Marie, Gerhardt, Max and Ravi connected into the meeting via a holographic link. The news about the sentient alien living in the artificial structures disturbed Ethan immensely, although he kept it to himself. It was just something else beyond the expected, something beyond his control. He had to work through his issues on his own and talk to Jade about them at the right time. The others sat in the conference room, fidgety and wanting to get started, all except Pia, who was in the medical infirmary, still recovering from her injuries. Looking around the room, Ethan saw various levels of excitement on the people's faces. He wasn't sure why they should feel that the discovery should represent good news, but he could appreciate that they wanted to find out more about the sentient Grubexl.

"Let's quieten down, shall we," Ethan said. "We have made a momentous discovery, something unexpected. Although, maybe we should have suspected something after finding the buildings. Maybe we will get one of the expedition members to provide a recount of events from yesterday." Ethan looked at John.

"I know that I was there, but maybe Celeste should report, since she communicated with Grubexl the most. I'm still amazed by Celeste's intrepid approach to the initial contact. She astounds me every day."

Celeste blushed. "What else was I meant to do? He was there, we were there. Were we meant to just wait for him or ignore him and walk away? It just seemed like the right thing to do." She looked up to her right. "We approached the site on foot after inspecting it from the air and then landed a reasonable distance from it. Grubexl waited for us and met us when we broke through the forest. He took a while to respond to my initial greeting, which he later explained. His translating machine had to adapt to the closest language it had in its system to English. Once the translator started working properly, our communication proceeded without a hitch."

"He knew of the planet and solar system we came from, mentioning Sol by name, which come to think of it, is a little disturbing, since we have only called it that probably for a few thousand years. He said that he was ancient, but wouldn't tell us how old yet."

"After that, he gave us a tour of the site and we saw where he lived and worked. He has a telescope able to filter out the daytime light from Tau Ceti and provide a view of the stars during the day and at night. He mentioned that he saw us arrive. He wants to see a star map of the sky."

"We then saw a stela, a jet-black slab about two metres high and one-point-two metres wide. It was about three centimeters thick. It didn't feel like stone, some kind of plastic, but it wasn't plastic either. When asked what it was, he said that he had come here through it, but he then wouldn't say anything else about it, saying that he would say more another time. He wouldn't talk about the drone either. He seemed surprised and quickly changed the subject, saying that he wanted to get back to his work, whatever that was." Celeste looked around at the others, waiting for questions.

"What did he look like?" Marie asked.

"Oh, similar to us. In fact, he avoided Hugo's question about why he looked so much like us. He was shorter than me, if that's possible, and slouched over as if he's old. He has two arms and legs but only four fingers and toes, including the thumbs which are opposing. He was bald and had no hair that we could see. His facial features are like ours, except he has no eyelids or ears. He was wearing an overall type garment of a material that I haven't seen before."

"Unusual to have a different alien species that looks so similar to us. His explanation would interest me," Marie replied.

"I notice that you say him. Is Grubexl male then?" Angelo asked.

Celeste looked at John, "I've said enough."

"We don't really know. He just looks male and speaks in a male voice, so we have assumed male at this stage."

"This is our first evidence of other sentient beings in the universe," Gerhardt's holographic image said. "It will completely re-interpret our understanding. What other species are out there?"

"Yes," Ethan looked at a point in front of him on the table for a second. "I'm concerned about what we tell our fellow human beings on Earth, and how they'll react. It might cause riots, and I don't know what else."

"We can't keep it hidden, at least not forever. It will leak out somehow if we try to keep it a secret," Hu said.

"You're right," John replied. "But that is something for our governments to decide. It will leak, despite the highest level of secrecy. We can't keep something like this under wraps for long, with all the people on this ship and whoever comes after us."

"So what should we do?" Ethan asked.

"We must report it back to my superiors. Let them sort out who to tell and when. Not sure what Hu should do. She has a responsibility to her government."

Hu looked at John. "I will abide by what this team decides for the time being. I only request that when you communicate this with your government, you request that they consider sharing the information with my government... and I feel, by default, the Russians. This is a joint endeavor."

"Excellent point," Ethan said. "That seems reasonable. Don't you think John?"

"Yes, it does. OK, we'll report it to our steering committee together with Hugo's request. It puts Hugo in a predicament though, if they choose to keep the information to just our government."

"Is that likely though?" Angelo asked. "Given our convivial relationship with each other at present, what strategic reason could they give to withhold the information from the Chinese and the Russians?"

"I'm just saying, it makes Hugo's position awkward."

"Well, they should have allowed no one from other nationalities on the expedition, if they wanted to keep the findings secret," Gerhardt's image stated. "There are several nationalities involved in the expedition, and one condition is an unconditional sharing of all information collected."

"You're right," Ethan said.

"Where do we go from here?" Max's image asked.

"What do you mean?"

"What do we do about further contact with this sentient being?"

Celeste raised her eyebrows. "We can't just ignore him. We need to continue the dialogue we started."

"Quite right," Marie's image said. "We need to find out as much as we can about him. Especially where he came from and how he got here."

Ravi's image contributed for the first time. "Maybe a more important question is, 'Why is he still here?'"

"An excellent point." Jade nodded her head.

"He's shown no aggression or sign that he will cause us any harm," Hu said.

Ethan looked around the room. "We seem to agree that we should have further contact with this alien. Since Celeste seems to have started a friendly relationship with him, maybe she should be the primary point of contact at this stage."

"He asked who the leader was when we first got there. It might be a good idea for you to meet him," Celeste said.

Ethan considered her point. "Maybe, but I don't want both of us on the planet at the same time. We are the two primary pilots for the ship."

"I'm sure we can sort something out."

"We'll discuss it. You continue with your contact for the time being. Is there anything else?"

The others shook their heads.

"OK, this meeting is over. John and Hugo, can you stay behind for a moment, please?"

The other members filed out of the conference room and Marie switched off the holographic link at her end.

Ethan got up and closed the door. "We need to decide what to tell Earth."

"We should keep it brief," John suggested. "We don't really know very much about the creature yet, anyway."

"I'm feeling very uncomfortable about this entire thing. It's too disturbing. If we had found a whole civilisation, it would be different, but just one?"

"Don't be so xenophobic." Hu had a slight smirk on her face.

"I'm not. I just don't like it. And this stela that Celeste mentioned."

"No point in jumping to conclusions, Ethan," John said. "Let's get more information first."

"OK, well, I'll draft something up and let the both of you review it before I send it to Earth."

"Sounds good to me," Hu said.

They left the room, destined for their other duties. Ethan scripted a report to Earth and sent it through the wormhole the same day.

A FEW DAYS after the initial encounter, Celeste prepared for another one with Grubexl. John and Hu stood waiting in the lander bay of the ship, waiting for her. Ethan stood with them as they waited.

"Don't take any chances," Ethan said.

"We'll look after her." John patted Ethan on the shoulder.

"I wish I could get down there to see it for myself. I don't like not knowing what we are dealing with."

Hu chuckled. "You have trust issues?"

"Of course not. You know what I mean. I'm not sure whether Celeste can see when she's being lied to."

"She's an adult Ethan. You trusted her to fly the ship, when some of us raised our eyebrows," John said.

"Celeste has a natural talent for that."

"... Natural talent for what?" Celeste said as she walked over to them. She held a bag and had a laser pistol strapped to her side.

"Nothing," Ethan said, blushing a little.

Celeste looked at Ethan for a moment. "I don't think I'll get a straight answer if I ask again, will I?" she finally said.

John and Hu burst into laughter as Ethan reddened more. "Just come back safely again, will you?"

"Will do."

Celeste, John and Hu went to the Lander and settled in their seats, John in the cockpit as pilot, and Celeste and Hu in the passenger cabin. They closed the hatch, and the Lander left moments later.

"What was that all about?" Celeste asked.

"Nothing, Ethan's just being a little over-protective of you, that's all."

"Oh, he thinks I can't look after myself, does he? Why do you think I brought this along?" Celeste said, as she tapped the pistol strapped to her thigh.

Hu smiled. "We will look after each other, between the three of us."

John landed the craft an hour later, bringing it down in the same location as before. They brought a small all-terrain vehicle with them to save walking the distance to Grubexl's abode. They bundled out of the Lander and into the vehicle.

"What's the bag for?" John pointed to the bag Celeste carried.

"Just a few things to show Grubexl. He wanted to see a star map, and I brought some other things that might interest him. It might loosen his tongue a little."

"You think he's keeping secrets?"

"Yes, don't you? He seemed to change the topic quickly sometimes when we asked too many questions."

"Hope you're right then. We need to find out as much as we can about him and where he came from."

Hu drove the vehicle to the site, with little but small talk between the three of them along the way. The vehicle crashed through the edge of the forest next to the buildings twenty minutes later. Grubexl stood waiting for them, as he had before. They hopped out.

"Greetings Celeste, Hu and John," Grubexl said.

"Hello," they all said to him.

Celeste frowned. "We've been having a minor argument. Does your species have what we call male and female and are you male?"

"We have male and female, and two other genders, but I am definitely male. I hope that clears up your argument."

John looked smug, "Yes it does."

"And you would be male also?" Grubexl asked John.

"Yes."

"So that would make you two female, yes?"

"Correct," Hu said.

"Come." Grubexl led them through to his accommodation building and pointed out seats for them to sit on. They sat. "I have prepared a little refreshment for us all."

They all looked at each other. Celeste wondered if they should trust whatever he was about to serve them. Grubexl placed a jug on the table with a green-colored liquid in it and four glasses. He went away and came back with a plate that had what looked like biscuits on it. They were round and eight centimeters in diameter, one or two high. They smelled of cinnamon and freshly baked, and Celeste wondered how he cooked them so quickly. He then sat down with them and poured a glass of the liquid for each of them. Raising his glass, he paused when he saw the others looking at the glasses in front of them.

"It is not poison. I will drink." He took a sip. "I assure you it is suitable for your consumption."

Celeste reached for her glass and hazarded a sip. "How do you know that?"

"I know more about you than you think."

"You only just met us the other day."

"I mean about your species."

"This is the first time humans have been here."

"Did you bring a star map with you?"

"Yes, I did." Celeste got her tablet out of the bag she brought, and produced a holographic projector. She set up the projector and had an image of the galaxy in their vicinity displayed a few moments later. She rotated the image and zoomed in, making the others feel slightly nauseous from watching the effect, highlighting Tau Ceti. "We are here."

Grubexl's eyes sparkled in delight. "Splendid. Where is Sol?"

"Here." Celeste highlighted Earth's star in a different color.

Grubexl leaned over to study the image. After a few moments he pointed to another star, "What do you call this star?"

"Alpha Centauri," Celeste said, looking at John and Hu with raised brows. "Why did you point out that one?"

Grubexl looked at Celeste for some time before answering. "You have been there, have you not?"

"We have."

"And what did you find there?"

Celeste felt reluctant to answer the question, but finally relented. "We found a planet, like Earth."

"What else did you find?"

"A grave of skeletons, much like ours, hidden in a cliff and a virus that killed several of us before we found a cure."

Grubexl nodded. "Yes, that would be right."

Getting frustrated with the one-sided flow of information, Celeste asked, "And how do you know all this?"

Grubexl looked down for a moment.

"We created that virus to speed up evolution. We interfered when we shouldn't have and had disastrous results."

"So there is more that one of you here."

"No, there is just me."

"Where are the others then?"

"They went back."

"Back where?"

"To my world."

"Which is where?"

"You would not understand."

Celeste sat back, folding her arms in irritation, "Try me."

"They used the black portal I showed you last time."

"But how does it work? Where does it go to?"

"It is a portal to another place."

"Like a wormhole?" Hu butted in.

"No, that is another primitive technology altogether."

Hu leaned back in surprise at the comment, considering they had only just mastered the ability to create a wormhole.

"Then what?" Celeste continued.

"It allows travel beyond dimensional space and time."

"Using other dimensions?"

"Yes."

"How do you generate the connection?"

"The generator embedded in the portal provided a passage through brane-space."

Celeste sat back, completed amazed by the revelation.

"That is only theoretical," Hu said. "No one has ever suggested how that would be possible or what sort of energy we would need, not to mention controlling where one might go using it. You could theoretically jump between branes. But that would mean that you could jump between universes, so to speak."

Having recovered, Celeste said, "Passage to where?"

"It is as your friend has said, to my brane."

"That does not explain why you are still here."

"I cannot get back?"

"Why not?"

"That is enough on that topic."

Seeing he would no longer proceed with that line of questioning, Celeste changed the subject. "You said before that your people were responsible for the skeletons at Alpha Centauri because you brought the virus. We estimated that the skeletons are two million years old. How could you have been here that long ago?"

Grubexl looked up at the ceiling for a few moments. "Yes, that would be about right. We are a long ageing species."

"How old are you then?"

"About three million of your Earth-years."

"That's staggering."

"Why are you so surprised? Do you think a species that can jump between branes could not work out the secret of ageing?"

"So how long will you live? Are you eternal?"

"No. The average age of my species is about five million of your Earth-years."

"Wouldn't you become overcrowded with living that long?"

"Time is different where I come from."

"We found that the virus at Alpha Centauri also came to Earth and infected us about that time. Did you go to Earth and do the same experiment?"

"We did, although the strain of virus was slightly different. It worked with you and slowly increased your brain capacity over many millennia. Whereas the other one acted too quickly, killing the species we tested it on."

"How do you know that it was effective with us? Have you been back to check?"

"Do you not have legends of beings from space visiting you?"

"They're just stories, fables, imaginings."

"They are true. In fact, one group stayed. They became infatuated with your female form of the species and joined with them, which is not allowed. They did it anyway. My people severely punished them when they found out. I believe the progeny became giants for a few generations before the gene pool dispersed sufficiently."

"That's true," John interrupted. "they recorded it in the bible, that's amazing. They called them 'sons of gods.'"

Having forgotten her drink until that moment, Celeste took a gulp of the liquid. It tasted sweet and somewhat like lime. It also tasted fermented. "Is there ethanol in this?"

"That is correct. It has about twenty-three percent."

"Wow, quite a punch. Better not drink too much or you'll have to carry me out of here."

The others laughed, including Grubexl, who laughed with a guttural boom in tone. "You get used to it," he said.

They all sat silently for a time. Grubexl studied the holo-image of the stars. Celeste watched him as she ate a biscuit from the plate. It was made of a cereal flour and other ingredients, which she couldn't determine. Cinnamon tantalized her taste buds as she chewed. She presumed the ingredients came from the planet. "You seem fascinated by the map. Have you been anywhere else in our galaxy?"

Grubexl stopped his study, jumping back as if she had caught him in the act, "Of course not."

"How did you travel from here to the other planets?"

"We brought ships with us, we could unfold once through the portal. They traveled faster than light. I presume you have discovered that means of travel. It would have taken you too long to get here otherwise."

"Do you still have a ship here with you?"

"No, they took it with them."

Being discouraged from talking about why his people had stranded him there before, Celeste went silent. "I feel like a walk. May I go for a walk?"

"Of course."

Celeste got up and walked out of the building. Grubexl accompanied her, and the others walked behind. They came to the portal again, and Celeste walked up to it. She touched it for a moment and it shimmered slightly as she placed her hand on it. She removed it with a start. "What was that?"

Grubexl, taken by surprise, said, "Just some residual energy buildup," but his eyes sparkled with excitement.

She looked at him with wide eyes and mouth open, shocked by the look he gave her. "We had better return."

They packed up their belongings and left, carrying many unanswered questions with them, returning to their Lander and the ship to debrief the others.

21

WHAT'S HE UP TO?

"It was the scariest thing I've ever experienced." Celeste shook as she recounted her time with Grubexl, and the unexpected shimmering of the stela.

"You came up against something that you weren't expecting. I don't know how to protect you from something like that." Ethan sat with Celeste in the conference room trying to calm her. Jade, Hu and John had tried unsuccessfully.

"You don't understand. It wasn't what happened that scared me, it was the expression on Grubexl's face."

Ethan frowned. "What do you mean?"

"It was as if he suddenly had hope about something. He passed it off as something benign, but I could tell that it was monumental to him. He wanted to jump at me."

"Why would he want to do that?"

"I don't know, but I saw it in his eyes."

"I think I should talk to him. I can't really associate with what you're saying without seeing him face to face."

"Please do. I'm too scared of him now."

"What do you think thing is?"

"I told you. He said it's some kind of portal. I suppose a wormhole of sorts to his home world."

Ethan rubbed his chin in thought. "It would be monumental to understand how it works. Imagine what we could do, if we could understand the technology and control it. We might be about to travel anywhere. Presumably one doesn't have to be here in the first place to establish a connection." He looked back at Celeste. She looked like the shy girl, lacking in self-confidence, that he saw when he first met her. He needed her as she was before the incident. "Go have a break. Take a few days off to relax."

"I'll be OK. It's just shaken me. I'll lie down for a while."

"OK, I need that smiling face back again."

A slight smile broke out on Celeste.

"That's more like it." Ethan rose from his seat. Celeste did likewise, and they both left the conference room.

"How's Celeste?" Jade asked when he returned to their cabin.

"Whatever happened shook her badly. She'll snap out of it. She will take the rest of today off and relax. But I need to go down there and talk to this creature. I can't get an appreciation for what we are dealing with by getting all my information secondhand. There're too many unknowns. Too many things could go wrong because we don't understand what we're doing, just like on Chariclo." He looked at Jade, brows crunched. His fear from Chariclo returned to him.

"I'm coming with."

Ethan looked at her face and saw from her eyes it wasn't a request. "Sure, I wouldn't go alone, anyway. I won't stop you, am I? I think I'll take Hugo with too."

"When were you thinking of going?"

"Tomorrow if you aren't doing anything else. I'll chase up Hugo and see if she wants to come with. Otherwise I'll find someone else."

Ethan, Jade and Hu sat in the Lander, flying down to the planet with Ethan at the controls early the next day. It glided through the atmosphere with ease as the M-drive controlled the descent to the surface. The verdant foliage underneath enriched Ethan's temperament as he gazed out the front window. The green turned to blue as water replaced land, the sparkle of reflected sunlight bouncing off the ripples and waves created by the wind. It constantly amazed him he was at the forefront of discovery for humanity. Nothing like that had really happened, for Caucasians at least, since mastery of sailing ships allowed sailing to the New World and beyond to see the wonders outside of the European landscape. Traveling over the campsite where Marie and the others still worked, Ethan wobbled the craft in greeting as it flashed by. They reached the landing site by the alien area half an hour later. Ethan steadied the Lander and slowly descended to the ground, a slight jar hitting solid ground moments later. He turned the systems off and continued sitting in the pilot's seat as he appreciated the experience of the flight.

"Are you all right?" Jade asked from behind him.

Ethan, the spell broken, looked around. "Yeah, I was just thinking about how much I enjoy all this."

Jade smiled. "Let's get going then, shall we?"

"Sure." Ethan unbuckled and rose from the seat, avoiding the instrumentation of the craft as he negotiated out of the cockpit.

Hu had already opened the hatch, and she started unloading the all-terrain, getting it ready for the journey. Ethan approached Jade and wrapped his arms around her. She obliged without protest. Ethan placed his cheek on her head and she rested her head against his shoulder, Ethan relishing the contact and love flowing into him.

"You two ready, or shall I go on ahead?"

Ethan and Jade laughed. "We're ready," Jade said and broke contact from Ethan, walking out of the Lander and to the vehicle. Ethan followed.

Hu drove the vehicle to Grubexl's dwellings, and they disembarked once they reach the place. As normal, Grubexl stood waiting for them when they arrived. Hu did the introduction. "Hello, Grubexl. I wish to introduce Ethan Richards. He is our expedition leader."

"It is an honor to meet you, Ethan Richards. I hope that we may discover many things together."

"It is an honor to meet you too, Grubexl. Please call me Ethan."

"Yes, Ethan, let us retire to my living area for refreshments."

"Certainly."

Ethan looked around as they walked to Grubexl's residence, his eyes taking in his surrounds. He stopped to feel the nature of the building walls. They were smooth with no joins visible. Even the corners seemed to have no sign of a joint, as if it were all one large construct. "What are the buildings made of?"

Stopping when he heard Ethan speak, Grubexl turned around. "A ceramic crystal matrix. It is very stable. It is also flexible, which allows for any sudden movement of the underlying ground."

"Do you get many earthquakes here?"

"Earthquakes?"

"Sorry, sudden slippage of the tectonic plates of the planet."

"Oh... no, not around here. I believe it occurs more frequently in other areas of the planet."

They continued walking and arrived at their destination a short time later. Grubexl invited them all to sit, and he brought over the same green drink as he had before, and the biscuits.

"I should warn you both," Hu said. "These are alcoholic. They throw quite a punch."

"Thanks for the warning," Ethan took a sip. "Wow, you weren't lying." He picked up a biscuit and started eating that, raising his eyebrows in appreciation of the taste. "Can you tell me more about how this transport device works?" Ethan asked once he had swallowed the food in his mouth.

"I am a biologist, not an engineer. I do not really know. It turns on when you touch it and then you walk through."

"How do you go to your destination initially, when there is no portal at the other end?"

"I do not know. The route designers set it all up. We just use it when it is ready."

"So you don't know what powers it."

"No, I believe that it involves something about what you would call strings."

"I wish I could talk to someone about that," Jade butted in.

"Do you work in such an area of expertize?" Grubexl asked.

"Yes, I do. We call it Quantum Mechanics."

"Why did you come here?" Ethan asked, regaining control of the conversation.

"We had a hypothesis we wished to test."

Ethan waited for Grubexl to continue, but when he seemed to not want to say more, he asked, "... and?"

"We wanted to determine the relationship between brain size and sentient intelligence."

"But why here, in this region of our galaxy?"

"Some exploratory teams determined that the species they found on Earth and at Alpha Centauri were suitable."

"What went wrong at Alpha Centauri?"

"We had an incorrect version of the virus."

Ethan felt angry with the revelation. "Costly mistake. You wiped out an entire species."

"These things happen from time to time."

Ethan became too furious inside to continue with that line of questioning for a time. He changed the subject. "Why can't you get back?"

Grubexl became uncomfortable. "I lost the ability to open the portal."

"How?"

"I do not know."

Ethan could see that there was something Grubexl wasn't telling him, but he was also sure that he would not get what it was from him either. He had one other topic he wanted to touch on before he went to look at the stela. "What was the drone that we saw the other day and why was it there?"

Grubexl remained silent for a time before he relented an answer. "It could be a sentinel. It guards me to make sure I do not move away from here. It may have thought you would remove me. Although the description your Celeste provided questions whether it is a sentinel."

"Why did it shoot an explosive at us?"

"I do not know. I did not think it possessed weapons. That makes me think it is not the sentinel."

"May I see this portal?"

"Certainly." Grubexl rose from his chair.

Ethan, Jade and Hu did likewise, and they followed Grubexl to the stela. Ethan looked at the jet-black surface, entranced by the smoothness it possessed, and yet it reflected little light. Grubexl, Jade and Hu stood a few metres away watching as Ethan studied the object, circumnavigating its footprint. He couldn't tell what kept it standing, as the profile it presented to the ground was too small to prevent it from toppling and it didn't appear to be embedded in the ground either. "Is this really in our universe, or is it some kind of extension from yours that is kept here somehow? I can't see how it would remain standing otherwise."

"I cannot answer with certainty, but I believe our world maintains its position. It is not something that originates from here."

Ethan nodded. He looked at the object again. Celeste had said that it changed when she touched it. He wondered if it would do the same for him. Going behind the stela where Grubexl couldn't see him, he touched the silky black surface and gently glided his hand over it. Nothing happened that he could see. Either it didn't work for him or it only activates from the one surface on the other side. He walked around, maintaining his contact with his fingers. The surface shimmered as soon as he contacted the front, a swirling cloudiness developed until he pulled his hand away. The object returned to its opaque state. Turning around to look at Grubexl, Ethan could tell he was ecstatic with excitement. He asked, "What just happened?"

"You activated the powering up sequence."

"I thought you told Celeste it was just some residual energy."

"That is what I thought then, but now I reconsider what happened, and I believe that you are powering the portal up."

"But how is that possible? I have no connection to where you come from. How can I power it up and you can't?"

"They can set it up to provide access by some and not others."

Ethan looked at Grubexl, eyes wide, incredulous. "How is that possible? We did not even exist when they set this up. How would it allow me to activate it, when it does not understand who I am and why I want to activate it? Surely, it doesn't just let anyone use it."

Grubexl frowned. "You make an excellent point. I... am unsure. As I said to the other's, some have visited and used the portal after I arrived, some just recently, relatively speaking. Maybe they provided the characteristics of your species to allow you to open it." Enlightenment flashed across Grubexl's face, as the skin where his eyebrows would have been rose. "Or maybe you have some residual genes from those who procreated with your women and it is picking that up."

Ethan considered his hypothesis. "Possibly. Jade, Hugo, you try. See if something happens when you touch it."

Jade and Hu stepped up to it. Jade tried first and touched the surface. She kept her hand there for some time, but nothing happened. Hu also touched the stela with an equally negative effect. "Guess we are not made of the right stuff," Hu said, a laconic smile on her face.

Ethan smiled. "Guess so. You may be correct, Grubexl. Whatever it is, it seems to only permit some to activate it. How long before it would be fully active?"

"You were almost there. The swirling cloudiness intensifies and increases in rotational speed until it flashes to a subdued white opalescence. It would permit transfer then."

"How? You just walk through?"

"Yes."

Ethan scratched his chin. "Is the transfer instantaneous, or does it take time to travel the distance?"

"We sense no lapse of time, only what it may take to walk from me to you."

"Incredible. Let's just leave it at that for now. I think we should go, and I thank you for your hospitality."

"You're welcome."

Ethan and the others walked back to their vehicle and hopped in.

Grubexl followed them and watched them drive off into the forest and out of sight.

Ethan ruminated what he had learned for a time as he drove back to the Lander, remaining silent as he did so. He finally asked, "What's he up to?"

"Good question," both Hu and Jade answered.

22

HIJACK

Loki's contact on the Tau Ceti expedition had just sent him a message about the alien Ethan and his team had discovered. He instantly saw the possibilities this may have for his influence, power and wealth to increase beyond measure, if he could negotiate a business deal with the alien. He had to see and talk to this being himself for that to happen though. He just had to find a means of getting there. He was certain that the Chinese wouldn't have a bar of him, so using the wormhole just would not happen, regardless of what he tried. There were just too many variables to control. The Russians would also be of a similar frame of mind, but Loki thought he could commandeer their ship, if he could work out a suitable plan. Their recent success in their hyper-drive development meant he would traverse the distance to Tau Ceti quickly. He would have to take care of juggling the consequences of commandeering the ship later.

He spent the following week getting intelligence from his sources and informants within the Russian system, using the information to develop a plan he felt would achieve his aim. Loki realized he could finally punish Ethan for his interference since his other plan seemed to have failed.

"Good morning, Loki," Eleanor said as he walked into his office.

"Good morning Eleanor, it's a beautiful day today isn't it."

Eleanor looked at him, wondering what he had to be happy about. "Yes, it is."

"I'll be going on a trip today, so you can take some time off, if you like. You haven't had a vacation for some time, have you?"

"No, I haven't. I wasn't expecting to now for a while either, but I will consider it then. I've always wanted to see the ancient ruins of Greece, or maybe the scenery of the outback of Australia. I'm told that is spectacular at the moment. They've received some substantial rain in the interior, so all the plants are in bloom."

"That sounds great. Please bring a coffee into my office?"

"Yes Loki."

Loki walked into his inner sanctum and sat in the plush leather chair at his desk. He looked at his messages and answered what he needed to. Eleanor came in and gave him his coffee. Reviewing his plan, he saw that all was progressing, and his ship was ready for departure. He was keen to get started. Having completed everything at the office by midday, Loki packed up what he needed and walked out, heading for his shuttle to the ship in orbit above him. He sat in the shuttle and the pilot sealed its hatch and took off. They rendezvoused with the ship a short time later. Going to his cabin, he made a call.

"Yes Loki."

"How are things going?"

"Ready to start phase one."

"Proceed."

The call ended. Loki sat back with a satisfied smile on his face.

～

～

～

THE TEAM of six made their way to a small cottage near Serov in the Ural Mountains. They wore black commando outfits and had infra-red goggles on. The time was just after midnight.

"Are the targets in place?" the leader asked through his radio mike.

"Targets in place," someone responded.

"Prepare to acquire on my word."

"Affirmative."

The leader crept to his allocated position. The lights in the street provided some illumination, but all was quiet. People were asleep at that time of night, especially on a weeknight. He looked around and saw the others in their positions. "Initiate," he said into the mike, as he lowered the goggles over his eyes. The streetlights went out moments later, and his vision sharpened with the reduced visible light. "Go."

The team surrounded the house. A team member tried the front door. It was locked. He bent down and pulled out his tools, manipu-lating the lock mechanism until it clicked. He tried the handle again, and the door cracked open. He opened it the rest of the way and entered with the leader and two others. The other two stood outside watching for trouble, guarding the house.

They swarmed through the rooms, disconnecting any means of communication, and converged at the bedroom door. One of them opened the door silently. The four crept in without a sound, two going to one side of the double bed and two to the other. The man and woman slept soundly, a snore coming from each of them in a steady rhythm. The leader counted down from three on his fingers. When the last finger bent over, one man on the other side and the one with him placed their hands on the man's and woman's mouths in unison. They both plunged a syringe needle into their necks and injected the contents. The disturbed victims woke in alarm, arching their backs and waving their arms, not knowing what was happening. They struggled for half a minute until the injected sedative took its effect and both slumped back onto the bed.

The leader nodded. One member lifted the woman, and

another lifted the man, placing them on their muscular shoulders with ease. Withdrawing from the room, they retraced their steps out of the house. The leader locked the door behind him as he closed it. *Poor security*, he thought. They rushed to the van parked nearby and piled into the back, as did the two guarding the house. The leader climbed into the front and sat in the driver's seat. He started the electric motor and silently drove out of the town to the location where the next mode of transport waited, thirty minutes away.

The vehicle stopped. They got out and carried the victims to the waiting shuttle, making them comfortable, but secure. Another van drove up five minutes later and deposited another person. The clandestine outfits vacated the shuttle, and the hatch closed, the shuttle taking off shortly later.

"Mission complete," the leader said to Loki through his comm, once he felt the shuttle rise from the ground and saw it disappear in the night.

A SHUTTLE MANEUVERED into the ship and steadied for a moment before it descended to the landing bay floor. The hatch opened moments later and six people entered with hospital gurneys, exiting again ten minutes afterwards with the three sedated captives. The shuttle exited the ship five minutes after that. Another shuttle arrived ten minutes later, depositing another two sedated people. That too left.

Loki stood watching the sleeping captives two hours later, as the sedative started wearing off and they stirred.

Apep opened his eyes and blinked to get the blurriness out of his vision. "What is the meaning of this?" he asked, seeing Loki and struggling with the restraints that held him. Galena moved slightly on the gurney next to him.

"Welcome," Loki said. "I am very sorry for disturbing your slumber, but I have something that I need you to do for me."

"Where am I?" Alexi asked from the gurney furthest from Apep in a groggy voice.

Loki looked over and saw Galena open her eyes. "Good, it looks like you're all safe."

"Loki," Galena said, eyes wide in surprise. "What are you doing? Haven't you interfered in our lives enough?"

Loki chuckled. "This will be very painless if you all do what you are told."

Apep, now wide awake, said, "What is it you want?"

"I want you to get me onto your ship and take me to Tau Ceti."

"Why?" Apep's eyes narrowed into slits.

"It is not of your concern. I thought I would give your new drive another outing. Now, we will get into the shuttle I have in the Landing bay and go over to your ship, where you will get them to welcome us on board. You will then take the ship to Tau Ceti and meet up with the expedition there."

"Never."

"Oh, I think you will. You have grown rather fond of Galena, haven't you? You wouldn't want to see her suffer pain... or worse?"

Hatred filled Apep's eyes and his jaw clenched. "I will kill you if you touch her."

"Do as you are told then, and all will be well. Now, let's be off."

Loki gestured to the others, and they wheeled the gurneys to the waiting shuttle and loaded them on board. They also loaded two other gurneys, the people still unconscious. Twenty men in combat outfits already sat in the cabin when they arrived, ready for the mission ahead. Loki joined them and sat in his allocated seat after telling the pilot all was ready. The hatch closed, and the shuttle left the ship moments later.

"Loki, we are approaching the Russian ship," the pilot said over the PA.

"Good, give me a moment," Loki replied. He looked at Apep. "Now, I will release you from your constraints and you will convince the captain of the ship to let us land. The life of your lover depends on it."

"But we have no authority to board the ship. They strictly regulate it," Apep lied.

"You will just have to convince them you have the authority." Loki grabbed Apep's arm and led him to the cockpit. He signaled to keep a pistol on Galena.

Apep looked back and gulped, despair in his eyes as he saw the terror in Galena's. He entered the cockpit, and the pilot gave Apep a headset. He turned a switch on and gestured for Apep to speak.

"Hello *Gagarin*, this is Apep Chernakov. Please respond."

"This is *Gagarin*. We acknowledge you, Comrade. What is your request?"

"I wish to come on board. Please grant permission."

A temporary pause broke the conversation.

"Hello Comrade Chernakov, this is Captain Gorbachev. This is highly irregular. I have no schedule for a shuttle."

Apep looked at Loki, pleading for direction. Loki looked back at Galena, malice in his eyes.

"I know this is unexpected, but Alexi and I need to come on board to check calibration settings on the hyper-drive. We can't do it from Earth."

"I wish people would provide the correct paperwork before things happen, OK then. We'll open the landing bay door."

"Thanks."

The pilot cut the communication.

"Happy?"

"I'll be happy when we are at Tau Ceti."

The gigantic door of the ship ahead of them slowly opened to allow the shuttle to land. It safely rested on the floor of the bay half an hour later.

"You guys know what to do. We must secure this ship before they send a distress call."

"Already done. We're jamming all frequencies from this ship," the leader of the group said.

"Let's take over the ship then."

The hatch of the shuttle opened and the twenty commandos streamed out to the shock of the personnel in the landing bay. They captured the ship, and it was in Loki's control two hours later with no drama. Loki ventured to the bridge of the ship when all was safe. He had Apep, Galena and Alexi in tow, well-guarded by his men. The captain sat in his command chair, sulking as they walked in.

"I am sorry," Apep said to him. "I had no choice."

"You will not get away with this, whoever you are," the captain said to Loki.

"We will be far away before anyone will even know that we are missing. Now, set a course for Tau Ceti."

The captain looked at Apep.

Apep sighed and nodded his bowed head. "Do as he says."

Galena sidled up next to him to gain what support from him she could, although her guard watched her with intense concentration.

The captain shrugged. "Prepare to disembark. Navigation set a course for Tau Ceti. Engineering, power up the hyper-drive."

The crew busied themselves with the tasks ordered and the ship left Earth orbit half an hour later.

23

LOKI ARRIVES

Ethan's comm unit sounded as he left the fitness centre on the ship, wiping perspiration from his face with a towel as he walked back to his cabin. He pressed the answer button, "Ethan here."

"Hi Ethan, this is the Command Center. We have just detected another ship entering the Tau Ceti system."

"What do you mean another ship?"

"A spaceship, it's coming towards us."

"Are you sure? Did it come through the wormhole?"

"No, it didn't come through the wormhole. They shut it to anything but communications at present. It just appeared."

"OK, I'll be there in half an hour. I need to shower first."

"No problem, it will take about three hours to get here, anyway."

Ethan disconnected, intrigued by what approached them. Was it an alien spaceship? He couldn't believe that they would encounter two different sentient species in one place. Tau Ceti wasn't exactly Grand Central Station. He freshened up and entered the Command Center forty minutes later. Celeste, already sitting in the pilot's seat, looked around when the door opened. She smiled when she saw Ethan.

"Any the wiser on what it is or who they are?" Ethan asked Celeste.

"No, they're still too far away to get a good visual image and they haven't communicated with us. I've refrained from sending anything until you came. I think that is a decision you should make, not me."

Ethan came over to the copilot's chair and sat beside her. "You're right. Would we get any response, anyway? Goodness knows what they use, if it's an alien spaceship. It can't be something from Earth, could it?" Ethan thought for a moment and a smile came to his face. "Unless..."

"What?"

"Unless it's Apep making one of his grand entrances, the sly dog. We can wait and let him think he's surprised us."

"Pardon me, but he has."

Ethan chuckled. He got his comm out and pressed a number. The person answered at the other end. "Hugo, come to the Command Center. I've got a surprise for you."

"What sort of surprise?"

"You'll find out when you get here." He hung up. Ethan called Jade to come too. He didn't bother about John, as he was fairly certain that Hu would bring him, anyway.

All three walked in ten minutes later.

"What's the surprise?" Hu asked.

"That," Ethan said, pointing to the screen. A dot was just visible, just up and to the left of centre.

"What is it?"

"A spaceship."

"What?" Hu, Jade and John all said at the same time.

"Exactly what I said when I found out. Now, it can either have one of two sources. It is an alien coming to say hello, or it's from Earth."

"Apep," Hu said, breaking into an enormous laugh that she found hard to control. "He has outdone himself this time. At least we know his drive works." The others smiled too. "Have you contacted him?"

"No," Ethan said. "I thought I would wait for him to contact us." They didn't have long to wait.

"Celeste, we have a visual comm request from the other ship," the communications person said.

Celeste looked at Ethan. "Shall we?"

"Of course," Ethan said, a smile appearing on his face to prepare for the link.

The communication person pressed a button and placed the feed on the primary screen. A head and shoulders view of Apep came on the screen, looking ragged and in no mood to spring a practical joke on his longtime friends. Galena sat just to the side of him, the look of fear in her eyes.

"Hello Ethan," Apep said, a cold timbre in his voice.

Ethan's smile disappeared. "What's wrong Apep?"

Apep looked around at someone and then returned to looking at the camera. "We've been hijacked."

Shouting started up from offscreen and Galena suddenly disappeared, being grabbed and pulled aside. Apep looked sideways, his face white and lips trembling as a bead of sweat appeared on his forehead. "You heard what I told you," came to the speaker from a voice off-screen.

A knot developed in Ethan's gut. He knew that voice. He felt afraid for Apep and Galena's safety, but a growing anger overcame him. "Put that monster on the screen," he said, his jaw tightening as he stared at the camera.

Several seconds went by before Loki came into view. Everyone, but Ethan, in the Command Center gasped. "Hello Ethan."

"If you hurt Apep or Galena, I'll kill you." Jade came over and placed her hand on his shoulder.

"Now, now Ethan, that's not like you. They won't come to any harm, so long as you do what I ask, and I get what I want."

"What do you want?"

"I want to see the sentient being that you've found."

Ethan's eyes opened wide, taken aback by the request. "How did you find out about him?"

Loki grinned smugly. "That's my little secret, now, do we have a deal?"

Ethan looked around at John, looking for some advice or support. He just shrugged and nodded to show that he couldn't see that Ethan had any choice. Ethan didn't want Apep or Galena hurt, but he didn't want to give in to the bully either. His head raced for a solution that satisfied both, but he couldn't see one.

Seeing Ethan's hesitation, Loki nodded to someone out of view. Two others came into view moments later. Ethan jumped from his seat and would have jumped through the screen if he could. "You bastard," Ethan yelled, seething with hate as he looked at Mark and Alice, both bewildered and frightened.

"Do you want me to show you I'm serious?" Loki asked.

Ethan took some deep breaths and sat down again, using all his energy to compose himself so he could think straight. Ethan turned back to him, "No, no... OK. What do you want us to do?"

"I want you to fly a shuttle over here and pick me and a few other guests up. We will then fly down and meet with this thing."

"Him."

"What?"

"It's male."

"Whatever."

"We'll get things ready and come over."

"No, just you, I don't want to see anyone else or we will remove them, and don't think I won't do it."

"I'm coming with too," Jade said, stepping into view. "You won't stop me."

"No," Ethan said, pleading when he turned to face her.

Loki was about to repeat his threat when he paused and thought. "Excellent idea, you can keep your husband in line. I will expect to see you on your way in an hour."

"We need longer."

"No, you don't. One hour." The screen went blank.

"How the hell did he hijack a Russian spacecraft?" Ethan yelled once the communication broke. "And how the hell does he know about Grubexl?"

"Good questions. One that we should answer with a little less emotion," John said, trying to get Ethan to calm down.

"Easy for you to say." Ethan glared at him for a moment and then took another deep breath and sighed. "Any ideas?"

"I don't know how he highjacked the ship, but we must have a mole amongst us, maybe the saboteur."

"No, not about that, about what to do."

"Oh."

"I can send a message to our people," Hu said. "Let them know what's happening. They might send a ship or two through the wormhole to arrest Loki."

"We can't do that. He might start killing people."

"They can at least put some pressure on him," John said. "He can only kill so many."

Jade gave John a shocked look. "They're our family and friends."

"I know, but we can't let him get away with this either."

Ethan thought for a moment. "Send a message to all three governments. At least tell them what's happening. I'm sure the Russians will want to know what's happened to their ship. We can work things out from there. What do I do? I have to get moving soon."

"That depends on what he will do, and how many people he will bring with him. I'm sure he won't be alone, and whoever he brings will have some firepower," John said. "You might just have to play it by ear."

"I won't go unarmed." Ethan said as he stood up.

"I didn't say you should. They'll probably search you, but you can only try."

"I might hide a few throughout the Lander, where they won't look." Ethan looked at Jade, "I wish you hadn't spoken up. It just gives Loki one more bit of leverage on me."

"I wasn't going to let you go on your own."

"I know. We'd better get moving."

Ethan and Jade left, headed for the armory to pick up a few laser pistols. They sat in the Lander half an hour afterwards, Ethan maneuvering it out of the landing bay doors and entered the bowels of *Gagarin* an hour afterwards, setting the Lander down on the bay floor. Ethan looked at Jade, his brow creased. "Here goes nothing." They stood and went to the hatch, Ethan pressing the button to open it moments later.

Loki and three henchmen, heavily armed, stood waiting at the far end of the bay, keeping Mark and Alice in front of Loki for protection against any trickery Ethan may have been unwise to attempt. Ethan and Jade walked out and down the steps. They stopped by the Lander and waited, Ethan gritting his teeth in fury and frustration at being so helpless. They shoved Mark and Alice forward and they walked towards Ethan, the others close behind. They stopped two metres from them.

"Hello Ethan," Loki said, a satisfied smile on his face. "I finally get my revenge with you."

Ethan frowned in confusion. "Revenge for what? How have I affronted you or caused you any pain that you didn't inflict on yourself?"

"You had the audacity to confront me at Iapetus and prevent me from achieving my goal. You made Jezebel a scapegoat for your fool-ishness and now you've caused me to lose even my empire. But now I have the chance for even more greatness."

"You're mad."

Loki turned to one of his associates, "Search them for weapons and then search the ship." Turning back to Ethan, he said, "I'm sure there will be some. You are a great adversary, but you're out of your league with me. You should have known your place and stayed there. Not to worry, it's all water under the bridge now."

The man came to Ethan and frisked him, finding the pistol hidden under his jacket. He removed it and proceeded to Jade, who balked at being touched by such a brute. She stepped away, but he grabbed her arm, to which Ethan started towards them to help her. The man swatted Ethan away with a solid punch to the jaw and nose, drawing blood. He had his own pistol out and aimed at Ethan.

"Don't," Jade shouted. "Ethan, it's all right. I'll submit." She braced herself and the man frisked her professionally, with no hint of lingering lust in his movements. He also found the pistol she concealed. He went into the Lander and they all heard various bangs and clatter as he searched that, coming out half an hour later with four more pistols that he had concealed in various locations.

"We are ready then," Loki said. "Lead the way Ethan."

Ethan looked at Jade and turned, leading the others into the Lander. He stood at the cockpit entrance with Jade as the others entered. Loki positioned Mark and Alice into the front seats of the Lander passenger area. Mark brought his eyes to Ethan's, "What's going on? Why are we here?"

"It's a long story, but it's not your fault Loki's a lunatic."

"You," Loki said, pointing to Jade. "You come sit with me. Gus here will sit with Ethan. That way we can make sure Ethan stays on the straight and narrow."

Jade looked at Ethan and Ethan at her. Fear welled up in her eyes. "Do as he says," Ethan said as he wiped some blood from his face with the back of his hand. He looked at Loki, "I'll kill you if anything happens to her."

"Just do as you're told, and everybody will get out of this in one piece," Loki replied with a jutting chin and a sneer.

Jade surrendered and went to a seat.

"Let's be off then," Loki said. "Let's go see this alien."

Ethan turned and went into the cockpit, followed by Gus. They both sat, Gus maintaining a pistol pointed in Ethan's direction. After conducting the pre-flight checks, Ethan closed the hatch and rose above the deck, exiting the spaceship moments later.

24

LOKI AND GRUBEXL

Ethan descended to the surface of the planet and landed the craft in the designated landing spot when they visited Grubexl. They all piled out of the Lander.

"We had been using a vehicle to go to the site, but there are too many of us to fit, so we must walk," Ethan said.

"I'm sure the walk will do us good," Loki said. "How far is it?"

"About an hour, I'll just get some water for us to use along the way."

"Gus can go with you and make sure you don't get any ideas."

Ethan gave Jade a fleeting look as he turned and went back into the Lander, Gus close behind. He went to the drinks locker and took out several canteens of water, handing some to Gus. They went to leave, "Oh, I forgot something," Ethan said. "You go ahead."

Gus stood where he was. "You get it while I stand here."

Ethan shrugged his shoulders and went back into the alcove. After a few moments, he came out with a bag.

"Open it."

Ethan shrugged again and opened the back, displaying its contents, a pile of energy bars. "Thought they might be useful to chew on along the way."

Gus grunted. They emerged from the Lander.

"Let's go then," Ethan said.

"Lead the way," Loki replied.

They plunged into the forest and started threading their way towards Grubexl, stopping a few times for rest and a drink and a bar to eat, for anyone who wanted one. Mark and Alice struggled in the tropical heat, not being used to the humidity and lacking fitness. Even Loki worked hard to keep the pace that Ethan set, but they finally emerged from the foliage with Grubexl waiting in his typical place by his abode.

Grubexl looked at Ethan and Jade and then at Loki and the others, particularly lingering his eyes on the henchmen and their weapons, a frown developing on his face. Looking back to Ethan, he said, "We meet again Ethan, but what is the meaning of this? Are they weapons?" he pointed at the pistols the henchmen had on Mark, Alice and Jade.

"I don't know what's happening. Loki here is determined to meet you. I don't know why. Yes, they are weapons."

"I see." Grubexl looked at Loki.

Wiping perspiration from his forehead with a cloth, Loki gave an all-conquering smile, "Greetings."

"Greetings."

"I did not believe it when I heard that they had discovered an alien. I had to see for myself. I wish to talk with you."

"I see. Your method seems a little unorthodox."

Loki chuckled, "I had to insist on Ethan bringing me here, and he needed a little persuasion."

"Well, let us get out of the sun and have a refreshment."

Grubexl led the party to his humble dwellings. Ethan wasn't sure, but he thought Grubexl had something up his sleeve. What it was, Ethan didn't know. He stayed content to see what panned out for the time being. There was little he could do, with so many of the others carrying pistols trained on him and the other hostages. Ethan sat down when they got to Grubexl's living area. The others did too, all except the henchmen who stood guard.

Grubexl went into his kitchen and prepared some drinks and snacks to share. He brought them out after ten minutes and placed the food and drinks on the table, inviting those present to help themselves as he did likewise. "Now, how about some introductions," he asked.

Ethan obliged. "These are Mark Richards and Alice Richards, my brother and sister, and this is Loki Mason, who shouldn't be here, but he insisted on coming."

"And the others?"

"They are here for my protection," Loki butted in.

"Protection against what?"

"Mainly against Ethan doing something rash."

"I see... and what is your business with me, Loki?"

"Let's make a toast first." Loki held up his glass, "To a fruitful friendship."

Ethan, Jade, Mark and Alice halfheartedly held up their glasses, but said nothing.

Grubexl said, "Indeed." He drank a large gulp of the alcoholic liquid.

Loki did likewise before his eyes opening wide and he started coughing as the effects of the fluid burned down his throat. "You didn't tell me it was alcoholic," he gasped.

"You didn't ask." A mischievous smile appeared on Grubexl's face.

Realizing the being might be testing him, Loki took on a warier demeanor. "You are the first non-human sentient species that we have encountered," Loki said, starting his sales pitch. "I see this as a marvelous opportunity for both of our races to come to a fruitful business relationship with each other. There are many things you could offer us we would find useful and I am sure we would have things that would interest you, knowledge of who we are and our technology."

Ethan rolled his eyes as Loki talked. Loki did not understand who he was talking to.

"Why would I have any interest in anything that you can offer?"

"Wealth and power."

"What good is wealth to me?" Grubexl sat puzzled. "I find your brain unusual. You think everyone, every species, would have the same values as yourself, and even if I had similar values, what I already possess far exceeds anything that humans could offer me."

Sensing that he would need to work harder to persuade Grubexl, Loki asked, "What would be a suitable exchange?"

Grubexl remained silent for some time. Loki almost continued with his spiel before he said, "You have no authority over this group of people."

"What makes you say that?"

"You need to threaten them with harm from these weapons to even get them to bring you to me. They sit here in contempt of you and I sense that Ethan here would kill you instantly, if he had the opportunity. I wonder if these people are here to protect you from him or from me."

Loki licked his lips at the rebuttal. "Ethan and I are friends."

Ethan burst into a laugh, "Yeah, best of mates."

Loki glared at him and then back at Grubexl. "You will trade with me."

"But you have nothing that I want. You have a higher opinion of yourself than is warranted. You haven't even bothered to find out who I am or why I'm here. At least Ethan is interested in these finer qualities of intelligence. You can't get me back to where I came from. The first woman who talked to me would be the only trade I could think of, but you are in no position to trade her. She doesn't belong to you."

"Who is that?" Loki demanded from Ethan, a feverish look in his eyes.

Ethan remained silent, knowing Loki's mind was unraveling, and any misplaced words might set him off.

Standing up, Loki went over to one of his men and grabbed the pistol. He aimed it at Jade. "Who?"

"Celeste," Ethan eventually said, watching Loki's movements carefully.

"Celeste? Celeste?" Loki searched his brain, trying to place the name. "Your astronomer, where is she?"

"On our ship."

"Get her down here."

"I need to go back to the Lander to contact the ship."

"That's a lie. I don't believe you would come here with no means of communication. Do I have to show my determination?"

Ethan thought the ruse was worth a try, but realized his options were running out fast. He noticed that Grubexl slowly rose and edged towards a table nearby, but didn't know why, except that it gave Ethan a line of sight with all three guards. He knew he couldn't take on all three before one of them, or Loki, shot him or someone else. He couldn't risk any rash actions. His one trump card had to remain hidden for a while longer. "No, you don't. OK, I'll contact the ship, but I need to go outside."

"Fine. Gus will shoot you if you try anything."

Ethan went out, closely followed by Gus. He eyed Ethan suspiciously, but let him do what he needed to do. Ethan opened his comm and contacted the command centre. "Hello, Celeste here."

"It's Ethan."

"Oh, are you all right?"

"Yes, nobody's been harmed yet, but Grubexl has asked for you to come here as a trade."

"What, I'm not a commodity to be bought and sold."

"I know that, but Loki might kill us if you don't come."

"Oh, what do we do then?"

"You must come down here." Ethan turned away from Gus to shield what he said to Celeste as much as possible. "You may need to bring some extra baggage to give you more protection since you don't have a choice."

"What do you... oh, yeah OK, I'll bring something extra along, just in case. It might take an hour or two."

"You can't help that."

"What does Grubexl want me for, anyway?"

"I don't know. He seems to have taken a fancy to you."

"Yuck, you're joking."

"No, he might want you to help open the portal, since you and me are the only ones that might have a chance of getting it open. Maybe he wants to go home."

"Get a move on," Gus said from behind Ethan.

"Yeah, OK."

"Who's that?"

"Just a hoon pointing a gun at me. I'd better go."

"Will get there as soon as we can get organized."

The comm link disconnected. Ethan turned.

"What were you talking about?" Gus asked.

"Just organizing what she needed to bring, since she might be down here for a while."

"Oh."

Ethan walked back inside. Gus followed.

They all looked up at the two. "She's coming," Ethan informed the others.

"Good," Loki said. "Now, what things would you have to trade?" he asked Grubexl.

"I don't know," Grubexl said. "You're welcome to look around."

"Let's... let's all of us look while we're waiting."

Grubexl shrugged as he led the others outside. He gave Loki a tour of his complex and confirmed there was little that might be of value for Loki to exploit. His mood darkened as the tour progressed until they reached the stela. "What's this?"

"It's my portal. It is how I got here, but I can no longer use it."

"Why not? Is it broken?"

"No. Access is just denied."

Loki's eyes brightened. "You mean that if we could get this working, we could explore where this leads to, or maybe set a tourism enterprise?"

Ethan closed his eyes, hoping Grubexl wouldn't mention that he seemed to be able to activate it.

Grubexl looked at Ethan, thinking.

"How do you know it works then?" Loki asked.

"Some of my people come through from time to time to check up on me."

Ethan gave a sigh of relief. The last thing he would do was go through the portal. He didn't know where it went or whether he would survive the journey or the environment when he got there. It would have to be a matter of life and death for him to go through.

Loki looked disillusioned again. He saw nothing that would make his name known for all time. "You must have something we can use."

"No." Grubexl stood silent, before saying, "Ethan said a drone shot at him the other day. You wouldn't know anything about that, would you?"

Loki chuckled. "I was hoping to scare him, or worse, but I see he came out of it unscathed."

"Not all of us did," Ethan said. "One of my team members is in a serious condition because of that. Who have you planted on my ship this time?"

"He has done this before then?"

"Yes, he killed my best friend last time. He seems to think it's my fault."

"He is deranged, isn't he?"

Ethan's eyes widened in surprise as Grubexl baited Loki. He would never attempt such a thing in his situation, but Grubexl had nothing to lose. Loki wanted something from him, so he had to behave himself. Ethan himself had no leverage to play Loki with.

"Not deranged," Loki said. "I just know what I want and insist on getting it. People who get in my way suffer the consequences. There is no stopping progress. Those who are at the forefront bask in its glory. Those who lag suffer the consequences."

Grubexl chuckled. "I hadn't realized we created such twisted minds when we gave you a boost along the way."

"Loki's tame, compared to some in our history. They are all remembered, but for the wrong reasons." Ethan said. He wondered if he could somehow catch the group off guard for a moment, but discarded the idea as soon as he thought of it. It was just too much of a risk. He had to wait patiently for an opportunity with a better probability of success.

"What's he talking about?" Loki asked.

"Grubexl and his colleagues helped us along our evolutionary growth. He created the virus we uncovered on Chariclo amongst other things."

The heat of the day started taxing Loki. "Let's go inside again, shall we? It's much more comfortable sitting in the shade."

They all went back to Grubexl's hovel and sat waiting for Celeste to arrive.

25

SHOOTOUT

"Hello? Anyone here?" Celeste said, raising her voice as she walked through Grubexl's compound.

The people inside Grubexl's abode turned their heads towards her voice outside. Ethan looked to Loki to see what he would do. It didn't take him long to find out. He hoped that Celeste had understood him when he talked to her.

"Let's all go outside," Loki said. "You two stay in here and give us some cover, in case she brought some company with," he said looking at his henchmen. They nodded.

Ethan and the others walked outside, Loki coming out last. "Hi Celeste," Ethan said. "Not sure what's supposed to happen now, but I'm sure we'll find out soon."

"Yeah well, I think I covered all contingencies in that area," Celeste said, looking directly at Ethan.

Grubexl walked towards Celeste. "Greetings again Celeste, I hope I have not disturbed you by wanting to see you again. I have found your company fascinating and wished to converse with you more. This... person would allow this to happen, so I took the opportunity."

Celeste looked warily at Grubexl. "I have no problem with talking to you, but I detest being blackmailed into it. I admit I haven't been for a while, but I've been busy and couldn't afford the time."

"I am sorry if I have upset you."

Loki looked towards the trees and surrounding buildings, searching for anyone else who may have come along to rescue his captives. "You came alone," he said to Celeste, his piercing eyes drilling into hers.

"Of course," Celeste said, maintaining a stoic face.

"You lie."

"I'm not. Why would I bring anyone else when I don't know who you have down here or how many?"

"I've looked into many faces in my time and I see deceit in yours."

"I have brought no one else with me, I swear."

Loki stood staring at Celeste for several seconds before he spoke more. "People will die, if you lie."

Celeste gulped, but stood her ground.

"So Grubexl," Loki said, turning to the alien. "I have completed my side of our deal. What can you offer me in exchange?"

"I'm not a commodity to be traded," Celeste said with a strident tone, her back arched and shoulders drawn back.

"No one's trading you," Loki said.

"Let me look," Grubexl said, shaking his head. "I will return shortly." Grubexl walked off to his workshop building and disappeared inside.

Loki's eyes darted to where Grubexl disappeared, around at the surroundings and back again repeatedly.

Mark and Alice stood next to each other, huddled together. Jade and Ethan also stood next to each other, but they stood fully alert. Celeste stood alone near Ethan and the others, but apart, her eyes looking directly at Ethan, trying to communicate her plans. Ethan couldn't really understand what her eyes were trying to say, but he hoped she had brought others with her. Celeste moved to a wall of Grubexl's house for protection, out of any direct line of fire between Loki and his two guards and anyone shooting at them from the exterior of the compound. Ethan looked at what she did and understood the intent of her actions. He started moving in the same direction with Jade.

"Where are you going?" Loki asked bluntly.

"Just wanted to lean against the wall, if that's OK with you." Ethan put a hint of sarcasm in his voice.

"You can stay where you are. We can see you much better there."

"Suit yourself." Ethan cursed Loki inside, but he couldn't do anything about following Celeste at present. He sensed something was about to happen, both from Celeste's look and her actions, as if all hell was about to break loose at any moment.

Grubexl reappeared with an item in his hands, studying it as he walked over. It seemed as if he was deciding whether he could afford to let it go. He stopped in front of Loki as he decided. "Here, this should interest your people." He held it out to Loki.

It was box shaped, about fifteen centimeters on all sides. Loki grabbed it and rotated it in his hands, looking at it in confusion. "What is it?"

"It's a communications device."

"What's so special about that?"

"You can communicate across space instantaneously. It doesn't matter how far you're away."

Ethan became interested in what Grubexl had brought out and walked over to Loki to have a closer look. "What good is one? Don't you need a transmitter and a receiver?"

Grubexl looked at Ethan. "Do you want me to do everything for you? Study it. You should be advanced enough to reconstruct the design for yourselves. It's a transmitter and receiver."

Ethan nodded. He would ask Loki for it, but he felt Loki would refuse to give it to him, believing he would steal it from him, even though Ethan was completely in his power at present.

Loki looked at Grubexl and then at the doorway he had come from with the device. "What else do you have in there?" He started walking towards the door.

Grubexl became alarmed. "Nothing of interest to you." He started moving to prevent Loki from going in the building.

Loki stopped and looked at his guards still bunkered in the house. "Shoot him if he interferes."

Grubexl stopped and glared at Loki.

"Put down your weapons and come out with your hands up," John said from somewhere in the surrounding vegetation. "I have you surrounded. You can't escape."

Loki stopped and looked at Ethan and Celeste with malice in his eyes, "This is you're doing. Whatever happens here is on your conscience." He looked at his men, "Shoot the man and woman over there first if anything starts, then the other three."

"No, you can't," Ethan said, fear instantly gripping him as he saw the danger they were all in, especially Mark and Alice. He couldn't live with himself if something happened to them. Why do these things always happen to him? He looked around in madness, trying to find another way out, a solution, but nothing came to mind.

"On the contrary," Loki shouted. "You had better put your guns down and show yourself before I start shooting people."

Silence hung over the people in the compound for a moment, like the stifling humidity that also surrounded them, waiting for a reply from John. "It will do you no good. You will not get away."

"You misjudge my planning," Loki replied. "You are the ones that won't get away. Do you really think I would come down to the planet with just the two guards I brought with me? There are others coming behind you as you speak."

"He's bluffing, John," Ethan said. "He doesn't have that many." Ethan realized he was putting himself and the others further at risk, but he felt things were already spiraling out of control. A spark could detonate Loki's insanity, whether he was the origin of the spark, or some unrelated warped occurrence, made no difference now. Loki had to find his treasure, and Grubexl's reluctance to reveal his technology could tip Loki over the edge, as easily as any actions or words from John or himself. He looked around frantically to find a spot they could rush to, if shooting started, but there was little shelter in the little open space amongst the buildings they all stood in. He tasted fear, a fear he had never tasted before, and thought it odd that it should taste metallic, fear for himself, fear for Mark and Alice and Celeste, but mostly fear for Jade, his one treasure, the one person in the entire world he would give his life for without hesitation. They were out in the open. Loki had chosen well. Celeste was the most protected of the lot of them. Jade clung to him for protection. He looked at her and saw fear in her eyes too, the same fear he tasted.

"What is the meaning of this?" Grubexl asked. "Is this all about having possession of me and whatever I may have? I can reassure you that whatever I have is rather boring and insignificant."

"It's not about you, Grubexl. Loki kidnapped people and is holding us hostage," Ethan said. "He's crazy for power and it's made him insane." Ethan looked at Loki as he talked, trying to judge what he might do next. Loki had madness in his eyes, and perspiration dribbled down his cheek. He took a handkerchief from his pocket and wiped his face. The gun he held pointed continuously at Ethan.

"This is madness," Grubexl said as he walked to a building close to him. Nobody stopped him or threatened him. Their concentration was elsewhere, as if they looked for something to come out of the sky at any moment, but didn't know exactly what that thing was. The tension in the air could cut steel.

Shots rang out in the direction opposite to where John's voice came from. They all turned to see what was happening, all except Loki's guards, who kept their attention on the hostages, but the buildings were in the way and no one could see anything. Further shots started resounding from the forest in John's direction moments later and Ethan started hearing bullets zipping through the compound as projectiles came in from the forest. More bullets started from within the compound. It seemed as if time had suddenly dilated, and things Ethan knew took only fractions of a second, took minutes to occur to his panicked mind. He heard screams and people falling and he fell, grabbing Jade and pushing her to the ground with himself on top of her to protect her with his body if he could.

Looking in Loki's direction, he saw his two guards scurry from their sheltered position in Grubexl's house to him, and pulling him out and away in the direction furthest from John and his people.

Ethan realized they must have created an escape corridor for them-selves and they vanished behind the building moments later. Shooting continued throughout the compound and in the forest for a time. Ethan couldn't tell how long it took before silence filled the air again. He didn't really think it was true when people described the dust settling after a gunfight, but, as the bullets stopped and the noise turned to silence again, Ethan looked and saw dust settling in the compound. Maybe his mind just imagined it to satisfy his thoughts, but it didn't matter. Whatever happened was over. Loki was gone, and the violence evaporated. Reality started returning to Ethan, as John and several of the security force from *Destiny* rushed into the compound.

Ethan looked over to the others. He saw Celeste sitting by the wall of the building, crying and scared. He saw Mark and Alice lying motionless on the ground, Alice faced away from him but Mark looked at him with lifeless eyes, wondering what had just happened. Ethan started shouting, "No..." but he then felt something sticky under him. He smelled blood and thought a bullet must have hit him too, but he didn't feel any pain. Getting to his hands and knees he looked for where the blood was coming from on his body, but under-standing hit him like a freight train as he realized the blood on his hands wasn't his, but Jade's.

26

YOU MUST GO THROUGH

Everything went blurry as Ethan tried to make sense of the world. He had blood on his hands, Jade's blood. He had failed. His entire life was a failure. Everything he ever tried ended in failure in some form. He failed his family, and they left him, and now they were dead because of him. He failed at Chariclo by allowing the release of a deadly virus, killing people he was responsible for, and now he failed the people here and most of all he failed Jade and she lay dead because of him. He had no will for life anymore. He couldn't protect her. His eyes looked around the compound as he still stood on hands and knees, but it seemed like a silent movie in slow motion. People in battle gear ran through the area, securing it from attack, John standing in the middle directing them. He walked over to Mark and Alice, bent over and touched each trying to find a pulse, his gaze searching for Ethan when he finished, his eyes glanced at him with pain, as he looked at Ethan. His eyes widened as he saw the blood on Ethan and Ethan saw him stand and run over, but it all looked like an ambling stroll to him in the dilated world he occupied. He saw Celeste coming too.

Looking down at Jade again, he saw red staining the ground

beneath her, but didn't smell the stench of death yet. Her eyelids flickered and reality seemed to change gear, invert, enter a different universe. Shouts and other noises returned to his ears. Everyone and everything returned to normal. "Ethan," she whispered.

Ethan started crying. He couldn't bear the pain. John rushed to them and bent over, looking at Jade to find her wound or wounds. "Medic," he shouted and moments later someone came over with a first aid kit. He listened to John and looked himself. Assessing the situation, he opened the kit and grabbed scissors, professionally cutting Jade's top off to expose the wounds better. Ethan couldn't keep track of the person's hands, they moved so quickly. They pulled out antiseptics and bandages, working on Jade as if he had been practicing his entire life for this one event, blood drying on his hands as he did so, not wasting time to put gloves on to protect himself.

After several minutes the medic looked up at John. "I've done all I can but she needs medical treatment on the ship immediately. She's bleeding internally."

"We'll get her to the vehicle and take her to the Lander."

"I don't want to move her too far. We need a stretcher to carry her."

"May I have look?" Grubexl said as he moved in for a better view. Ethan hadn't noticed him coming out of his hiding spot. Grubexl held an instrument Ethan had never seen before.

Ethan saw concern and weary sadness in Grubexl's eyes as they looked down at Jade, as if they had seen death far too many times in the past. The medic moved out of the way slightly as he yelled over to another person to get a stretcher. Grubexl squatted and rotated a knob on the instrument. Lights flickered on. A few seconds later, Grubexl waved the thing over Jade's torso and brought it back to his eyes for viewing the screen on the front. His brow furrowed. "How long will it take you to get her to your doctor?"

"Three maybe four hours," John said.

Grubexl shook his head, "She does not have that long." He looked at Ethan.

Ethan knew his failure would be complete. He sat on the ground, looking at Jade, despair in his eyes as the meaning of Grubexl's words sank in.

"There is only one way to save her," Grubexl said.

It took a moment for the words to have any meaning to Ethan as they penetrated the fog of despair in his mind. He looked up. "What do you mean?"

"She will not last long enough to get to your ship based on the readings I have. There is only one way to save her. My people can save her, but you must go through the portal."

Ethan's head jerked to the black stela standing fifty metres away. "I can't go through there. What's on the other side? How do I know you aren't lying? There's probably nothing but a void wherever it leads to, if you can even go through it as you say."

"It is up to you. Everything I say is true. You will emerge from a similar portal at the other end, and my people will be there waiting. They always guard the portal. They have the skill and equipment to attend to Jade, but you must go now before it is too late. They cannot resurrect the dead. You must go through."

Ethan looked at Grubexl, trying to find out from his expression if what he said was true. He looked at Jade as she lay unconscious on the ground. He couldn't go through the portal without testing it, could he? It went against everything he had drilled into himself. 'Test first before committing,' had always been his motto since the explosion that almost killed him at the laboratory testing the warp bubble equipment. Grubexl could be wrong. They might get her to the ship in time. Could he risk that? At least they would die together if Grubexl lied, and the pain in his heart would cease. He didn't know if he could still live, if Jade died on the way to the ship. What would he do without her? He suddenly understood the pain Hu must have gone through when her partner didn't return to her. Could he break that rule? Could he take the leap of faith being asked of him to save Jade?

A man came back with a stretcher and placed it on the ground next to Jade.

"Can you get her back in time?" Ethan asked the medic.

The medic looked at Jade and then back at Ethan. "I can't guarantee that." He shook his head.

Ethan looked at Grubexl. A genuine concern seemed to flow from his eyes.

"Let's get her on the stretcher," the medic said.

"No," Ethan said as he broke his gaze with Grubexl. He looked at John. "I'll take her through the portal."

John looked concerned and braced himself. "If you're sure," he finally said.

"I'm sure." Ethan stood up, wiping some dirt from himself. He looked at Grubexl. "Will the portal stay open once I open it, or do I have to have my hand on the surface all the time?"

"Once it is open, it will remain open for thirty seconds after you take your hand away or you enter it."

Ethan nodded. "Put her on the stretcher and take her over to the portal," he instructed the medic. He walked over to the portal and looked at it, wondering if he was making the worst mistake of his life, maybe his last. The medic and another carried Jade over and placed her on the ground just behind Ethan. John and Celeste came over and stood by him. Grubexl stood nearby.

Celeste placed a hand on his arm and rubbed it. "You'll be fine. This is what you must do."

He looked at her. She had a reassuring smile on her face. He nodded again. The stela towered in front of him, like an impassable sentinel, blocking his path until he said the right password. He took a deep breath and breathed out slowly to calm himself. Lifting his hand, he placed it on the stela, as if he was placing it on a biometric hand scanner. The surface slowly changed and shimmered. The opalescence brightened until the stela surface became pure white. The white seemed to implode and disappear as if sucked into the blackness from the middle to the edges. It finally stabilized as a star field over the surface and Ethan's hand threatened to disappear into the face of the stela. His eyes bulged in amazement, and his heart pounded. Ethan looked at Grubexl, who nodded that all was ready.

Ethan looked at Jade lying still on the stretcher and took another deep breath. He took his hand away, and the portal held as Grubexl said it would. He quickly placed one arm under Jade's shoulder and the other under her knees and lifted her up, positioning himself in front of the portal. "See you all soon," he said as he took his leap of faith and walked into the void beyond.

27

THE OTHER SIDE

Ethan held Jade tightly in his arms as they journeyed to the unknown. He felt light-headed, as if the vacuous environment he traveled in made him slightly intoxicated. They stayed in the nexus between worlds for an unknown period before they came out of the other end, almost stumbling as he emerged from the connecting portal.

A ring of beings greeted their arrival. All looked similar to Grubexl. Several held objects that Ethan knew could only be weapons, and they trained them on Jade and him. He blinked as he stood still, Jade still lay in his arms, bewildered at the incomprehensible scene in front of him. He said the only words he could think of. "Help me, please."

Two of the beings seemed in charge and they looked at each other as Ethan spoke. They recognized the meaning of the sound, so one went away and came back. He played with the dials on the front of an instrument and Ethan saw it was like the one Grubexl used when conversing with them. "Greetings," the creature finally said. "We are surprised to see the portal used."

"We desperately need your help. Grubexl said that you can heal Jade here. She has been shot," Ethan replied.

Both beings looked at Ethan and then at Jade. One said something to the other, and it went away and came back a minute later with the same instrument Grubexl had used to analyze Jade's condition. He moved to Ethan and Jade and scanned her, looking at the readings afterwards. His eyes widened, and he said something to the others. Two of the guards rushed off and came back with a gurney moments later. "Please, place her on here." The alien said. Ethan complied. One strapped her on and rushed her down a corridor. The two beings in charge followed, as did Ethan, once he recovered from the shock of where he was.

"Where are you taking her?" Ethan asked the others, as he trotted to catch up.

The two walked at a brisk pace. One turned its head, "To the hospital."

They all came to a blank white wall moments later. The one who talked to Ethan placed its hand on the wall, and it shimmered like the portal. It opened and the being pushing the gurney went through, follow by the other two aliens and Ethan, reappearing in a hospital area. A being in a white gown met them and looked at Jade and then at the instrument the other being had used. It nodded and said something. They pushed the gurney into a room with a white slab in the middle of it. The slab had lights and controls on the side and a hinged transparent half-cylindrical cover over the top. The slab was two metres long and one point two metres wide. They placed Jade on the slab and closed the cover, sealing her in, as if she lay in a transparent sarcophagus. The doctor played with the controls like he played a piano. He said something to the others, as the atmosphere in the machine went white, hiding Jade from view.

"What's happening?" Ethan asked, confused over everything in front of him.

One of the original beings looked over and frowned. It came over. "I am sorry we have not informed you. Your mate is close to death, but we can save her in time. She is in a healing machine." It looked over to the other being and said something. It came over too. "There is nothing else we can do now, but wait," the first one said. "Come, let us go for refreshments and we will talk."

"I want to stay here with Jade."

"It will take time. You cannot do anything to speed up the process, and nothing will change if you are here or not. The doctor will inform us when the healing is complete."

"I still want to stay."

The first being looked at the second, frustrated at Ethan's insistence to stay. "Very well. But let us go outside of the room so the doctor can conduct his duties without interference. There is a window you may observe from."

Ethan looked around the room. It was empty except for the machine, but he saw the waist height to ceiling window next to the doorway they entered the room through. He nodded and walked out with the other two. An alcove interrupted the smoothness of the opposite wall with seating and a coffee table in it. Ethan felt sure it hadn't been there when they arrived, but he may not have taken notice, distracted by the intensity of the earlier situation. They gestured for Ethan to sit, which he did, tiredness suddenly hitting him as he closed his eyes, rubbed them and opened them again.

One of them left and came back a few minutes later with a tray with drinks and some food on it. It had another translation device with it too. "Please drink and eat," it said.

Ethan obliged. He grabbed the glass with the drink in it and took a sip. It tasted sweet, like coconut milk, and soothed his throat as he gulped it down. He took another couple of gulps and placed the glass back on the table, leaning back in the seat and closed his eyes again to rest for a moment. The two beings stood opposite him when he opened them. They seemed to study him.

"How did you activate the mechanism?" one of them asked.

"I don't know. Grubexl believes that my genes may have remnants of some of you, who came to our world a long time ago."

The being nodded, but then looked stunned as if it realized something. It said, "Excuse our rudeness. We have not introduced ourselves. My name is Antixl, and this is Poloxl." Antixl pointed to the other one. "We welcome you to Earth."

Ethan's jaw dropped, "Earth?"

Antixl chuckled. "Yes, we know that you also have a world called Earth. We will explain later. What is your name?"

"Oh, I am equally rude. My name is Ethan Richards, and the woman is Jade, my wife. You are both male, I presume?"

"You are correct. How did this happen to your Jade?"

"We recently discovered how to travel faster than the speed of light and we traveled to the planet Grubexl is on, finding Grubexl there. Another of our species found out about Grubexl and wanted to use him for his own purposes. He threatened us, and there was a gun battle. They shot Jade and some others in the crossfire." The memory of the shootout angered Ethan for a moment.

Antixl nodded. "It seems you have the same troubles with personalities we had millennia ago."

"We have had many wars in the past. We probably will again. It just seems to be who we are."

"So, Grubexl told you to come through the portal?" Poloxl asked.

"Yes. He examined Jade as you did and concluded we didn't have time for us to treat her ourselves. He told me that the only way to save her was to go through the portal."

Antixl and Poloxl looked at each other. "Maybe there is hope for him yet," Antixl said.

"We shall see," Poloxl replied.

"How long will it take for the healing to work?" Ethan asked.

"Several hours, I'm afraid. Do you wish to go to some accommodation in the meantime?" Antixl asked.

"No, I'd like to stay here, if that's all right with you. I want to be present when it is finished or if something happens."

"As you wish. We must leave you for a while and attend to our other duties, but please press this button here and one of us, or both, will come to your assistance." Antixl pointed to a button on the wall in the alcove.

"OK. Thanks."

"We wish the best for you," Poloxl said and nodded, as did Antixl before they both walked off, leaving Ethan to his thoughts and fatigue.

Ethan sat back and closed his eyes again as he felt his depression return to him, as it had in similar situations in the past. He shook it off and told himself that he wasn't to blame and he couldn't have done anything differently. Feeling edgy, he opened his eyes again and stood up, walking over to the window to look at Jade in her sarcophagus. It was still opaque from the gasses inside, hiding her from his view. He stared at her as his thoughts returned to Loki, gritting his teeth. Every time his path crossed with Loki's, something terrible happened. Jake died the first time and now Mark and Alice and this. Revenge suddenly flared into Ethan's emotions as he contemplated what he would do to him. Could he kill Loki in cold blood, as he wanted to do? He suddenly realized he couldn't, not in cold blood. He would if he had to defend himself or Jade, but he couldn't see himself executing anyone, no matter what evil the person had inflicted on him. Loki still lurked on Caerus, unless he got back to the Lander that had brought his other soldiers down. But where would he go? Would they allow him back on the Russian ship? That depended on whether he still had control of it. Ethan thought John would request more troops through the wormhole for support and to capture Loki, but that would take time. He realized he didn't know how long he had been on this strange mirror Earth. Looking through the window gain, he saw nothing had changed except where the doctor stood, so he sighed and walked back to the seat and closed his eyes again.

He woke up with a jerk, as someone shook him. Ethan realized he had been asleep and opened his eyes, rubbing the sleep from them. He looked up and saw the doctor beside him with his hand on his shoulder. He smiled at Ethan and said something he didn't understand, but he waved him to follow him. Ethan rose, stretched the kinks from his muscles and went with the doctor back into the room. He stopped when he saw Jade sitting on the slab, his eyes misting up with joy as she smiled at him. The doctor smiled too. Ethan ran over to Jade and hugged her for what felt like an eternity. Releasing her, he held her shoulders and looked into her eyes, "You're alive."

"Obviously, but where am I?"

Ethan chuckled. "You're on Earth."

Jade frowned. "It doesn't look like Earth, and who is this guy apart from looking like a doctor."

Ethan quickly wiped the teardrops that had accumulated around his tear ducts away. "We went through a portal and entered another place, where Grubexl comes from, but it is also called Earth."

"That must be how we called our planet Earth then."

Ethan looked at Jade's body where the bullets had penetrated. They had removed the bandages and he couldn't see where the bullets had passed into her. It was as if she had never been shot. "This is amazing."

Jade suddenly looked self-conscious as she sat semi-naked on the slab. "What happened to my clothes? Why are they all cut up?"

"Don't you remember?"

"I remember shots being fired and then pain and that's it."

"You were shot twice, here and here." Ethan touched her body where he remembered the bullet holes were. "The medic cut your clothes away so he could treat you."

"Oh, I thought you may have become impatient with me."

Ethan laughed.

"What am I going to do? I can't walk around like this."

"We'll think of something."

"What happened next?"

"What?"

"What happened after I got shot?"

"Oh, Loki ran off and..." Tears came to Ethan's eyes again, but tears of pain. "They killed Mark and Alice."

"Oh, Ethan. I'm so sorry." Jade reached over and pulled him to her so she could hug him. He let her and felt her warmth against him.

Regaining control again, he said, "And you were bleeding. The medic said you had internal wounds and needed a doctor straight away, but Grubexl examined you with some scanner and said you wouldn't make it back to the ship in time. So he convinced me to go through the portal to get help here. It was that or watch you die."

"That was rather risky."

"As I said, it was watching you die going back to Destiny, which the medic thought was probable, or take a risk. Either we both died trying to go somewhere, or Grubexl told the truth, and what was this end would save you."

Jade looked into his eyes as she stroked his cheek. "Well, I'm glad you took the risk and we're both alive to tell the tale."

"So am I."

The door opened, and Antixl and Poloxl walked in, Poloxl carrying a package.

Ethan and Jade looked over. Ethan said, "Jade, I'd like you to meet Antixl and Poloxl. Their quick actions saved your life."

"I can't thank you enough," Jade said.

"It was our duty," Antixl said. "And it pleases us you have made a full recovery. Ethan was very distressed when you both appeared."

"The doctor noticed damage to your clothes," Poloxl said. "We have brought some clothing to replace them, if you desire." He held out the package he was holding.

"Why, thank you. I couldn't possibly walk around in these." Jade gestured her tattered clothes.

Antixl and Poloxl laughed. "It would seem that the females of your species have similar attitudes to presentation of appearance as ours."

Ethan laughed along with them, but Jade huffed. She opened the package and a full-length gown unfolded when she held it up. "This is beautiful."

"It is our current fashion."

Jade hopped off the slab and looked around for somewhere private to change, but found nowhere.

Seeing Jade's dilemma, Antixl said, "Oh, please forgive us for our rudeness. We will turn around if you desire."

Jade blushed, "If you don't mind." Antixl and Poloxl turned. Ethan stayed looking at her. "You too."

"What?" Ethan said innocently. Jade glared impatiently. "OK," Ethan said in submission and turned.

Jade quickly changed into the gown and she said, "You can turn around again," a minute later. The gown fitted her perfectly, hugging her body like it had been tailor made for her.

The others turned around.

"You look magnificent in that," Antixl said.

"Our females will be jealous," Poloxl said.

Ethan just winked.

"Do you feel well?" Antixl asked Jade.

"Yes, no one would believe someone had shot me."

"Then come, let us leave and go somewhere to relax and refresh before further talking." He held out an arm to usher Jade and Ethan forward.

They accepted Antixl's gesture and walked out of the room. Poloxl took the lead, and they walked back the way they had come, reaching the hospital portal moments later. They traveled through, much to Jade's consternation, and to the area they had arrived at. Continuing through another corridor, they saw that the walls and ceiling were smooth and smokey-blue. The floor made a slight noise as they walked along it and it held the impression and pattern of tiles, although it was smooth, but non-slip. An arched exit appeared a little further ahead, and they emerged into an enormous courtyard, green lawn carpeting most of the central area. It reminded Ethan of a country estate. The air smelled fresh. Pathways radiated from their location in various directions. They took one that went slightly left, Steps intercepted their path a hundred metres later and they descended them, continuing their walk for another hundred metres. Birds sang from the trees ahead of them. The trees hid their view of what lay behind them until they pierced their barrier, and a lake opened up before them, its expanse preceded by a rotunda on the lake's shoreline, with a small jetty projecting into it.

"It's beautiful," Jade said.

Poloxl looked at her. "It is. We take pride in maintaining its appearance."

They mounted the four steps leading to the interior of the rotunda where a table and chairs awaited them, the table bearing a jug and glasses. The same green looking liquid sat in the jug they had tasted when with Grubexl.

"Please sit," Antixl said.

Ethan and Jade sat in chairs next to each other. Antixl and Poloxl sat opposite. One of their kind came from somewhere and served the drinks.

"Have you had this before?" Poloxl asked.

"Yes, we have," Jade replied. "Grubexl served it to us. It is very alcoholic."

"Yes, it is. I wondered if he managed to manufacture it where he is. Now, what would you like to know? I am sure that you have many questions."

Jade and Ethan looked at each other, before Ethan asked, "Where are we?"

"You have traveled between branes and are now in a different universe. The properties of physics are still the same as in yours, otherwise coming here would have destroyed you, as we would have been by going to yours."

"So the multiverse is true," Jade said, "and the portals are a link between the two."

"In a manner of speaking."

"Physicists will have a field day when they find out about this." Jade suddenly became scared. "You will allow us to go back?"

"Of course. We will not keep you here against your will."

"I take it that both places being called Earth is not a coincidence," Ethan said.

"Correct," replied Poloxl. "When we went to your planet and conducted our experiment, we instilled the thought in your species to consider your planet as Earth."

"So Earth was the first place you conducted your experiments on the human brain size."

Antixl sighed. "And we meant it as the only place. Grubexl wanted to conduct a further experiment on a different planet with a much-accelerated growth rate. Totally illegal. He conducted the experiment before we could stop him, with disastrous results. He wiped out the entire species. That is why he remains there. He is exiled, imprisoned in your universe for the rest of his existence."

"We found the skeletons of the other species on our first expedition," Ethan said.

"You did?" Antixl had a look of fear. "Was the virus still present?"

"Yes, it killed several of our people when it infected them. It also infected Jade, but we developed a cure for it before she died, thank god."

"We are pleased. We tried removing the remains so they wouldn't be found, because of that very reason. We were not sure how long the virus might linger."

"You are two-million years old then?"

"Yes, even older," Poloxl said. "I am almost four-million of your years old. I am near the end of my life, but I might be fortunate to live to five."

"Amazing."

"Tell us about your species. How have you developed?"

"We have just developed faster than light space travel. That is how we met Grubexl and found the other dead species. We are obviously a long way behind the technological advancement of yourselves. We populate our solar system on various planets and moons, but have a long way to go before we have truly established permanent settlements. The main issue is the lack of breathable atmosphere. We have been fortunate in discovering planets in our expeditions with atmospheres that suit us, or almost suit us."

"Is that what the devices in your nostrils are for?"

"Yes, the atmosphere on Caerus, that is what we have called the planet Grubexl is on, is only fifteen percent oxygen, which is just below what we need to survive. These enrich the air we breathe so we get enough oxygen."

"Sensible." Poloxl paused for a moment as if considering whether he would say what he intended to. "We could supply you with the ability to breathe without them if you wished. It might change your appearance slightly though, and it would be permanent for you and any of your offspring."

"What sort of change?"

"You would grow an additional organ on your head, something hardly noticeable with your hair to cover it. It would photosynthesise the carbon dioxide, like your plant life, but the oxygen is retained in your bloodstream. The organ also accumulates the excess for later consumption."

Ethan and Jade looked at each other, not sure what to say. "We will consider it," Ethan finally said.

Jade had a question. "You seem to be male, like Grubexl. Where are the females in your species?"

"They are around. They are not as beautiful as you though." Jade flushed from embarrassment by the compliment. "Your species seems to have developed a visually appealing female form. You are lucky. Our females remain in the background. Not that we don't find them attractive. We do."

"That is why some of your species came and propagated with us, then."

"Yes, that was embarrassing. It should never have happened. They were a little too amorous in their youth, I'm afraid. We exiled them on your planet, and we shortened their lives. It would not have been appropriate for them to live amongst you as long as we do."

Jade remained silent. She was out of questions for the time being, as was Ethan. They finished their drinks.

"Would you like to inspect some of our facilities?"

"I would be interested in that," Ethan replied.

They all rose and Antixl and Poloxl spent the next two hours showing them various things of interest and how they worked, to the utter fascination of Ethan in particular.

"You must be tired and hungry," Antixl said. "Since it is becoming part of you usual night cycle, I believe. You are welcome to stay and feast with us and stay your night. You are welcome to stay as long as you want."

Ethan looked at Jade to see what her thoughts were, and then said, "We would love to have a meal with you and stay the night. We will consider how long we stay when we wake up."

"Excellent."

28

GRAND TOUR

Ethan and Jade woke the next day refreshed. The previous evening's meal had been the banquet Antixl promised and had Ethan's stomach bursting at the seams. Other members of their species were present, including females. They paid particular attention to Jade. Ethan had to agree that the females were far inferior in beauty to Jade, although everyone was inferior to her. He decided he would call them Terrans, since they name their planet Earth too.

They refreshed themselves in the bathroom facility attached to the bedroom and went to find some breakfast. Two Terrans met them at the door of the bedroom and ushered them to a dining room where they feasted on a sumptuous breakfast. Antixl and Poloxl met them as they finished eating.

"We hope you had a refreshing sleep," Antixl said.

"We did, thank you," Jade responded. "But you will have to stop feeding us so much. We will put on too much weight."

The Terrans in the room laughed. "We just wish to give you a good impression of us," Poloxl said. "Please come this way. We wish to give you a tour of our planet, if you believe that would be of benefit to you."

"That would interest me," Ethan agreed.

"Follow us." The Terrans led Ethan and Jade out of the building they occupied and into a garage area, where several open top vehicles sat. They led them to one and invited them to join them in the vehicle. Ethan and Jade entered and sat down. Another Terran already sat in what Ethan presumed to be the driver's seat. Poloxl motioned for the driver to start. The vehicle lifted off the ground by an anti-gravity drive system and left the garage, picking up speed as it rose above the ground and out of the immediate area of the buildings they stayed in.

"Where are you taking us?" Ethan asked.

"We will take you to our capital city where you will see our life as we pass the day," Poloxl said. "I have arranged a visit to one of our technology centers and then we will visit a medical facility, a different one than we were at yesterday."

"We will mostly be interested in your technology centre. We are both involved in that line of research ourselves. The medical facility would be of more interest to others in our teams, if they were here."

"Very well. We require you to attend the facility for a brief time. Our people wish to examine you." Poloxl saw Jade become apprehensive, and Ethan also had some concern. "Do not be afraid. We will not harm you. Our research people wish to examine the long-term results of the test we conducted, that is all. I am sure that you appreciate the value of documented evidence of the results from an experiment."

"We feel a little like specimens being examined," Ethan said.

"That is not our intent."

"Tell me, have you traveled to universes other than ours?"

"We have attempted to, but have had no success. The connection failed when we tried. Our scientists believe the physical properties were too dissimilar to ours for the connection to be stable. Your universe is the only one we have established a stable connection with so far."

"How vast is your civilisation?"

"We have expanded our presence across two galaxies in our universe, so you see we have a minuscule presence."

"It is far vaster than us, although we have a lot of catching up to do."

"Precisely."

They sat in silence again as the ground below rushed by, the trees and grasslands providing plenty to look at along the way. They crested a hill and a vast city appeared, the perimeter quickly approaching them. Ethan estimated that an hour had gone by. Ten minute's time the vehicle slowed, and they landed at a building, inside a small alcove, to protect the vehicle for the elements. Two Terrans stood waiting for them as they disembarked.

"Greetings Poloxl, Antixl," both Terrans said.

"Greetings Miloxl, Juzixl," both Poloxl and Antixl replied. "I present Ethan and Jade to you," Poloxl continued.

"Greetings Ethan and Jade," both said.

"Greetings," Ethan and Jade replied.

"It is our honor to escort you through our facility to present our humble technology to you," Miloxl said.

"It will be our honor to inspect your facility. I am sure there is much we can learn from your experience," Ethan replied.

Juzixl said something to the others that Ethan couldn't understand, and they smiled. Seeing Ethan and Jade out of the conversation, Antixl advised, "Juzixl just said that you are very polite."

"I see."

"This way, please."

They spent almost two hours looking through the buildings that made up the facility. They entered one enormous room where huge furnaces smelted material Ethan had not seen before. It involved a continuous process, and a coppery-colored metal exited the end of the machine, although Ethan knew it wasn't copper. "What metal is this?" Ethan asked.

Miloxl smiled as Poloxl translated the question. He said something back to Poloxl. "Miloxl says that unfortunately he cannot disclose the composition of the material. The base component has a high number of protons and is usually unstable, but we have stabilized it with the addition of alloying elements. It is very strong and long lasting. We use it for most of our construction purposes."

Jade leaned forward at the mention of stabilizing an unstable element, as she and other scientists had been working on the stability problem of Astatine with no success, or answering why it was stable on Iapetus and not on Earth. She asked, "We have a problem with the stability of one of our elements. We call it Astatine, and it has eighty-five protons. Would you have any suggestions on stabilizing it?"

Poloxl translated the question to Miloxl and Juzixl. They had a long intense debate over the answer until Poloxl finally nodded. "They say that they cannot tell you too much, as that may interfere with your normal development. They can tell you what they have already mentioned, that alloying can change properties of materials."

Jade nodded. "I understand and thank you for what you have told us."

After looking at the smelting operation, they walked through more manufacturing sections of the facility where machines, instruments and many other devices were being made and assembled. Ethan could have spent days there, but realized he probably would still have understood a minuscule fraction of the technology he had seen. Their hosts were keen to move on though, so he and Jade obliged and entered the vehicle for the journey to the medical facility. They entered the principal building and looked at the research being conducted, gene modification to cure various afflictions, engineering novel food supply and immense machines that dissected the body into three-dimensional images down to the cellular level.

"Marie will be envious of what we've seen here," Jade said, as she marveled at the advancement in the technology.

They neared the end of their tour of the facility, and Poloxl asked, "Have you considered the offer we mentioned yesterday about providing you a slight modification, so you wouldn't need artificial enrichment of oxygen in the atmosphere?"

Ethan looked at Jade, who looked a little apprehensive. "We really haven't talked about it. You've kept us so busy, we haven't had time

and we were so exhausted last night, we dropped off to sleep immediately."

"Not to bother. There is plenty of time. We will not keep you
occupied so much. You can then enjoy our planet more and ponder
your choices."

"Thank you."

They went back to the same estate they arrive at and had dinner
with just Poloxl and Antixl.

"You are welcome to arrange for the vehicle to take you anywhere
at all. Just make your request known to one of the staff and they will
arrange it for you."

"Thank you," Ethan replied. "How vast is your civilisation here
and what does the planet look like?"

Poloxl rose from the table and went to a side table by the wall. He
slid open a cover and pressed a button which exposed a console.
After some manipulation, a holographic image of a planet hovered
over the dinner table. "This is Earth."

Ethan and Jade rose and examined it. "It's very different to our
Earth and yet it looks similar, familiar," Jade said.

"You populate the areas in red?" Ethan asked.

"Yes, that is correct. And we are here," Poloxl said as he pointed to
a large blot of red.

"What is the population of your planet?"

"Six hundred million."

"So little?"

"It used to be much larger before expansion to the cosmos, but it
reduced and we have settled with the current number as a sustain-
able one for comfort and the good of the planet. Anything larger and
the energy consumption heats the planet up to unacceptable levels
over time."

"I feel this is an issue we are dealing with now. Our world is vastly
overpopulated, and I believe that is one reason for our push to
explore our galaxy."

"It is a common problem."

"You have seen a similar pattern with other civilizations?"

"Yes, it has been our observation that by the time a civilisation reaches a critical mass of survival, it has developed the technology to relieve the pressure, by reaching out to other places."

Ethan looked at the image of the planet for a while longer.

"Do you have other races in your species?" Jade asked.

Antixl and Poloxl looked at each other and then back at Jade. "We do not understand the question," Antixl said.

"We have several races on Earth, different variations of Homo-Sapiens, but we are all the same species. Just as an example, some have white skin like us, some have dark brown skin."

"I see. No, we do not. We engineered that variation out of us a long time ago. It interfered too much with our development."

Silence descended on the group and Poloxl shut down the holograph.

"It is time for us to leave you," Antixl said. "We will not see you tomorrow, so you can do whatever you like, unless you wish to speak with us or wish to return to where you came from."

"Thank you for your hospitality," Ethan said. "I think we will enjoy having some time to explore your planet, while we are here before we return."

"As you wish. I wish you a pleasant sleep."

Poloxl and Antixl left, and Ethan and Jade went off to bed.

They spent the next few days trekking to various locations of the planet and exploring them. They usually returned to the estate exhausted by the activity, but thoroughly enjoying what they saw.

29

RETURN

Ethan and Jade spent over two weeks on the alternative Earth, enjoying the serenity of everywhere they went and the experience of seeing unfamiliar things with everything they saw. They sat in the rotunda by the lake late one afternoon, enjoying the balmy temperature and the view of the sun descending in the western sky, a glass of the green alcoholic drink in their hands.

"This is like a second honeymoon," Jade commented.

Ethan looked at her. "It didn't start off that way."

"No, I suppose it didn't." Jade frowned.

Ethan sighed. "We need to think about going back. We can't stay here forever."

Jade looked out over the lake before answering. "Back to what?"

Her question surprised Ethan, but now that he thought about it, he wondered the same thing. What would they find when they returned? They had only been away two weeks, so he presumed everyone would still be around. But what would have changed. He gritted his teeth for a moment. "I wonder if they've arrested Loki yet."

"What happened to him?"

"He ran off once the shooting started. His mercenaries picked him up, more than likely."

"You don't think he's still lurking around, do you?"

"Anything's possible with him when it involves wealth and glory."

They sat in silence for a moment.

"You still haven't answered my question," Jade said.

"What question?"

"What are we going back to?"

"Exploring I suppose."

"I'm getting sick of exploring. What's left for us to explore, anyway? We've traveled to other stars. We've traveled across branes to another universe. How would we top that?"

Ethan sat in thought. He really didn't know what Jade was driving at. Did she want to settle down back on Earth and just do a regular job? He didn't think he could do that. "What are you suggesting?"

"I've always wanted to live on a farm and grow my own food, be my own boss. I've been thinking. With Caerus, we would have the entire planet as a farm. There would always be something new to discover there. It would be better than getting shot at every time we go somewhere. But what do you think? How much further do you want to reach?"

"I'm not sure. Life's been hectic and a slower life would be interesting for a time."

"Who said anything about slower? I think we'd be run off our feet."

"I mean slower than in not being at the forefront of what we do."

"It wouldn't prevent us from having some vacations now and then, if we get itchy feet. We have friends in high places."

Ethan laughed. "We can't just ask John if we can borrow *Destiny* every time we want a vacation."

"Why not?" Jade asked in a mocking tone.

Ethan went quiet again. Was Jade right? Should they stay on Caerus? They would be the first to colonize another planet then. "What should we do about the genetic modification Poloxl and Antixl suggested?"

"I don't know. They suggested they wouldn't be very visible and it would mean we wouldn't need to use the enhancers anymore. I wouldn't miss seeing the back of them. It would be an enormous help if we stayed on Caerus. Wouldn't it?"

Ethan pondered the thought. "Let's see if they can show us a hologram of what we might look like first."

They spent the rest of the evening watching the sunset and the wildlife settle for the night, before returning to the residence to do the same.

They contacted Poloxl and Antixl the next day, asking if they could see a holograph of what they might look like with the modification. They made the images and provided to them to see.

"They're right. You can't see it much. Our hair would cover it completely if we grew it," Jade commented. Throwing her fear away, she said, "Let's do it. We have never shirked an opportunity for something new, why stop now."

Ethan reached for her and hugged her. "That's what I love about you," he said.

They contacted Poloxl again and advised him they wished to undergo the treatment. The decision seemed to delight him, and Antixl was very excited about the entire thing when he met them later. They went back to the medical facility where the procedure went ahead without an issue. It took several days to complete. Ethan and Jade looked in the mirror.

"Now, that's a fashion statement," Jade said, as she inspected the aureolean membrane haloing her head from ear to ear.

Ethan laughed. "It is rather unique," he said, inspecting himself in the mirror.

The time of departure came. Poloxl and Antixl met them and led them to the portal. Ethan walked in silence and introspection. They arrived in front of the doorway to their own universe.

"What's the matter, Ethan?" Jade asked.

"What if Loki is there waiting for us? What if he somehow overpowered the others and has control of the area and Grubexl?"

"You seem to be afraid of this Loki," Antixl commented.

"He's evil and ruthless," Ethan said.

Antixl and Poloxl spoke with each other in their own language for a moment, and Antixl left. He returned a short time later, "Here, have these," he said, handing two small belts to them and a small cylinder made of metal. The cylinder was the size of a pen and black, but it had a small button at one end.

"What are these?" Ethan asked.

"Put the belts on, please," Antixl requested.

Ethan and Jade complied.

"When you touch this circular patch at the front, a force field will encase you. The projectiles we found in Jade cannot penetrate it. You touch the patch again to turn the field off. This will protect you from this Loki creature."

Ethan and Jade's eyes opened wide in surprise. Ethan tried the operation. He hardly noticed any difference, but could just see a translucent edge around him. It disappeared when he touched the patch again. "And this?" he asked, holding out the cylinder.

"That is a weapon. The button activates it. Point the other end at the target and press the button to fire it, but please only use it if you need to. We do not condone violence and we give this to you reluctantly."

Ethan nodded. "We will remember." He stayed deep in thought for a while longer. "Can I request another favor?"

"What is it?" Poloxl asked.

"If we find it absolutely necessary, can I bring Loki to you, to stay here in exile until he dies or shows genuine repentance and a change in attitude?"

Antixl and Poloxl looked at each other and discussed the request in their language for a minute before Poloxl replied. "This is acceptable to us."

"Then, we thank you for your hospitality and are ready to leave you," Ethan said.

"It has been our pleasure. Please return whenever you wish to converse with us again. We have adjusted the settings of the portal so that either of you can activate it, but no one else can anymore, so you two will be the first and last to ever see the other Earth for now." Antixl said.

"Why is that? Why have you precluded anyone else?"

"Our people have discussed the issue and we think this is not the time for extensive migration of beings between universes. A time may come when the situation changes and we open the portal again."

Ethan looked at Jade. "Shall we?"

"Lets."

They activated the portal and walked through. Moments later they emerge from the portal on Caerus, expecting to see someone to meet them. The only one in front of them was Grubexl. He stood about twenty metres away, a smile on his face and expectation in his stance. "I see that you are well," he said to Jade.

"Where is everyone?" Ethan asked as he searched for anyone in the compound.

"There is just me. The others could not wait for you to return, so they went to do other things. They are still on the planet somewhere as far as I know."

"How long have we been gone? It's only been three weeks, hasn't it?"

"You have been gone for three months. Time is different where you went."

Ethan started walking around and then he took a deep breath. "Hey, notice something? We can breathe like normal."

Jade also took a conscious breath and smiled. "Yeah, we can."

Looking back at Grubexl, Ethan asked, "And has Loki been back?"

"I have not seen him since the altercation."

"Do you know if they captured him?"

"No, I do not. Your... John told me two weeks ago they were still looking for him. He has not returned to the ship he arrived in or made any other contact, apparently."

"Not even to get a look at your store?"

"No."

"Well, let's hope he died then."

"Ethan?" Jade said.

"Well, that would be the best for everyone, wouldn't it?"

"What should we do now?"

"We should contact the ship. Let them know we're back. We don't have any comm though."

"John left one with me so you could make contact when you returned," Grubexl said. He walked off and into one of his workshops, returning a minute later with the comm in his hand. He gave it to Ethan.

Ethan contacted the ship. "Hello *Destiny*. Is anyone there?" A minute went by so he tried again, checking the comm worked.

A further minute went by. "Is that you, Ethan?" the familiar voice of Celeste asked.

"Yes, it is."

"Oh, I'm so glad to hear from you. And... Jade?"

"Jade is fine. Other members of Grubexl's species met us and they patched her up."

"That's great."

"Can someone come and pick us up?"

"Sure. I'll get something organized and let you know. Hugo will be pleased. She will probably pick you up. She has been in a depression ever since the incident."

"I'll wait for you to call back then." Ethan cut contact.

30

LOKI'S EXILE

E than and Jade talked to Grubexl about what they had seen and done while on the other Earth as they ate and drank with him, waiting for the Lander to come to pick them up. Grubexl seemed very pleased they had been successful in their journey to his home planet. Ethan felt his interest was a little more than just catching up on news from there though. He said he knew Antixl and Poloxl, but didn't say much more about them or his relationship with them. They heard a noise outside and went to stand up to investigate.

Loki appeared at the doorway, disheveled and crazy eyed, a pistol in his hand as he looked first at Ethan and then Jade. He looked surprised when he recognized her. "I thought you'd be dead."

"I'm obviously alive," Jade said, her eyes wide as she looked at the pistol.

"You don't look too good," Ethan said. "Why don't you put the gun down and get some help? We can take you back to Earth."

"I will get what I came for and return in glory."

"You're crazy."

"No, determined. Now Grubexl, if you will lead me to your store of equipment," Loki said, waving with the gun for Grubexl to move.

Grubexl looked at him for a moment. Ethan could see he was thinking things over in his head. Grubexl finally said, "Why settle for what I have when you can have much, much more?"

Ethan and Jade looked at him, horrified. Ethan suspected what Grubexl would say next, and he didn't like it, although it would be one way of getting him through the portal.

"What do you mean?" Loki asked, a calculating look in his eyes.

"That stela over there, Ethan here can bring life into it."

"He can? How? What good will that do?" Loki looked at Ethan with delight at the prospect of even more being in his possession.

"He needs to touch it." Grubexl thought for a moment, looking at Jade. "Jade has to be with him though."

Both Ethan and Jade frowned, a little confused by Grubexl's remark. Since Ethan couldn't think of why he would have said it, he played along, assuming that Grubexl had some plan to get them all out of their predicament.

"Show us how this works then," Loki said, gesturing for Ethan and Jade to go to the stela.

Ethan and Jade looked at each other and went to it. Jade held Ethan's arm as he placed his palm on the surface of the object. The face clouded over, but Ethan maintained his contact. The surface suddenly collapsed and his hand disappeared for a moment until he pulled it out again, the sensation still unsettling, even though he knew what to expect. He looked at Grubexl, who had a satisfied look. "What now?" Ethan asked.

Loki stood delighted with the prospects of the opportunity. "Go through," he said to Ethan.

"Are you crazy? I'm not going through there."

"Go through or I shoot Jade." Loki's face looked more insane by the second. Ethan realized he was having a serious mental breakdown and it wouldn't be long before he became completely unhinged.

"If you go, I go," Jade demanded.

"Suits me," Loki commented.

"But we've already been there."

"You've already been and returned? That is magnificent. I see an opportunity for a prosperous tourism business between here and there. Many people will pay for such an adventure."

"You fool. Do you think the people at the other end will allow anyone to come and go as they please? They'll shut the portal down completely if you offend them." Grubexl said.

"They'll see reason."

"You think you can wave that at them like you are me? They will disarm you before you realize it. Greed doesn't motivate everyone." Grubexl turned again and stomped off.

"You're playing with fire," Ethan said. "You'll get your fingers burned." He fumbled for the weapon the Terrans had given him, rotating it between his fingers in his pocket, wondering if he should use it. He waited, but moved his other hand to the patch on his belt to activate his force field. He unobtrusively motioned to Jade to do the same, which she did. Grubexl looked at them in surprise when he saw the surrounding fields, but said nothing.

"Hello, is anyone around," they all heard from the forest area. They looked towards the source of the voice. Celeste, Hu and John emerged from the forest, looking for some indication of life.

"Stay back," Ethan said.

Loki swiped the butt of the gun against Ethan's head, making him see stars for a moment. Apparently the force field didn't include protection against large objects. The welt of a bruise started appearing. John, Hu and Celeste instantly retreated to the cover of the forest.

"Welcome back," Loki said as he moved behind Ethan and Jade's bodies for protection.

"Put your weapon down," John shouted from the trees. "There are more than us three."

"I don't believe you this time. You had no reason to suspect I'd be here."

Ethan knew that Loki was right. He doubted that John, Hu and Celeste had brought anyone else. He had to think fast before anyone else got hurt, but he had no ideas.

"I still have my agents in the background, waiting for my orders," Loki advised.

Ethan looked around, alert by the revelation, to see if he could locate where they were, but they remained well hidden. He still held the weapon in his pocket, his finger close to the trigger button, but not knowing whether to use it. He wanted to see who lurked in the background and where.

"Leave them go," John shouted.

"Fire," Loki replied.

A hail of bullets came from behind the buildings towards John and the others, whizzing uncomfortably close past Ethan and Jade. John returned fire and a battle lasting several minutes played out. Ethan's temper started rising at Loki and the insanity of the whole situation. He wanted no more of his friends dead. Pushing Loki to the ground, he disarmed him and pulled his alien weapon out, pointing toward Loki's minions and pressing the button. A beam of light shot out. Ethan waved the beam around as it sliced through the building. He heard one shout of pain soon after and then another and the firing stopped.

John came into view a little later, wary of further attack. He ran between the buildings, Hu and Celeste following close behind. They disappeared, but came back into view a few minutes later and walked up to Ethan and the others. "I don't know what that thing is," John said, "but it made quick work of the men firing at us. They're both dead."

Being distracted by meeting each other, they didn't notice Loki moving and grabbing the pistol lying on the ground, Ethan having forgotten to take it away in the heat of activity. He stood up suddenly and pointed the pistol at Ethan. "You've caused me enough problems. Now you die." He fired the gun, and the bullet flew towards Ethan, but stopped dead in its flight when it hit the force field. It fell to the ground. Loki's eyes widened, and his pupils dilated, and his madness reached its crescendo. He laughed a manic laugh and started firing at anything until Ethan shot the gun from him with his weapon. He evaporated half of Loki's hand too. All seemed calm again except for

Loki, shouting out in pain, holding the stump of his hand. Ethan had a good mind to whack him over the head to shut him up. He had enough of him and decided what to do with him.

Grubexl moaned in agony, as red blood seeped from the injury in his side. Celeste rushed to him, concerned over his condition. "We must help him," she yelled to John and Hu.

They came over and John looked at his wound. He frowned. "I'm not sure what we can do. It looks serious."

"Can't we get Angelo down here?"

"He may not have that long."

"What about the portal?"

"He can't go through it. They have blocked his access," Ethan said.

"Do not concern yourselves," Grubexl said as he opened his eyes to slits. "My life is draining from me. It is maybe fitting that I am prevented from returning to my world. I have not yet paid the penance for my sins."

Celeste raised his head into her lap as she sat on the ground, a tear trickling from her eyes. "What do you mean?"

"My people were content with what they had accomplished with you humans on Earth, but I was not. I had to take it a step further on another world. So I produced a mutated form of the gene and released it on a similar species to yourselves, but it was too potent. I wiped out the whole species before I could produce a cure."

Celeste's eyes widened. "Chariclo."

"Yes. That is my sin of which my people have said I must repent. I never accepted that I did anything wrong, but they said it was against our ethics, against our principles. Why? Was it not the same as what they had done on Earth? They were not sure of the outcome. Did we have a right to interfere in the development of another species in any universe? Maybe not, although it worked out in your case, or did it? What would the outcome have been if we didn't interfere... the same?... Or different? We will never know." Grubexl coughed, blood dribbling out of his mouth, mixed with saliva.

"Can't we do anything for you?"

"It is time for me to leave. There is a door in my workshop. A spoken word locks it. The key is... come closer Celeste." Celeste bent down and leaned over him. Grubexl whispered something and suddenly convulsed in a spasm before turning limp and lifeless.

Celeste cried.

Ethan looked at Grubexl and Celeste, sadness overwhelming him. The first alien modern humans had ever seen had been killed by the same humans. So very typical of humanity, even if Grubexl's death was accidental. A sudden anger percolated from inside him and boiled over into outrage. "You," he shouted, pointing at Loki. "You wanted to see these aliens and their world. That's exactly what you'll do."

Jade looked at him, frightened by his anger. The others looked at him in shock from the outburst. Ethan strode over and grabbed Loki by his good arm and yanked him up. Loki's crazed eyes looked at Ethan, a sudden fear flowing from them as they saw Ethan's anger. He had no energy to resist Ethan. Ethan pulled him over to the portal and activated it again.

"No," Jade said, once she realized what Ethan meant to do, but she was too late. Ethan walked into the portal, dragging Loki behind him.

THEY CAME out the other end, little time having passed, even though they had traveled the vast void between universes. Guards met them as before. Loki cringed in fear as he looked at the beings in front of him. "Can you please ask either Poloxl or Antixl to come," Ethan asked.

One guard went off. Poloxl came five minutes later, looking puzzled as he saw Ethan and Loki. "Welcome again Ethan, but why have you returned so soon?"

"Remember that favor I asked when we left?"

"Indeed."

"Well, I am asking you to fulfill it. Please take this monster and lock him up. He doesn't deserve to live in our universe any longer."

Poloxl looked at Loki and back at Ethan. "Are you sure?"

"Yes. Maybe he'll repent and realize his sins in time, but he will just cause more problems if he stays with us. I might be tempted to kill him, and I don't want to be in that position."

"Very well." Poloxl gestured for two of the guards to take Loki away.

"No..." Loki yelled as they dragged him along, his eyes frantic with fear.

Ethan's anger started subsiding once Loki disappeared from his sight. He calmed down and thought of what to do or say next. He looked at Poloxl. "I'm deeply sorry to put you in this position, but I'm at a loss with him. I will come and check up on him from time to time. If you feel he has repented, I may take him back with me. You can contact me as well if you think he is ready. On another matter, I must inform you that Grubexl is dead. They shot him in the crossfire while Loki's men tried to kill some of my people."

Poloxl looked horrified. "That is disturbing news. We never intended for him to die in that way."

"Sometimes our actions have unexpected results." Ethan looked around, not sure what to do next. "I'll get back. Too much time will pass otherwise."

"Yes. We will be happy to see you again, but please do not bring any other criminals through."

Ethan laughed. "No, I won't. I don't wish to stretch our friendship. Till we meet again." Ethan held out a hand.

Poloxl looked at it for a moment, not knowing what to do. His face lit in realization and he extended his hand, grabbing Ethan's for a handshake. "Till next time."

Poloxl activated the portal and Ethan went through back to Caerus.

31

A NEW BEGINNING

E than walked through the portal on Caerus moments later. No one was there to welcome him, but he heard a noise from inside the house Grubexl had used to live in. "Hello," he said in a raised voice.

Jade ran out a second later and ran to him. "You're back," she said before kissing him.

They parted. "Maybe I should go away more often," he said with a grin.

"Don't you dare."

"How long was I gone?"

"A day."

"That long? Well, they'll keep Loki until he comes to his senses, if he does. I don't think they were pleased about it, but they said they would."

"It frightened me when you took Loki through. I've never seen you so angry."

"I was just fed up. I couldn't take him any longer. It was that or shoot him, and I didn't want to do that."

"Come inside and have something to eat. Grubexl left a multitude of food to eat."

Ethan walked to the house next to Jade, his arm around her waist. "Where are the others?"

"They've returned to the ship. I'll contact them in a minute, but I want you all to myself first."

"Did you stay here overnight?"

"Yes. I didn't know when you'd return. It's comfortable here, actually. And with not having to worry about breathing, I could have a decent look around and think about what life might be like here."

"So you still want to stay here?"

"Of course."

"What happened to Grubexl?"

"They took him back to the ship. Gerhardt wants to do an autopsy on him to find out how different he is from us."

Ethan had returned late in the morning and Jade contacted the ship midafternoon once they had some time together.

A Lander touched down nearby the next morning, Jade persuading the others to let her have Ethan to herself overnight. Hu and John came to meet them and took them back to the ship. Ethan and Jade were unsure how their new gland would react to the increased oxygen level on the ship, but it didn't prove to be a problem. The photosynthesis process must have adapted. Celeste, Apep and Galena waited for them as they emerged from the Lander. They all hugged Ethan and Jade when they met them.

"Just like old times," Ethan said. "This calls for a party."

They all laughed and agreed.

They congregated in the lounge later in the day, together with Angelo, Marie and the others in the team, telling each other all that had happened.

"What's on your heads?" Gerhardt asked.

"This?" Ethan replied. "They're membranes to photosynthesise carbon dioxide to oxygen. It supplements our supply in our bloodstreams so we don't need the enhancers. The Terrans genetically changed us to grow them."

"What on earth for?" Pia asked. She had recovered from her injuries.

Ethan and Jade looked at each other and then at the others. Jade said, "We've decided to stay here and become the first colonists of Caerus."

"What for?"

"It seems like a good idea. We both feel we've had enough traveling and exploring. You'll probably get in less trouble without us, anyway."

"We will miss you," Apep said. "We will not get in trouble together anymore."

Jade and the others laughed. "You're welcome to visit us anytime, now you have your own ship. It seems you can get here at a moment's notice. We'll return to Earth now and then. I'm sure we'll need various supplies from time to time."

"Well, you have reached for the stars, Ethan," Hu said.

"I suppose I have. Do you have your ship back, Apep?"

"Yes. The other terrorists surrender when Loki not return. They lose pay packet."

"They won't like time in prison."

"Better than dead."

"Does that mean I get to have *Destiny*?" Celeste asked with a sheepish grin.

"You might have to ask John about that," Ethan said. "But I suppose I won't be needing it anymore."

"We'll see," John said, with a feigned stern face.

They continued chatting for some time. Ethan became silent, looking at his glass as he rotated it in his hand. He looked at Angelo, "What happened to Mark and Alice?"

"They're in our morgue. We will return them to Earth for burial."

"Of course." He turned to Jade. "We need to return for that."

Jade reached over and rubbed his arm.

The party drew to a close in the evening. Being too late to return to the planet, Ethan and Jade stayed on board and returned the next day, taking their luggage and belongings with them. Celeste and Hu came down with them.

Celeste walked into the building that housed the safe where

Grubexl had stored his equipment. Ethan went with her. She touched the door and wondered if she had heard Grubexl correctly. Deciding to try, she stood back and said, "Earth."

The door slid open. Ethan and Celeste looked into the vault in amazement and then at each other. Ethan shrugged his shoulders and went inside. Four shelves lined the far wall with things on them he had never seen before. Other equipment stood against the other walls.

Celeste came up behind him. "This will take years to investigate," she said.

"Yes, it will. I might get the Terrans to tell me what everything is, so long as they don't confiscate it when they find out."

APEP AND GALENA left on the *Gagarin* a week later, returning to Earth. The others stayed for another two months, exploring other areas of the planet. Ethan and Jade went back to Earth to bury Mark and Alice and move their possessions. Jade's family were at a loss to understand why Jade would want to live on another world. They placated her parents with the promise of frequent visits. *Destiny* too eventually left, but many other scientists came through the wormhole to continue research into the planet. The news about Grubexl, the portal and the other universe on the different brane spread like wildfire in the scientific community on Earth, much to Ethan's and Jade's annoyance. Many scientists came to examine the stela. They asked Ethan to activate it many times, but he refused, not wanting to disturb the Terrans with inquisitive scientists. *They will just have to work out their own theories*, he thought. He didn't tell them about the vault, as he felt he should find out what was safe for humanity and what wasn't before he let anyone look at it.

Loki's disappearance didn't cause much fuss, to Ethan's surprise. The company seemed to just shrug its shoulders and move on, as if to say, 'Good riddance.' The problems in the business seemed to evaporate once Carson took over as the new CEO.

The Russians investigated how Loki had hijacked their ship, but, as there was no one to prosecute, nothing more came of it.

John and Hu married a year later. Ethan and Jade returned to Earth for the wedding and enjoyed meeting all their friends again.

Life set into a routine for Ethan and Jade soon after return from the wedding. They sat out on a bench next to a building one evening, watching the sunset, enjoying a wine they brought back with them. "We must learn how to make this," Ethan said.

"You think you can make it as well?"

"I doubt it."

"Let's just settle with getting some shipped from Earth now and then, shall we? There are plenty of people coming here and we have a good stipend from the government for what we're doing."

They sat in silence.

"It's lonely sometimes," Jade said, a slight depression seeping into her.

"Hey, we've got each other, and we are the first inhabitants of Caerus. We even have the headdress to show for it," Ethan said as he placed his arm around her shoulders.

Jade laughed despite her mood. "I love you."

Ethan reached over and they kissed and hugged. "I love you too."

They looked at each other and Jade asked, "What will we call ourselves?"

Ethan thought. "What about Cetusians?"

Jade smiled. "That will do."

～

～

～

"WAHHH... WAHHH... WAHHH."

Ethan held up the tiny wriggling baby as he finished delivering it, a smile of joy on his face. Jade, exhaust by the labor, smiled with perspiration dripping from her. The labor had caught both of them by surprise and they didn't have time to arrange transport back to Earth for the birth. The first ever Cetusian had been born on Caerus three years after Ethan and Jade first set foot on the planet.

∼

The End

Read another exciting adventure from John Wegener.

Type https://books2read.com/Halwendes-Redemption into your browser.

Thanks for reading this book. If you loved the book and have a moment to spare, I would appreciate a quick review on the site that you purchased the book from, as this helps new readers find my books.

Subscribe to my Newsletters and receive three free episodes of The Chronicles of Gatacus Todd.

Type http://subscribepage.io/g4r4f8 in your browser.

ALSO BY JOHN WEGENER

Books

Reach For The Stars Trilogy

FTL

Centauri

Ceti

Reach For The Stars Box Set (Books 1-3)

Loki's Fall

Zodiac Series

Scorpius

Libra

Halwende's Legacy Series

Halwende's Redemption

Halwende's Resurrection

Halwende's Reincarnation

Halwende's Legacy Box Set (Books 1-3)

Solar Dawn Series

Lunar Rift

Other Stories

The Dark Ages

SAGI

Short Stories

The Love Particle

ABOUT THE AUTHOR

John Wegener grew up in the Adelaide Hills of South Australia. He now expresses his imaginative dreams by engaging in writing after a 34-year career as a Chemical Engineer in the steel industry, which has taken him to many countries and allowed him to experience many cultures. John currently lives in Wollongong, Australia with his wife and children.

Click on johnwegener.com to find more of my books or read his blogs. Type subscribepage.io/g4r4f8 to subscribe to my emails for more stories and information.

www.ingramcontent.com/pod-product-compliance
Lightning Source LLC
Chambersburg PA
CBHW071828020726
47502CB00004B/1279